The Walled Garden

Barry W Litherland

For Jon,

On your birthday,
30th September 2016

Barry

Chapter One

Detective Chief Inspector Jack Munro looked up. Modern pine desk, modern swivel chair, new slim computer screen, freshly painted walls, new carpet - he frowned disconsolately; old Jack. From within his office he could see Aaron Marks confidently scrutinising the screen of his new computer, his black stick propped against the side of the desk. It was summer and the sunlight was firing beams through the open windows of Portskail Police Station. They struck him fiercely. Jack mopped a sweating brow.

He prised himself unwillingly from his chair and walked across the room. 'It must be my age. I'm leaner, smaller and lighter than you. You'd think I would sweat less too, but no.' He looked at the black stick and frowned. 'Don't you think it's time you got rid of that thing? It's merely an affectation. You don't need it.'

'I've grown used to it. I feel undressed without it. But never mind that now. Take a look at this. It's the CCTV footage from Strathan Tower.'

Jack leaned forward and peered at the screen.

'It wouldn't win any awards, would it?' he muttered, 'a walled garden at night, lots of dark flowerbeds, and nothing happening. It's like one of those arty foreign films.'

His sharp eyes moved restlessly across the screen and then settled on something towards the centre. He pulled up a chair and looked more closely.

'That's better, much more interesting. Now we have characters and the beginning of a plot. My professional attention has been engaged. I take it that this is our principal suspect.'

Aaron Marks nodded. He looked up and his grey eyes met the darker eyes of the older man. 'I think we could safely say that we wish to find this man in order to eliminate him from our enquiries. He isn't afraid to be seen, is he, standing in the centre of the garden and looking directly at the camera?'

'Perhaps he wants to be seen. What would you say - about five feet ten, 13 stone, perhaps in his thirties? It is a he, I think.'

'The clothes don't help us much,' Aaron added, 'Dark jeans, dark hooded top, dark everything.'

'We won't get a clear picture of his face either. But I do admire the slow theatrical manner in which he turns his head towards the camera? It's quite Gothic, especially the way the hood falls lower over his face as he moves. You can never quite see him, not in any detail.'

'It's clever, very clever.' Aaron paused, reviewed the footage and paused again. 'It's quite purposeful and carefully choreographed. He knows the cameras are there and he's using them quite deliberately.'

'It's wonderfully theatrical. Here we have an actor, a rather melodramatic actor, putting on a show. He is expecting someone to see this and to wonder who it might be. But why, I wonder, and who is his performance directed at? Is it a live performance, do you think, or was it planned to be viewed later and at leisure?'

'Now look at this,' Aaron said. He pressed a key and hurried the footage to another point. 'This was the second night, taken a few days later. What do you make of that?'

'Same scene, same hooded figure,' the older man murmured, 'but, wait a minute. Hold the picture there. Yes, I see what you mean. It would be easy to overlook if we weren't such gifted professionals.'

'And if I hadn't been trained by a master of his craft, yes I know.'

'As long as you remember your obligations, my boy, but no, you're right. It looks like the same person. He's even dressed the same; but that is most definitely not the same person. 'He - and I say that with some reservations - must be three or four inches shorter and considerably lighter.'

'I think they also look slightly younger, don't you think?'

Jack nodded. 'Perhaps; but look how the head moves slowly and the hood drops over the eyes. They must have rehearsed this together. This scene is almost identical to the first. How very strange and how very amateur; I think we should arrest everyone in the local theatre group. I wonder who the audience is supposed to be.'

'It must be someone who could see the live performance or someone who has access to the recorded footage and it's certainly someone who understands its significance.'

'So who could that be, the owner of the house or one of his friends or a member of staff? The list can't be that long. '

They were silent for a moment.

'Look again, Jack. There's something else in this second recording. Look, there in the back corner, beside the fruit bushes.'

After a moment, 'No, I can't see anything else. What am I looking for?'

'Just watch closely. There! Did you see that?' He pointed at a dark corner of the screen.

Jack shook his head. 'Run it again.'

'Perhaps,' Jack murmured, 'Perhaps. What do you think? Is someone watching the watchers? Is it a hidden accomplice, perhaps?'

'It looks like there's something in the darkness beside the bushes. If it hadn't moved I'd never have seen it. I'm not sure it's a person; it could be an animal, even a bird, but something moved.'

Jack stretched out his aching back.

'It could be nothing more than a casual encounter between a few leaves and a passing breeze. Perhaps it's the ghost of Strathan Tower; there must be one. All these old houses have a ghost or two. Well, which ever way you look at it there's something menacing about these events. You don't expect to look out of your window on a dark evening and see someone staring up at you. How many times did Mr. Deitch say the garden had been entered? Three times before they put up the CCTV and twice after? It's very strange!'

'It became rather more menacing this morning, don't you think?'

'It did indeed.' Jack turned away. He wiped his forehead with a large, white handkerchief. 'I hate this heat. It's out of place in Portskail. Go forth, my boy, and investigate. Take Rosie with you. She has always been a better judge of character than her owner. See what your little springer spaniel makes of the principle players. If she growls at anyone, bring them in for questioning. I trust that dog implicitly. In your absence I shall discover what I can about the owner of the hall. I didn't like Mr. John Deitch; there was something shifty about him'

Aaron stared at the screen for a moment then looked away. He was thinking about John Deitch. Jack was right - there was something rather unsettling about John Deitch. It was hard to catch his eye and harder still to retain a hold on it. When his eyes finally settled on something - perhaps the view beyond the window of his study - his expression conveyed wistfulness, melancholy and resignation. It was the look of a man who had given up.

After a few minutes Aaron closed the computer and gathered his coat and stick.

'I'm going back to Strathan Tower,' he called. 'I need to talk to the gardener and cook. I'll speak to Deitch again too. I can check which of his friends were actually in the house when the figures were seen. I wonder if the cook is back at work yet.'

Poor Mrs. Davidson, cook and housekeeper to Mr. Deitch, what a shock it must have been. When she opened the front door and stepped out to take her early morning stroll she was greeted by a grotesque and most unpleasant sight. During the night someone had hung a body from the broad branch of a sturdy sycamore. The noose was tight round the neck and the head was at a strange angle. Arms and legs hung loosely. There was a knife wound in the chest and blood, lots of blood. In the top left hand pocket of the tweed jacket was a single sheet of writing paper – a sheet of expensive and distinctive blue vellum. There was one word written on it in large, black letters - GUILTY.

The fact that the body was nothing more than an effigy created from sacks stuffed with newspapers and then clothed, surmounted by a balloon shaped head with painted eyes and a wide, smiling mouth, did little to detract from the horror. Nor was she to know at that point that the blood was animal rather than human. The housekeeper emitted a loud shriek ran quickly back to regain the security of the old house. There, with beating heart and breathing more rapidly than was good for her, she awaited the house owner who was already hurrying down the stairs.

John Deitch paced outside. He saw the cause of her distress and realised at once that he had little option now but to call the police. It was a decision he took most unwillingly.

Aaron Marks and Jack Munro found the local, uniformed police already present. They interviewed John Deitch. He was the sole occupant of the hall that night, his friends having returned home the previous day. The housekeeper, who had remained overnight in a room set aside for her occasional use, was now at home in the village and was sedated. She could not be disturbed or interviewed until later.

Over the next half hour the full story of the events of the previous few weeks became clear. First there had been the disturbances in the garden, trivial but annoying; someone had dug holes, as if burying something. Then, on two evenings, figures had been seen in the garden and had been captured on CCTV. Now matters had escalated and this grotesque effigy had appeared over night. Aaron removed the CCTV footage to study later, back at the office.

'I have a bad feeling about this, Rosie,' Aaron murmured, as he drove north to where the old hall stood in its isolated grounds on a rocky promontory beyond the village of Strathan. 'It feels like the beginning of something; but the beginning of what, I wonder? It takes a rather strange sort of person to engage in acts like these.'

On the back seat of the car Rosie, a small, brown and white springer spaniel, lay on her side. She yawned and flicked her tail. Her thoughts were elsewhere. Aaron would take her for a run on one of the tiny beaches they would pass on their journey north; she would chase her ball and rush into the waves. Then there would be a steamy, warm ride in the car and relaxing sleep.

Chapter Two

When Aaron arrived at Strathan Tower he headed straight to the spacious, walled garden. There he sat down on a bench to consider the strange events which had occurred at the hall. He was in no hurry. It was high summer. Softly scented roses bloomed against the rough, grey stone behind him and other varieties in white, pink and red filled flower beds. Round them wound a soft grey gravel path which then passed under twin arches of clematis and between hedges towards more garden areas where sweet peas clung to netting and marigolds bloomed in narrow borders. Over another dividing hedge lay the vegetable garden.

Aaron glanced to his left towards the tower house which stood beyond the garden, adjacent to a small copse of trees. Through these trees the drive curved from the gate towards the wide arch of lawn and the gravelled front of the house. A single window, high in the west tower, looked down on the garden.

Rosie sat at his feet. Occasionally she raised her eyes and softly whimpered. Eventually Aaron became aware of the sound and reached down to stroke her flanks. She licked his hand affectionately.

'Well, Rosie,' he murmured and his grey eyes softened in a smile, 'What do we make of this?'

Rosie was inclined to make very little of it. She lay down with her head between her paws and emitted a long sigh. Patience was going to be required. Her nose twitched. Over the wall and across an expanse of lawn lay a track which led down to the beach. Rosie could smell the sea and the beach. That was where she wanted to be, chasing a ball across rock and sand, not here on a leash in a garden. She sighed again and closed her eyes. For now she would have to wait.

Aaron rested back against the stone wall and closed his eyes. He was almost camouflaged against the stone and the creeping roses. He studied the patterns the sun made behind his lids then opened his eyes and looked towards the house. His attention was drawn again to that one window, on the top floor of the tower just beneath the parapet. He imagined someone standing there, looking out over the garden.

'I wonder who was in that room,' he mused. 'I must check.'

He was about to close his eyes again when he was disturbed by a voice calling from his right where two long greenhouses, set in the corner of the garden, marked the domain of the gardener.

'Hey! You over there! Can I help you? What are you doing here?'

A man, about thirty and with a tangle of dark, curly hair approached him. He brushed his hands together and then wiped them on a t-shirt. He was not tall but of a stocky build and sunburnt and weathered like a piece of driftwood.

'Ah, Robert Wilkie, I assume.' Aaron stood up and held out a broad hand. He smiled. The young man was suddenly dwarfed by the taller figure. Rosie stood up and eyed the stranger suspiciously. She made no move towards him.

'We don't have dogs in here!' the young man said. 'Mr. Deitch doesn't like dogs.'

Aaron reached into his pocket and removed a wallet from which he extracted a card. The young man looked at it and then stepped back.

'Ah,' he scratched the dark curls and smiled apologetically. 'I thought you would be up at the house. We're all a bit jittery at the moment with these things happening.' He looked down at Rosie with obvious distrust. 'Even so,' he mumbled, 'we don't usually allow dogs in here.'

'She's a police dog,' Aaron reached down and caressed her ears.

'She doesn't look much like a police dog.' Wilkie scratched his head and fine dry dust fell on his shoulders.

'Plain clothes, she's a specialist.'

'Ah,' Wilkie seemed reassured. His dark eyes softened into a smile. 'You mean like those dogs trained to smell out bombs and drugs and bodies.'

'Something of that sort; though she's rather more on the intellectual wing of the force. Can you show me where the ground was disturbed?'

'Where do you want to begin?'

'Let's approach them chronologically. Start with the first one, shall we?'

Aaron picked up the black cane. Rosie shuffled unwillingly to her feet and shook herself. Aaron leaned lightly on the cane as he walked, as if out of habit.

'Were you injured in the line of duty?'

Aaron shook his head. 'An eighteen stone prop forward and an over ambitious run for the line. The immovable object won.'

'Will it get better?'

'The specialist says it should do; my wife says it already has and my superior officer believes this cane is an affectation. I suspect they are all right in their way. How long have you been working here?'

'I'll have been here twelve years this Autumn. I was seven years with Mrs. Waterson before she sold up. She was nice, very old school, a real lady. I've had five years with the current owner.'

'John Deitch.'

Wilkie nodded, without enthusiasm.

'You don't like him particularly?' There was a silence. 'This is just between me and you, I won't be writing anything down. I've already formed my own opinion. I spent some time with him yesterday. Rosie has her own view too.'

'He isn't an easy man to like,' Wilkie said, 'though he's not without his good points. Emma Varley, - she's his private assistant, and friend - she seems to understand him.'

'I'll see Emma Varley later. She has an apartment here and a house in the village, I believe. Are Emma Varley and Mr. Deitch in some sort of relationship?'

Wilkie laughed. 'No, nothing of that nature; they seem to like each other's company, that's all. Mr. Deitch was very sociable when he first arrived, especially during the first year. But he gets bored with people, it seems to me. There aren't many visitors nowadays, just a few regulars, old friends'

'Is he good to work for?'

Wilkie paused. 'I don't want to speak ill; he pays me regularly and he leaves me pretty much alone...but you never quite know what to expect next from him. He can be pretty sharp sometimes; then another time he's full of smiles and humour as if he's making a special effort. Much of the time he just seems bored, bored and depressed.'

'That can't be easy. Are there many people working here?'

Wilkie shook his head. 'There were more in the old days when the Watersons were here. In those days the house was at the centre of a small estate. There were a lot of social functions too, garden parties and the like. It was quite lively. Then the estate and the farmland were sold off bit by bit until only the house was left. Then that was sold too. There's only me and Ruth Davidson, the housekeeper, who are still on the permanent staff. I look after the garden and grounds and Ruth has the house. We hire extras from the village if we need it or if Mr. Deitch has visitors staying. Other than that there are just two cleaners, villagers again. They come in three mornings a week.'

'You liked Mrs. Waterson, the previous owner?'

'I've known Mrs. Waterson since I was a child. I'm a local man, you see, born in the village. I've lived here all my life. I was at school with Agnes Waterson, her daughter. Mrs. Waterson sent her children to the local school. She wanted Agnes to belong here, just as she belonged here. Well, when I finished at college I came back here to work and I've been here ever since.'

'Then things changed and now you work for Mr. Deitch?'

'Things always change,' Wilkie said quietly.

Aaron noted the shadow that fell momentarily over the gardener's face. 'Where does Mrs. Waterson live now?' he asked.

'She has a house in the village. It's the large, white house you meet as you descend the road to the harbour. It's at the top of the hill just before the final bend, set back amongst trees.'

They paused by a flower bed which seemed to be close to the very centre of the garden.

'This was where we found the ground disturbed the first time. I arrived her one morning just as usual and there was a small mound of earth. At first sight it looked like a very tiny grave. Someone had cut flowers from the bed over there and laid them around it.

'So it looked a bit like a grave for a pet,' Aaron mused, 'or a child?'

'That's what Ruth – Mrs. Davidson - said.'

Rosie sniffed the soil and then pulled towards the path.

'Is she on to something?'

'No, she wants to play ball on the beach. There's nothing for her here. Where was the next one?'

They walked across the garden to another bed. Another tiny grave had been found here. It was discovered exactly a week later, half hidden by blackcurrant bushes.

'The third one was near the south eastern corner. Same shape, same size, and flowers spread around it too!'

'And each one appeared just a week after the previous one?'

Wilkie shook his head. 'The first appeared one Friday and the second one the following Friday. The third one appeared the following week, only that was on the Wednesday. Maybe he knew we were watching.'

Aaron stood by the second location and looked around. In two corners of the garden he could see close circuit cameras set on the wall top and angled towards the centre.

'When did those go up?' he asked.

'It was after the first disturbance. Mr. Deitch wanted it done at once. We had them in place within a couple of days. He said he wanted the culprit caught. It was unnerving for the friends who were staying. It wasn't pleasant to think there was someone wandering around the garden at dead of night, he said. He was starting to look pretty unnerved himself. It was thanks to the cameras that we caught sight of our vandal.'

'How long after the disturbances in the garden did the figure appear?'

'The first appearance was a few days after the first disturbance - on the Monday, I think.'

'So the first grave – for want of a better word – was found on the Friday morning and the figure was sighted on CCTV on the following Monday night?'

Wilkie nodded.

'How curious,' Aaron murmured. He glanced back towards the house. 'It would appear that, having advertised his presence, the visitor entered the garden with no other purpose that to be seen from the window in the tower or caught on camera.'

Wilkie scratched his head. 'I hadn't thought of that. I suppose that's why you're a detective and I'm a gardener. You think he stepped out of the shadows in order to show himself?'

'Yes. I've been looking at the footage. It looks like that.' He glanced round. 'So the night time visitor was here five times in all, three times digging holes and twice posing for the camera.'

Wilkie nodded. 'It's a strange way to behave.'

'Yet he was never seen when creating the graves.'

'No.'

'Did you see the footage?'

'Only briefly, Mr. Deitch wanted to know if I recognised him.'

'Did you?'

'No.'

'We keep saying him. Are you certain it was a man?'

Wilkie was quiet for a moment. He scratched a tousled head. More dust fell. 'I hadn't really thought of that,' he said. 'I just assumed it was a man because of…well, you know.' He nodded towards the arch of trees and the driveway as if indicating something that required no greater elaboration. 'That's not a particularly feminine thing to do.'

Aaron nodded. 'It would seem an obvious conclusion to draw,' he said. 'Unfortunately, I'm not allowed to make assumptions without further corroboration. Rosie wouldn't let me. Nor will she allow me to assume that only one person is involved.' As if on cue Rosie looked up and wagged an upturned tail. Her eyes softened. 'See, she's pleased I remembered my training. Now, tell me about the objects you found.'

Wilkie had the look of a man trapped in uncertainty. He tried a nervous smile and then chuckled loudly. 'She's the brains and you're ...'

'...the brains too - exactly so! There is no room for brawn in our partnership.'

The chuckle burst into a loud laugh which took a moment to subdue into a good natured smile. Wilkie was growing to like this detective. D.I. Marks was not at all what he had expected.

'I nearly missed the first object. Mr. Deitch insisted I dig up the ground just in case someone had buried a dog or a cat there. It seemed a bit of a stretch but you never know do you? There are some strange folk about. I spent half an hour digging until I'd cleared the loose soil. There seemed to be nothing. I was about to start heaving the soil back in – and not without a few mutterings, I can tell you, - when I saw a small box. It was the sort of box you might get in a jeweller's shop for a wedding ring. It was half protruding from a clod of heavier soil.'

'Did you look inside it?'

'I was under strict orders to bring anything I found directly to Mr. Deitch. Nothing was to be disturbed. It was pretty clear I wasn't to open it.'

'So what was inside?'

Wilkie laughed loudly.

'I couldn't help myself. I took a quick peek. It was a bit disappointing. I've watched the television programmes; I was expecting a severed finger or something ghoulish like that, but it was just a lock of hair, although that was strange enough.'

'An adult's or a child's would you say?'

It was quite long and it was fair. I took it for an adult.'

'Did you see Mr. Deitch open the box?'

'He glanced in the box and went very pale; I suppose that's to be expected though.'

'Such things usually have special significance to the person who sends and to the person who receives,' Aaron said. 'Of course it's far from certain that Mr. Deitch was the intended recipient. I can't make that assumption.'

'Rosie wouldn't let you,' Wilkie suggested.

'Precisely so; you understand our relationship perfectly.'

They crossed the garden towards a narrow arch which led to a gateway in the East Wall. The wrought iron gate was strangely decorated with a flower emerging from a large and flourishing letter W which itself carried leaves of wrought ivy and honeysuckle.

Aaron stopped to look at it.

'Mrs. Waterson commissioned that,' Wilkie explained, 'not long after she took over the running of the estate. That must be, oh, twelve or thirteen years ago, when her husband died. It was in memory of him. You'll find a lot of things around the garden and grounds that she built or planted or designed in his memory.'

'Very tasteful,' Aaron murmured. 'Has Mr. Deitch made many improvements?'

Wilkie could not restrain a grunt of cynicism.

'He buys all his good taste; or Emma Varley provides it. He's got precious enough of his own.'

They passed through the gateway and across a gravelled drive and a manicured lawn towards the wide entrance of the house.

'What did you find in the other holes?'

'Well, I can't say for certain because they were all in boxes like the first but I believe the second was a small, gold chain with a curious design cut into a tiny pendant. It looked like initials interwoven, perhaps a C and a J. The third was a plain, gold wedding ring. It was broken where the gold had worn thin. Do you think it was him - you know,' He indicated towards the drive again, 'the dead guy?'

It was Aaron's turn to laugh.

'I don't think our effigy has got the brains or the guts, do you? I'd like to meet the person or people who strung him up, though,' he said. 'Have you any ideas who they might be?'

Wilkie shook his head. 'I don't move in those sorts of circles,' he said, 'at least not knowingly. You can never tell though, can you? People are strange and unpredictable. I prefer plants, they're easier.'

'And I prefer dogs,' Aaron nodded.

'Whoever strung up that effigy must have something to do with the things I found in the garden, though.'

'It would seem a reasonable supposition,' Aaron smiled. 'But Rosie thinks it's better to wait and allow the evidence to accumulate.'

Wilkie looked at Rosie who nonchalantly scratched an ear. 'What do you think they mean?'

'They might indicate loss – a marriage, a child, a relationship – it's hard to know.'

'Who was the effigy intended to represent, I wonder?'

Aaron shook his head. 'Mr. Deitch didn't appear to know. He assures me there was no reason why it should be him. But of course one can never be sure.'

'What do you do next, if you don't mind me asking?'

'Well, our garden visitors are most definitely still out there and I would dearly like to meet whoever they were. For now though all I can do is gather information and wait.'

'Wait?'

Aaron smiled. 'There's a lot of waiting in this job. My boss hates it. He finds it frustrating. He likes it when the lines join to make patterns and the patterns create a shape. Then he can begin to control events.'

'Does he always find his patterns and shapes?'

'Pretty much so,' he said. 'He's like Rosie when she's on a scent. He doesn't give up. None of us give up once we are on a scent.'

He parted from Wilkie at the entrance to the house and made his way back indoors.

'Mr. Deitch won't want you taking Rosie in there!' the gardener shouted. 'He doesn't like dogs.'

Aaron waved a hand back over his shoulder and made his way slowly into the house.

Chapter Three

Aaron made his way up the stone stairs and Wilkie, after watching him disappear into the interior of the old house, turned back to the garden and the vegetable plot where he was working. As they reached the first floor the carpeted, stone steps widened onto a wide, wood panelled corridor. On the wall at the top of the stairs, facing him and looking down towards the door, was a portrait of the new owner of Strathan Tower. It had evidently been painted only a few years previously. His short, slim stature and pinched, ageing face were immediately recognisable as were his brown eyes, his immaculately brushed dark hair and his finely manicured hands. It was a curious portrait. Here was a troubled man seated at a desk. Above the desk a window looked out over the castle wings and the sea. The sitter looked ill at ease as if caught at a moment of indecision. He looked like a man dressed in borrowed clothes, uncomfortable with his wealth and fine surroundings. Aaron looked at the signature of the artist; it was Emma Varley.

To his right the corridor led towards an elegant dining room and the lounge; to his left it led to the drawing room, a private study, some secretarial rooms and a newly installed games room. Aaron turned towards the drawing room.

'Mr. Deitch?'

There was no answer. Aaron opened the polished, oak door and looked inside. The drawing room was carefully and expensively furnished. The paintings, the ornaments and the floor and wall coverings exuded wealth. Aaron felt as if he could hear money dripping from the ceiling and trickling down the wall. Yet it seemed strangely hollow.

'No photographs, Rosie,' he murmured, 'and nothing personal. It's all empty wealth. Not at all like our house.' He looked round. 'There are no memories here, not his at any rate.'

He heard someone moving in another room beyond the drawing room and passed through an ornate door to find himself in a small study. John Deitch was seated at a mahogany desk, his chin resting on one hand, a pen held in the other. He gazed out of the window towards the sea. This was evidently where the portrait had been painted. Deitch turned slowly as Aaron entered. He did not move from his seat but casually indicated a chair. He glanced at Rosie but said nothing.

'Did you speak to Wilkie?' His voice was quiet, lethargic and his dark eyes buried in shadow. He spoke unwillingly as though any attempt at speech took energy he was unwilling to waste.

Aaron nodded. 'He was most helpful although he couldn't add a great deal to what we already know. I would like to speak to Mrs.

Davidson, if I may, and perhaps to any other people who work regularly in the house. Also, could you let me know who was staying here on those five days and, in particular, who stayed here on the nights when the figure appeared in the walled garden?'

John Deitch moved his hand listlessly to indicate a piece of paper on the desk and then gazed once again from the window.

'I thought you would need it.'

Aaron picked it up. It was a short list. It contained just five names.

'The house was empty when the garden was disturbed on the first occasion. I was alone. My friend, Mr. Conlon,' he drawled the word slowly and smiled as if amused at some hidden irony, 'came to offer me support and was here on subsequent occasions. Miss Varley was here as usual. Mr. Jarrett was here for a pre-arranged business meeting.'

'I see, so Mr. Conlon, Leigh Conlon, was here throughout.' Aaron paused for a moment. 'He wasn't here on the most recent occasion though, was he, when the effigy appeared?'

Deitch shook his head. 'No, he wasn't here that night. I was alone.'

'I shall need to speak to him. Did any of your guests see the figures in the garden?'

Deitch looked casually at his watch.

'Emma Varley; she was in the tower room which looks out on the garden. She screamed rather dramatically I'm afraid, and woke us up. By the time I reached her Mr. Conlon was already there. On the second occasion Conlon was staying in that room. He saw the figure,

I believe. He called Jarrett who was in the next room but by the time he arrived it had gone.'

'Jarrett? Oh yes, Roger Jarrett. I see his name. He is…?'

'Jarrett is my solicitor. He was here to conclude some business dealings and stayed over. He had travelled up from the city.'

'I'll probably need to speak to Leigh Conlon, Emma Varley and Roger Jarrett.' Deitch nodded without emotion.

'It was you who called the local police, I believe,' Aaron continued.

'They inquired, they checked, they found nothing and they left. The CCTV footage wasn't particularly helpful, some figure in the dark I could not recognise. I was advised to wait and see if anything further occurred. Something further occurred and here we are.'

Aaron was struck again by the lethargy in his gestures and his voice. It was as though nothing that had happened or might happen was of any significance. He spoke like a man who was tired, so tired that he could feel no curiosity about what was happening, no engagement with the events. His dark eyes showed no interest. Deitch raised his hand and waved it gently to and fro and sighed. 'Here we are.'

'We've looked at the footage. Did anyone else see it?'

'Conlon,' Deitch said. 'I have no secrets from Conlon.' He laughed as if he had said something amusing.

'You've known each other long?'

Deitch frowned for a moment. 'Known each other? I don't suppose we've ever known each other. We travelled the same path for a while then we parted. But as you see our paths continue to cross.'

'And Emma Varley?'

'Yes, I shared the footage with Emma.'

'Have you known her long?'

'She is a more recent acquaintance than Leigh. Perhaps Emma and I do know each other, after a fashion. Our acquaintance dates back to just after to my arrival here. She is an artist. Her studio is just outside the village. Hers is the good taste you see around you. Emma assisted me with the purchase of all the furnishings that I required for my new home and to enhance my new status. I couldn't have managed without her. Now she stays here as my personal assistant and my friend. She has a house in the village but she also has an apartment here. It is helpful to me. I often work until late.'

For the first time Aaron heard a flicker of life in his tone and his words. They were like a tiny flame emerging momentarily from a dying ember.

'You are quite sure no-one else has seen the CCTV footage?'

'Wilkie saw it. If it was someone local, Wilkie would know. Jarrett left the next morning without seeing it. I saw no reason to involve him.' The tone of indifference had returned. 'I was about to write their addresses for you and their telephone numbers and emails.' He turned back to the desk again for a moment and wrote quickly on a piece of monogrammed note paper. 'You may contact them as you wish. Emma Varley is working in her studio today. She has a commission. She is a fine water colour painter, you know, very fine, but she also paints in oil and acrylic. She will return here tomorrow or perhaps the day after. Conlon is staying for a few nights in our Highland capital. He never stays anywhere long. Once, many years ago, he had a home in Portskail. He may still retain it as a permanent residence or a pied a terre, I don't know. We don't talk of such things. We don't communicate much between his visits. I prefer it that way.'

'It seems a strange relationship.'

Deitch shrugged. 'No stranger than many, I think. He emails or telephones if he is planning to visit. He arrives, stays a few days and departs.'

'That seems rather secretive,' Aaron commented.

'Indeed. Conlon keeps his secrets. He's like many businessmen in that respect. He's rarely to be found in the same place for more than a few weeks. Is there anything else you need of me?'

'You've had some time to reflect. Have you any further thoughts about the identity of the intruder in the garden or who may have been responsible for that piece of grotesque theatre outside?'

'I've not gone through life without making enemies but I hardly think they would return at this juncture to threaten me. Besides, as you say, it's all rather boringly theatrical. If someone wanted to hurt me I'm sure there would be more immediate ways to achieve that end.' He paused for a moment and then spoke quietly as if addressing himself. 'If I could return to the beginning of my life I would make different choices. But we must all suffer for our inability to make true amends for our misdemeanours, don't you think?'

He waved his arm again as if to dismiss both his enemies and any concern they might have aroused in him. He turned back to his desk and wrote some details on the piece of paper. When he finished he handed it to Aaron. Aaron noticed the finely manicured hands, the long fingers, the white cuffs protruding from beneath a grey jacket, the gold cufflinks.

'These are the details I possess. Mrs. Davidson is in her living quarters on the top floor. You will find her quite easily. Emma Varley is at her studio. Is there anything more you require?'

'Did the sheet of blue vellum writing paper mean anything to you?'

Deitch shook his head slowly. 'It's a common enough brand,' he said. 'Even Jarrett uses something like it for some of his legal work. It carries no significance for me. The word, of course, strikes deeply. 'Guilty'. We are all guilty to some degree, I suppose. I immediately considered my own past life and reflected on any harm I might have done. It was not a pleasant experience but it has passed now.'

He stretched out a hand to be shaken. Rosie grumbled deep in her throat. Sometimes an outstretched hand was a threat.

Chapter Four

Aaron made his way along the corridor towards the west tower. He found a narrow, stone staircase spiralling up to the top floor. Mrs. Davidson was in a small sitting room which overlooked the front of the house. She rose abruptly from the chair in which she had been seated and cast her magazine hurriedly on the table. She brushed her sleeves as if removing some dusty coating and held out a delicate hand to Aaron. Rosie wagged her tail briskly. Mrs. Davidson had a smell of food about her.

Aaron smiled. Mrs. Davidson was not at all what he expected. For some reason, probably related to childhood story books, he expected a cook housekeeper to be plump and rosy with strong arms and a ready supply of chins. Mrs. Davidson was more like a tiny bird. She did not walk across the room, she flitted. She nodded her head sharply and her eyes were bright when she looked at him. Now she held her hands clasped in front of her expectantly.

'I've been waiting,' she said. 'I don't usually have too much time during the day but Mr. Deitch told me to hold myself in readiness.

He said you would want to speak to me, interview me. It sounded very serious and complicated. I do hope I don't have to remember too much. My memory is not as good as it should be. See,' she said. She flitted to the table and picked up a small notebook. 'Oh dear, I seem to have lost my pen; how very frustrating!' She showed him the book. 'This is my memory nowadays. It was Emma Varley's idea. She said, 'Ruth Davidson, your memory needs a little support. You should write things down in a book.' So I do, you see, - when I can find a pen.'

'It looks like a very good idea,' Aaron smiled, 'It's certainly one which has been useful to my profession over the years.'

Mrs. Davidson looked at him uncertainly and broke into a light laugh, like bird song.

'Of course,' she said, 'how silly of me. Now, do sit down and tell me what you want to know.'

She perched on the edge of her armchair and Aaron took a more comfortable seat opposite her.

'Tell me how you came to find the effigy. Tell me exactly what you did and what you saw.'

'Oh dear, yes; oh dear indeed; now, let me find my book. I wrote it down, you see, as soon as I came back to my room. It was rather a shock, rather too much of a shock for someone of my age. Now, here it is.' She picked up a pair of spectacles from the table and perched them on her nose. 'She opened the notebook. 'It was ten minutes past six in the morning precisely. I know that because I had just listened to the news headlines on the radio before I went downstairs. I like to walk briskly down the drive for half an hour before I begin my work. It sets me up for the day. I always do it, no matter what the weather.'

'You live in the hall?' Aaron asked.

'Oh no, no, not at all, but when Mr. Deitch has guests or if there is some work that keeps me late I sometimes stay in the housekeeper's bedroom. It isn't at all often, perhaps once every two or three months. Andrew, my husband doesn't like it. He has to make his own tea, you see. Andrew is not a modern man, not at all modern. He can boil an egg but little more than that. But when Mr. Deitch asked me to help finish the kitchen accounts and to prepare for visitors this week I just had to tell him. 'Horace,' I said, 'you'll just have to make your own tea. Heat something up in the microwave, for goodness sake. Don't be so helpless.'

'Horace?' Aaron looked puzzled.

'Oh, I often call him Horace. He really is a Horace, you see, even though he is called Andrew. Now, let me return to my notebook. Ah yes, I opened the front door and took a nice, deep breath of fresh air and I turned towards the walled garden. Then I took a few steps across the lawn towards the drive. It was then that I saw it. It gave me quite a start. At first I thought it was a guy, like you have on bonfire night. I thought some local children had been playing a silly trick. It was only when I approached it that I saw the ghastly rope and the - well, you know - the knife wounds and blood and so on. It was really quite ghastly.'

She looked at her notebook. 'That was at 6.18 precisely.'

Aaron smiled. 'And it was then that you shouted out,' he suggested, 'and brought Mr. Deitch running down the stairs.'

'Oh no, not at all; I may look like the sort of person who would scream at the slightest thing but I assure you I am not. I haven't screamed since primary school when a ghastly boy called Billy McCrae put a live toad down the neck of my blouse. He's an electrician now and quite a respectable man but he was a horror as a child, a horror. To this day I find it difficult to turn my back on him. No, it was not the effigy that made me shout out. Nor was it the rope or the blood. It was something else entirely.' She shook her head emphatically.

'What was it?' Aaron asked.

'When I looked round I was sure, quite sure that I saw a dark figure slip away beneath the furthest trees where the shadows are deepest. It was a momentary glimpse, almost peripheral, but I am sure there was someone watching me. At first I imagined it must be Wilkie – Robert Wilkie, our gardener – but it was too early even for him. Silly as it may seem, I am also of the impression that he was quite dark complexioned although that may have been no more than the nature of the morning light. I was also quite sure he had been waiting for someone to come out of the hall and find the effigy where he had placed it.'

'You said 'he'. Are you sure it was a man?'

'Oh yes. It's surprising how much you can see in a few seconds, especially when you are sufficiently scared. It was a man, not an old man, I think; he was quite agile and he moved very quickly.'

'And he had dark skin or a dark complexion.'

'I think so.'

'Thank you, Mrs. Davidson. Do you think you could show me exactly where this figure was standing?'

Mrs. Davidson nodded, - a bird pecking seed.

'Just one other thing,' Aaron said. 'Have you told anyone else about this figure?'

'Only Mr. Deitch and Wilkie. Mr. Deitch told me to wait until I had spoken to you before I said any more. Of course I told poor Horace when I got home but that's all. Mr. Deitch went back indoors to wait for the police. Wilkie stayed with me.'

'Mr. Deitch didn't look at the effigy?'

'Only from the steps; he didn't want to - oh, dear, what was the phrase he used? He didn't want to contaminate the scene.'

Aaron frowned. 'Could you lead Rosie to the scene?'

'Oh yes, will she follow the scent do you think?'

'I doubt it, unless he had her ball in his pocket. But she would like to see it nonetheless.'

Mrs. Davidson's laugh was shrill and bright. 'Of course,' she said. 'Follow me, Rosie.'

She led them to the front of the house and out into the wide circling drive. They crossed it and traversed a close cropped lawn to reach the edge of the narrow band of trees which accompanied the drive for a short distance towards the road. They approached the sycamore from which the effigy had been hung.

Mrs. Davidson stopped. 'I was standing here,' she said. 'I didn't want to get any closer to it, not once I saw what was on it and beneath it. Well, you wouldn't, would you? It's not a pleasant sight to greet you in the morning before breakfast. Why do people do such things, do you think? Can they not be content with what they have? I said the same to Horace. 'Why can people not be happy with what they have?' I said, 'It was a beautiful morning. It was quiet and peaceful. It was a day when it was a pleasure to be alive. So why spoil it? Andrew thought they must be bitter or angry or just plain nasty.'

'Where was the figure who was watching you?' Aaron interrupted her gently.

'Oh yes, indeed, yes,' Mrs. Davidson laughed and clasped her hands together. 'Well, let me see. I was standing precisely here.' She moved two steps to her right. 'I saw him through there, beyond the birches, close to the fence enclosing the paddock. He was still for a moment and then moved to the right, into the tangle of trees. I lost sight of him almost immediately.

'Did you hear anything?'

Mrs. Davidson shook her head. 'I think he must have reached the end of the fence and then cut across the field to the road.'

'Unless he doubled back and followed the edge of the walled garden towards the shore,' Aaron suggested. 'Of course that would have been rather risky. He might have been seen from the house.' He looked round. 'I think I'll take a closer look,' he said. 'Thank you, Mrs. Davidson. I won't keep you any longer. I'm sure you have things to do.'

Mrs. Davidson shuffled away, her head turning to one side and nodding. A blackbird on the lawn mimicked her movements. She walked hesitantly for a moment and then more briskly towards the door. The blackbird flew, calling, into the walled garden.

Aaron walked through the trees and followed a wire fence. Beyond it three ponies moved unconcerned across the grass, pausing to crop the turf. One looked towards him and shook a soft mane.

Aaron stopped at the corner where the fence ended. He looked towards the road and then back towards the hall and the shore. Rosie sniffed the ground at his feet, her tail wagging, her head moving side to side as if in pursuit of a scent.

'What do you think, Rosie?' Aaron murmured. 'Which way did he go?'

As if in answer to his question or perhaps to a question of her own Rosie sniffed the air and turned towards the sea and the shore.

Chapter Five

Emma Varley returned to her living quarters on the top floor of Strathan Tower the following evening. Her commission was finished, her interview with Aaron had been concluded and her time was suddenly her own. She returned with a sensation of warmth and some pleasure. The apartment and the hall felt very much like home to her nowadays. She spent more of her evenings in those rooms than she ever did at her house in the village.

The lounge was a room which seemed designed to reflect the person who inhabited it. There was little furniture but each item seemed to have been selected to convey to a visitor the taste and judgement of the inhabitant. There was nothing ostentatious about Emma Varley or her room. Everything suggested an educated and refined judgement of what was most suited to her surroundings. Her choices were impeccable. Nor was the importance of comfort neglected. The room was warm and homely and was enhanced by the selections of ornaments and paintings and vases of fresh flowers which graced walls and surfaces in just the right number to enthral a visitor.

Emma Varley was growing gracefully older. She had never married. Opportunities for love had arisen during her early life but none had amounted to anything. Her tastes had been developed over fifty years of refined isolation. She still loved the colours and the textures that had enticed her in her youth and directed her choice of clothing, but now in shape and design they fitted perfectly to her age and nature. She had remained as slender as she was as a young woman and moved in a manner which suggested a restrained and regulated energy which lingered just below the surface. Emma Varley had decided views on many issues, especially with regard to the arts and to design, but she tempered that with a quietness of expression which rendered the firmness of her opinions a pleasure to hear.

John Deitch appreciated her delicacy and refinement. He trusted her judgement implicitly and was happy to allow her to manage the refurbishment and furnishing of his home. He felt inadequate to make such decisions himself but he knew when the outcome was a success. John Deitch at first appreciated the skills that Emma displayed; later he came to rely on them. Finally he found he disliked making any decision without consulting her.

He was with her now, lounging on a softly cushioned sofa and listening to her as she spoke in firm, familiar tones. He allowed the book he was reading to fall beside him.

'I liked that young policeman,' she said. 'He had a way of listening which made you feel he was interested not only in what you were saying but also in who was saying it. We spent as much time talking about my paintings and the village as we did about the events up here. Yet he missed nothing. He was particularly incisive.' She smiled and looked up. 'I liked him even more when he bought one of my watercolours. It was a good choice, one of my best. It was for his wife. She's called Andrea. They have been married for just over three years and they have a little boy called Jacob; he's one year old. You see how much I know of him. He is obviously very much in love.'

John looked at her and smiled. 'Does he still believe in such things, do you think?'

'Yes he does and so do I, so we'll have no more of your cynical talk, John, if you please.' She looked at him sternly above a pair of narrow silver rimmed glasses. Besides, you believe it too. You're just frightened to admit it. You've been led to believe that love, tenderness and caring are weaknesses and we know who's to blame for that.'

He laughed. 'Indeed, I was taught by a master. Conlon believes that such emotions are there to be exploited. I've spent so many years suppressing them in myself that I distrust them even when they appear in others.'

'Hush! Hush!' Emma Varley interrupted him. 'We've agreed that Conlon and the past are best left to lie. You have time ahead of you and can choose your own direction. I just wish we could rid ourselves of the presence of that ghastly man.'

'He has me on the end of a rope,' John said darkly. 'I can never escape him. All it requires is one pull on that rope and I would be brought down. He has me tied in to things from which I can never extricate myself. We were partners for all those years and I never realised he had built in such layers of self protection. If the edifice ever really crumbled it would be around me that it would fall. Of course I'm safe from any risk provided I behave as he expects. Only Conlon himself can really harm me and it's in his interests to keep things as they are.'

'You would be far better without him. You don't need him.'

John smiled. 'It's fifteen years since I broke up our partnership and yet I'm tied to him as completely as if we had never parted. Even this house is his. I merely lease it from him for my lifetime. I'm afraid I have to put up with his visits and the constant reminder of a past I would like to forget.'

Emma frowned. 'Sometimes I think you would be happier if the whole edifice came crumbling down. I think you've had quite enough of Leigh Conlon. However, if the moment ever comes, I think you should bring it down yourself rather than wait for him to do it.'

'Perhaps, perhaps, but in the meantime I shall continue to do what little I can to make amends and to prove myself a better person than I have been in the past.'

'Indeed you shall,' Emma Varley looked at him, 'and I shall be here at your shoulder to make sure you do and I shall speak to you as clearly as your conscience.'

John threw back his head and laughed and for a moment felt the weight of years fall from him. 'You are very good for me, Emma,' he said, 'but tell me about your interview with Aaron Marks.'

Emma Varley had explained to Aaron how she had clearly seen the figure in the garden and how she rather wished she hadn't. It was quite unnerving, she said, and for a moment it had quite shocked her. She was quite, quite convinced that he was looking directly at her. It was a foolish fancy, of course. He was merely looking in the direction of the house and the window. She cried out, a fact about which she was most apologetic.

'You have rooms on the top floor, I believe, but that night you stayed in the tower room. Why was that?'

'When Mr. Conlon comes to stay he chooses which room he stays in. That night, for some reason, he insisted that he would stay in my apartment. Mr. Conlon is not a reasonable man. He exerts his authority simply because he can. Perhaps he felt I needed reminding of his power; perhaps I expressed an opinion too strongly or disagreed with him over some minor point. It would take nothing more than that for him to act in such a manner.'

'I am surprised that Mr. Deitch didn't insist you retain your rooms.'

'It was a small sacrifice for me to make to ensure Mr. Conlon was happy with his stay. There was no point in causing trouble for Mr. Deitch. Besides, I quite like the tower room. It's very quiet and on a clear night the view of stars over the garden is particularly splendid. There was a partial moon that night too.'

'Did you recognise the figure in the garden? Was there anything even vaguely familiar about him?'

'No,' she told him. She thought for a moment. 'No, I'm afraid I didn't. He didn't seem concerned about being seen, though. In fact I think he wanted to be seen. He looked up towards the tower. Perhaps he was looking directly at my window, I don't know. I couldn't see anything of his features because of the hood but when I reconsider the scene it occurs to me that he was waiting for a light to appear in the window before he turned – unless the light merely caught his attention.'

'Do you think he knew that it was you in the room?'

'Was the performance for my benefit, do you mean? Oh no, not at all. We had planned to give the room to Mr. Conlon. It was only later that we made changes to accommodate his wishes.'

'So the figure would have been expecting Mr. Conlon to see him rather than you.'

Emma nodded. 'Yes, I suppose so. In which case, he was successful because it was Mr. Conlon who arrived promptly at my door when I shouted out so foolishly. He looked out of the window. A moment later the figure moved slowly backwards and was lost in the shadows.'

'How did Mr. Conlon react?'

'He continued to stare for a few moments. He didn't move from the window. Then John, Mr. Deitch, arrived and they ran down the stairs and out into the garden. I saw them from the window. Of course, they found nothing.'

'I believe you watched the CCTV footage?'

Emma nodded. 'Yes, I saw both recordings. It was something of a surprise. Everything – every movement, even the way the head moved and the hood fell over the face, - everything was the same; but…'

She paused.

'But...' Aaron prompted.

'Well, the second figure seemed noticeably shorter than the first. I'm almost certain it wasn't the same person.'

Aaron asked her about the small graves dug in the garden but there was little she could tell him about them. Nor had she been present at the hall when the effigy was strung up from the tree. She had no idea who might have done such a thing.

'Did you see the items that were buried in the garden?'

She nodded.

'Were you aware of any significance associated with them?'

She wasn't. Aaron Marks had repeated the list quietly under his breath, slowly, as if thinking aloud. 'A lock of hair, a broken wedding ring, a locket with entwined letters.'

'Did he ask you about anything else?' John sat forward on the sofa. He looked troubled. His eyes moved from Emma to the ground, to the table, to the window and back again.

'We speculated for some time about the significance of the items. They were all very personal, you see, and suggestive of love and relationships – the ring, the locket, the hair. He wondered if the person who dug the graves had experienced a loss which was somehow related to the hall or to its residents. Perhaps he had lost his wife or child. There was nothing I could tell him.'

John looked suddenly pale and old. He turned away.

'Did he ask anything else?' he enquired as if from a distance.

Emma shook her head. She didn't confess that they spent some time talking about John Deitch himself or that she corrected some of the misapprehensions Aaron had acquired about her employer and friend.

'At heart Mr. Deitch is a very kindly man, you know,' she said. 'In his younger days he didn't always act in accordance with his true nature but he's had time to reflect and to repent. He has changed considerably and he has done a great deal of good. I believe we should give people a second chance don't you, inspector?' she asked.

Aaron smiled. He didn't answer. He'd seen too many victims to be able to make such a judgement. Forgiveness was not in his gift; it was for those who had suffered.

'As he was about to leave,' Emma said, 'he asked me about the local community. He wanted to know how well I knew the previous owners of the Tower. Of course I could tell him very little about their personal circumstances. Mrs. Waterson isn't someone who confides in people outside the family. I explained that our relationship had been largely professional and that over the years I had helped with some small purchases for the hall. I told him about the watercolour she commissioned for the entrance hall which, I believe, now graces the entrance hall of the White House.'

'And then?' John asked. 'He bought a painting and left?'

'Yes. I like customers who actually buy things.'

They were silent for a moment.

'Do you think our midnight visitors intended that they should be seen by Conlon?' John asked quietly.

Emma nodded. 'It would seem reasonable. He was there on both occasions. The room was intended for him. Of course we can't rule out the possibility that it was mere coincidence.'

'If that were the case we would need to assume that the garden visitors were actually aware that he was visiting and that he would be in that particular room.'

'That' Emma murmured, 'would imply that someone in the house complicit. I would rather not believe that.'

John smiled wearily. He leaned back and yawned. 'Unfortunately Leigh wasn't here on the night that our effigy appeared. That knocks a rather large, gaping hole into our theorising, don't you think?'

'Indeed.' Emma was quiet for a moment. 'I'm glad. I don't want to be suspicious of people.'

John shook his head. He stood up and walked listlessly towards a small shelf of CD's. He chose one and inserted it into the player. Bach emerged quietly and gradually filled the room. John sat back down and closed his eyes.

'I think we shall wait,' he sighed. 'I would be very surprised if that young detective hasn't come to exactly the same conclusions. I would also be surprised if he doesn't make a few enquiries into the background of our esteemed friend and, alas, into my own. I expect he will speak again to everyone who works here, including you, and that he will come to a negative conclusion as to any complicity. I find it difficult to believe that Ruth or Wilkie would act in such a way. The casual staff and the cleaners, of course, are a different matter. I think our detective will discover whatever there is to be discovered. He may uncover too much.' He smiled at her.

'Then isn't it time to do what you have spoken of so many times? You should speak to him. You will never be at peace until you do, you know that.'

John slowly rose to his feet and walked across the room and then back again.

'I know,' he said, 'I know what you say is true but I'm unable to do that. I'm far too deeply implicated in a whole series of matters of which I was largely unaware. I would be risking everything.'

'This tower of cards will come tumbling down one day, whether you like it or not. Perhaps it would be better to be the one who removes the first card.'

'Perhaps, perhaps, but I shall wait a little while yet. Leigh Conlon will over reach himself one day. I must await my opportunity. I have some small amount of evidence that would worry him if he knew about it. Perhaps these strange events will drive him to some precipitous action. Who knows? I shall wait and I shall watch.'

'I don't want to see you get hurt,' Emma sighed softly.

'And I do not wish to distress my only friend. But now, I must go. It is time you were left in peace and I'm tired, very tired.'

He leaned forward and kissed her gently on the cheek.

'Good night, my dear,' he said.

Chapter Six

Leigh Conlon was not a man to appreciate menacing figures in gardens at the dead of night. He didn't like mysteries either. He liked to understand what he saw because what he saw and understood he could control. Leigh Conlon liked to be in control. Whatever he could control he could manipulate – that was Leigh Conlon's view of the world and he used it to good effect. In the early days he had suffered some momentary pangs of something that resembled a primitive conscience but they never achieved maturity and Conlon quickly mastered the dark art which vanquished such temporary inconveniences. He learned, through habit and repetition, to eliminate all feelings of compassion or empathy in his dealings with others. It was business, he told himself, and in business one had to be single minded, one had to be ruthless.

'Collateral damage is inevitable,' he said to himself. He took primary damage for granted. You had to hurt people, damage people, ruin people, if you were to succeed. It was best not to think about them. That was another important lesson learned early.

Sometimes, he had to admit, he rather enjoyed the process as much as the outcome. There was something exhilarating about destroying someone. It was the final victory, the moment of supreme power. Sometimes, later in his career, when he was bored and listless, he went out of his way to ruin someone. It relieved the tedium that came with increasing wealth. He would lay plans, plot, conspire, tempt, control and eventually destroy. Then he would celebrate another victory, another demonstration of his supreme skill.

It was like that, years ago, with the bearded idealist, Harmison, the greedy, gullible Barden and the desperate Gill. It was also like that with Major Richard Waterson. The Watersons were just the sort of people Conlon detested, modest yet confident, reserved yet self assured. They were comfortable with themselves. They had wealth but they didn't flaunt it; they had status but they didn't exploit it; they had influence but they didn't abuse it. They were liked; they were respected. The first time Conlon met Major Waterson he despised him. It was as if the few words that Waterson had spoken had been a gauntlet thrown into his face. Major Waterson was everything that he, Conlon, could never be.

Waterson had been a formidable opponent, knowledgeable, hard working, incisive, a man who would not be easily fooled or easily tempted. Conlon played a long game but he was confident of ultimate victory. Major Waterson had a weakness. His was a generous nature; he trusted people and he was trusted by them. He had integrity and he was respectable. Conlon had no such limitations.

Major Waterson was brought to the very precipice. Ruin lay ahead. His health, previously robust, suffered and he died of a sudden and very violent stroke. Conlon felt cheated by his death. Even worse, the major had secretly invested a sufficient sum for his family to retain the estate and to continue their lives, albeit in rather reduced circumstances.

Conlon couldn't accept defeat. He turned his attention to the estate, to Mrs. Waterson and to her son, Marcus, who was then in his mid twenties. Mrs. Waterson proved to be a robust barrier to all his machinations. She had heard enough to distrust the name of Leigh Conlon. There was no opportunity to practise his wiles with her. He turned instead to her son. Conlon's artificial charm, his generosity and his exciting social connections seduced the young man into dealings which left Conlon wealthy and Marcus in considerable trouble. Only by selling Strathan Tower and entering into sordid negotiations with Leigh Conlon could Mrs. Waterson clear the debts and save her son

Marcus could not face the prospect of remaining at home and took up a position overseas in a firm run by an old university friend. He was affable and generous like his father but he was burdened by the same fierce pride. He was adamant that he would not return until he could repay every penny he had lost.

However, the immediate outcome was that Leigh Conlon became the owner of Strathan Tower. He immediately offered the lease on very generous terms to his one time partner, John Deitch, who was looking for somewhere to live where he could use his wealth to good effect. It was a solution that suited them both. Conlon liked to retain a hold on people. Deitch may have retired from their business partnership many years before but he could not be allowed to fly free. His wings had to be carefully clipped. A debt like this could be useful.

It was in a hotel lounge in the regional capital that Aaron met him just a few days after the events at the hall. Conlon was suspicious and tight lipped; he said no more than he had to and weighed each word as if there were a price attached to it.

'Can you describe the events of that evening?'

'I heard Emma Varley cry out. It must have been about one o'clock in the morning.'

'Where exactly were you when you heard her shout?'

My apartment was on the top floor. I was walking up the stairs. I'd just poured a brandy and was taking it to my room.'

Aaron waited but Conlon seemed disinclined to continue. Aaron waited. Eventually, with a sarcastic smile, Conlon spoke again.

'By the time I reached Emma Varley she had regained some composure and was standing by the window. The lights were off. The only light was from the moon just above the trees. She pointed down into the walled garden.'

Once more he paused. He was playing games. The same unpleasant smile hovered around his lips.

'Please – do continue.'

'She told me there was a man in the garden staring up towards the window. It was rather ghostly, she said. It gave her quite a start. 'Is he still there?' I enquired. I found it ironic that any man worthy of the name would be peering at Miss Varley in the dead of night.

'She turned and pointed and I leaned towards the window and looked. There was the figure just as she had described. As I watched, he turned slowly away and melted into the darkest parts of the garden. He was lost in the depths of dark foliage. It was a man, most certainly a man. There's little more to say. It must have shocked Emma Varley to imagine a man would stare at her bedroom window. Perhaps she was flattered.'

His laugh was cold and malicious.

'The corridor light was switched on and John Deitch came into the room. He was very pale, I recall. He must have feared for her safety. He has taken an incomprehensible liking to Emma, you know. We walked down to the garden together. We searched but there was nothing to be seen, not so much as a footprint, nothing. We spent twenty minutes walking all the paths but whoever it was had most certainly gone, probably out of the small doorway near the greenhouses.'

'Had you seen the figure before?'

'No.'

'Was there anything familiar about him?'

'No.'

'What about the second night?'

Conlon shrugged and feigned a disinterested yawn. 'I imagined it was the same person. The night was darker and the moon was smaller. It was hard to imagine more than one person wandering about a walled garden at night.' He laughed slowly and without mirth.

'Can you think of anyone who might feel they had some reason to create such a melodramatic spectacle?'

'No.'

'Do you think it was directed at you?'

Conlon looked at him sharply. 'No-one would dare. I thought it was probably nothing more than a tramp looking for somewhere sheltered to sleep or someone drunk from the village, someone who had taken a dislike to the owner.'

'Did the effigy suggest anything to you?'

'No, I wasn't there so I gave it little thought.'

'What about the objects buried in the garden?'

'I have no thoughts on the matter and no opinion. It was rather odd, rather tasteless, but I could say nothing else.' He shrugged again and turned away, busying himself folding his newspapers. 'It was all rather melodramatic, rather tedious and not worth thinking about.' He turned back to Aaron; his eyes were blank and cold despite his smile. It was a smile that offered no warmth and no hint of a thaw.

Aaron shook hands and left.

Chapter Seven

When he reached the pavement outside, Aaron wiped his hand on his coat. There was a slimy, slippery quality about Leigh Conlon that he could not quite define. He was repelled by it. There was something horribly cold behind that façade, something closed and shuttered behind the false smiles and the phoney bonhomie. Everything about him from the carefully styled hair to the smart suit and expensive shoes to the very words he used and the manner in which he used them made him think of oil.

Rosie was lying asleep on the back seat of the car. She lifted her head and yawned and turned heavily round to nuzzle her head in his hands.

'He was lying to me, Rosie, and he was playing silly games. That man was hiding something.' He stroked her head gently and her eyes narrowed and then closed. She turned round and lay down. 'I don't trust him.' He started the engine. 'I wonder what the real connection is between Conlon and Deitch. Let's hope Jack has some news for us.'

He sat for a moment, thinking. He watched a few cars pass. 'I think he was anxious. I don't know why I think so, Rosie, but there was something in his manner, something just beneath his oily surface that wasn't comfortable. I felt as if I was poking a stick in a wasp's nest.'

In the absence of anything more substantial to support this assertion Rosie opted to make no contribution. Her eyes remained closed; she snored gently, rolled on her side and stretched her legs. She dreamt of beaches, of seaweed smells and chasing a ball.

The road to Portskail led over bleak and empty moorland blighted by periodic invasions of forestry, their barren uniformity marking a strange contrast with the subtle changes of shape and hue presented by grass and heather moor. For long periods he was accompanied by a fresh rolling river throwing exuberant white waves down gentle, rocky slopes. When he reached a long narrow loch with an ugly damn he pulled up. It was time for Rosie to get a little exercise along the sand and shingle shore.

It was another hour before the road wound up a long hill through broadleaved trees and then dropped steeply towards the ferry port of Portskail which lay below him like a closely guarded secret. He turned along the shore and passed the hotels and shops opposite which a number of tourists were looking out towards the fishing boats in the bay and the rocky mountain ridges and sharp, grey peaks beyond. The ferry was just loading. In half an hour it would sail out towards the open sea beyond the loch, a picturesque addition to an already beautiful scene. Cameras would click; another memory among thousands of others.

Jack was in the back office when he arrived. Aaron had barely flung his coat over the chair back before he emerged. His eyes were sharp and every movement conveyed restless energy. Jack was on a scent. You could always tell.

'Our Mr. Deitch would be a worthy quarry if I were of a hunting disposition,' he said, 'and Leigh Conlon would be even better. Yet neither of them has as much as a parking ticket against their names. They are spotlessly clean.'

'Then why would we want to go hunting?'

'Shadows, my boy, shadows; there are so many shadows around them - shadows of corrupt business dealings, scams, fraud, extortion, blackmail. There's nothing that implicates either of them directly, of course, but the shadows, yes, the shadows of the crimes are all over them. I can hear echoes too –...And if you listen closely – did you hear that?' He cupped his hand theatrically round his ear, 'You can still hear the cries of the people they harmed.'

'Am I to turn out my hunting gear?'

'Oh yes, Aaron, yes indeed. Let's dig a little, apply a little pressure here and there, and see what crawls into the daylight.'

Chapter Eight

Sleep did not come easily to John Deitch after the disturbances in the garden and grounds. Despite his apparent indifference, the events of the previous weeks had concerned him deeply. During the daytime he could maintain an aspect of indifference and discard any worrying thoughts as he performed his small number of daily tasks. When he walked down to the shore, which he did most days, his mind was absorbed by the gulls and waders and the breaking waves, the smell of seaweed and the slippery rocks. Only occasionally did unwelcomed thoughts intrude. On those occasions his stomach would lurch uncomfortably.

'Do you have any enemies?' the detective had asked him.

He shook his head. 'In business you always make enemies but none who would do something like this.'

He smiled grimly now. It was the wrong question. 'Have you ever acted towards someone in a way that might provoke such hatred?' That would have been a much harder question to ignore. It was a question which haunted him. The list was not a short one. His had been a long and treacherous road to wealth and respectability. Faces from the past rose before him with appalling clarity. People he had given little thought to for years now imposed themselves upon his mind, - Harmison, Barden, Gill. Things he had done which he had buried deeply in the darkest depths suddenly returned. He found himself slipping back to those evil days at the beginning when he first met Leigh Conlon and their ghastly partnership began.

'Will I never be free of it? If I could only go back and change the things I've done – Harmison, Barden, Gill.'

It was much worse at night. Often now he would wake, perspiring heavily, unable to breathe, desperate to break out of the lonely darkness around him. He fumbled with his bedside lamp. He needed to fill the room with brightness, no matter how artificial. He had to drive away the shadows before he saw again what had once been his future racing towards him at a terrible speed, before he saw again the terrible consequences of the choices he had made, before he watched again, in awful clarity, as he performed those irreversible actions he performed in that small, breathless, urgent moment he once called the present.

At the time those choices seemed so unimportant, so harmless. Time would wash away their consequences. He would be able to do good things when he was wealthy to atone for the few misdeeds that occurred here and now in the present. He saw those opportunities flying towards him from the brightness of a selfless future.

He was older now and wiser. He knew now that as the future roared towards him and drove past it ceased to maintain its speed. When he looked behind him into the past, the consequences of his actions had not receded. They lay immediately behind him, they loomed over him. They formed a huge bulging, lugubrious, opaque, seething mass. They trailed tentacles of consequences past him and wrapped themselves round all that was to come. They would only fade when he died and when those he had hurt also passed away. His good deeds, which he had hoped would dissipate and destroy this hideous mass, made little impression.

'I've tried to be a better man,' he murmured as he rocked to and fro on the side of his bed, 'I want to put things right but I can't. My future is contaminated by my past. I can't escape it.'

He thought of Harmison, Barden and Gill. He wanted to see them, to apologise, to make some recompense but he feared the consequences, he feared the critical eyes, the accusing fingers and the looks of disgust. And he feared Leigh Conlon. Most of all he feared Leigh Conlon. He shook his head; it was impossible. He could not face the awful reality of what had happened to those he had betrayed.

No, sleep did not come easily to John Deitch.

One night, just a week after the appearance of the effigy and having slipped into an unusually deep sleep, he awoke suddenly. He was immediately aware of the moonlight softly illuminating his room and dispersing some of the shadows and the darkness.

He leaned down to reach a small bedside table where he kept a jug of water. He poured a glass and took a sip. As he did so, he raised his eyes and glanced around the room. He emitted a stifled cry and drew back quickly. He was not alone in the room. In the corner, adjacent to the window and staring diagonally across towards the opposite corner, a dark figure was standing. He neither moved nor blinked. His hair was dark and combed back, his jacket was funereally black. His arms lay limp at his sides. He was wrinkled and old.

All this John Deitch saw in the two or three seconds which passed before he drew himself beneath the covers and lay motionless, frozen still, unable to move, not daring to make a sound. Even his shallow breathing seemed horribly loud. He waited, expecting at any moment the hand of a ghostly killer would grasp the duvet and slowly pull it back. His heart pounded uncontrollably.

It was the eyes and the aged pallor of the face that caused him the most terror. The eyes did not blink; they did not flinch. They just stared. Even in the pale moonlight Deitch was sure they were of an icy, dead grey, incongruously and deeply set in that deathly face.

Moments passed. Deitch slowly calmed himself. There was no-one there he told himself over and over. It was a dream, an illusion, nothing more. How could there be anyone in his room at that time of the morning? The house was securely locked; the alarm was on. It was impossible, absolutely impossible for anyone to have entered the house, climbed the stone steps, walked along the corridor and ascended the second flight of steps and entered his room without disturbing the alarms. It was a trick of the moonlight, a momentary illusion, a flight of fancy merging from an incomplete dream. He need only look. The figure would be gone.

Slowly he raised the corner of the duvet. Even more slowly he eased himself up. He turned his head slowly until he could glimpse the room beyond. The moon had passed behind a cloud now and the room seemed darker. He breathed a soft sigh of relief. There was nothing to see; it was a dream, a ghastly dream.

He reached a trembling hand for the glass and took another sip. Beads of sweat formed on his forehead. He pressed the cold glass against his brow. At that moment the moon emerged from its cloud cover and a wisp of pale light entered the room through a crack in the curtain. And there it was again, a cold grey, upright figure standing in the corner of the room. He had turned very slightly and he was staring now, not across the room towards the far corner, but directly at him, John Deitch. For a moment, those cold grey eyes met his and penetrated him like cold, ruthless, accusatory blades. Then clouds covered the moon and he was there no more. He receded into the darkness and vanished like the words in a closed book.

Deitch wanted to shout, to call out for help; but there was no-one in the house. Mrs. Davidson had returned to her own home in the village and he had no guests. Emma Varley was in her house in the village and wouldn't return until the next day. There was no-one to hear him. He lay still and he did not move until the first light of morning gradually lessened the gloom then he slowly sat up and waited. Only when he knew that the sunlight had dispersed the shadows in the room did he cautiously ease back the curtain.

There was nothing to be seen. The room was unchanged. It was just as it had been when he retired the evening before. He slowly swung his legs over the side of the bed and stood up. His legs felt weak and his whole body trembled. He flung the window curtains back and looked out over his estate. Everything was as it should be. The sun was flickering through the trees and its shadows drew familiar, strange patterns on the walls. He dressed and made his way downstairs.

'A dream,' he muttered, 'it must have been a dream, a waking dream or a nightmare drawn by my half conscious mind. I've been thinking too much about the past, that's what it is.'

He looked at his watch. It was already eight o'clock. Mrs. Davidson would be in the kitchen. She began work at seven thirty. By now she would be preparing breakfast. Not for the first time Deitch considered how much better it would be if he had someone resident in the hall. Emma Varley spent much of her time there but not enough. Mrs. Davidson preferred to go home when she could and he could hardly replace her. She had been there for years and she was good at her work and discreet.

He felt the need for human company at that moment more than he had felt it for years. He headed directly to the east wing where the newly refurbished kitchen was installed. He could hear the radio and he could hear Mrs. Davidson moving about. There was something warm and familiar about it. He pushed the door open and walked in.

Mrs. Davidson was not alone. Wilkie had just arrived and had taken up a customary chair in the corner. A mug of tea steamed in one hand and a slice of toast in the other. He stood up as Deitch entered.

'Good morning, Mr. Deitch.'

Mrs. Davidson was standing by a long, oak table. She was setting out plates and cups, some on a tray which was obviously destined for Mr. Deitch in the breakfast room and others for herself and Wilkie.

She flitted to the stove and checked eggs and bacon and then the toaster.

'I'm a little behind hand this morning, Mr. Deitch, I'm so sorry; and here are you coming down to collect your own breakfast and you find Wilkie sitting in the corner and we're gossiping away as if time is of no matter. Breakfast will be with you shortly sir, very shortly; oh dear!'

Deitch shook his head impatiently.

'It's of no consequence, Mrs. Davidson. I didn't come down here to hurry you along. I merely...I was just...I wondered if the newspapers had arrived yet. There are some prices I wish to check.'

Wilkie looked at him curiously. Emma Varley collected the newspapers at the shop in the village if she was not staying in the hall. She always placed them on the small, deal table which lay within the entrance hall. Otherwise they were delivered from the shop in a small, white van which arrived a little later.

'They don't usually arrive before nine, Mr Deitch, but Wilkie can check for you, if you would like him to.'

'No matter, no matter; but I think I shall join you for a few minutes if you have no objection. Could you pour me a cup of tea, Mrs. Davidson? And perhaps, since I am already here, I shall have my breakfast in your company this morning. It smells delicious.'

Mrs. Davidson glanced nervously towards Wilkie. John Deitch pulled up a chair beside the long table. He drummed his fingers on the smooth, wooden surface and seemed preoccupied. Wilkie stood up.

'It's time I got to work,' he said, brushing a few lingering crumbs from his jaw and wiping away the remnants of his tea. He looked disconsolately at the eggs and bacon frying on the hob.

'Have you been in the walled garden yet this morning?' Deitch asked.

'Yes, Mr Deitch, I generally walk through that way in the morning and unlock the greenhouses and sheds. I usually make a start on a task or two and check the grounds. Then I head over here. Mrs. Davidson is kind enough to make me a slice or two of toast for breakfast.'

'Wilkie is a typical bachelor, Mr. Deitch.' Mrs. Davidson was pleased to have something to say, some contribution to make to a conversation which, because it was unexpected, was awkward and clumsy. 'He can make a breakfast for himself well enough but he prefers to have it made. And I enjoy making it for him. He is very good to me and Mr. Davidson, you know, very kind. Mr. Davidson's arthritis prevents him from doing some of the heavier work in our own little garden and Wilkie often comes by to help. I don't know what we would do without him. I often say to Mr. Davidson, 'Horace, I don't know what we would do without him. You can't manage the garden any more. Wilkie is a good friend to us.'

Deitch tried to smile. It was a weak flickering effort which died in its infancy. 'You must stay and have your breakfast, Wilkie,' he said. 'There were no disturbances in the garden I take it, nothing out of the ordinary?' There was a tremor in his voice which did not pass unnoticed. Again Mrs. Davidson and Wilkie exchanged glances.

Wilkie shook his head. 'Nothing, Mr. Deitch.'

'You checked the grounds?'

'I walked round the paths and the drive. There was nothing out of the ordinary. Everything was quiet.'

'Good, good. On second thoughts, Mrs. Davidson, I shall take my tray and go to the breakfast room. It's pleasant to eat breakfast whilst looking out over the shore. The weather seems set fine today. I may go for a walk later. Tell Emma Varley to come straight up when she arrives. I have some matters I need to attend to. I think we shall invite some guests for the weekend. Some company would be pleasant, I think. Yes, some company.'

'Shall I carry the tray for you, Mr. Deitch?' Wilkie asked.

'Oh, indeed no, I shall take it myself, Wilkie. Thank you, Mrs. Davidson, thank you. Good morning, Wilkie.'

He took the tray and backed awkwardly through the door.

'Well, what do you make of that?' Mrs. Davison turned to Wilkie with a bewildered look.

'Fear,' said Wilkie, 'He's frightened of something. That man knows more about these happenings than he's ready to admit.'

'Oh, I do hope it's all over now. I do so dislike such unpleasantness. It's not what we're used to in a quiet little backwater like this. I hope that horrid Mr Conlon isn't one of the guests. That man makes my flesh creep.'

Wilkie frowned. 'That Mr Conlon has a lot to answer for,' he said, 'and answer he will, one day.'

In the breakfast room, John Deitch sat and stared across his uneaten meal at a point on the wall. He saw nothing; he heard nothing. He was pre-occupied with something which he worked round and round in his head like a stubborn morsel of food in his mouth. Eventually he became aware of the room and the cold food and the shadow that had passed across the room as the sun slipped nervously behind a cloud.

He turned abruptly and walked into the study where he picked up a phone.

'Jarrett,' he snapped, 'It's John Deitch. There's something I need you to do for me. I want you to find an address...Harmison – I want to know where I can find Harmison.'

Chapter Nine

If you emerge from the drive of Strathan Tower and turn to the left, away from the village and towards the main road to the north, you very soon pass a small, well hidden parking place with a number of picnic benches and tables. It is surrounded by deciduous trees, silver birch, rowan and alder between which the benches are set. A number of marked walks radiate from it passing through an area of forestry and along the banks of a river, a popular haunt of fishermen in the season. There are benches set here and there along the bank where, when the sun shines, the occasional walker rests and enjoys the views over the languid water and across the heather moor towards distant hills and mountains.

It is a picturesque spot, frequented more by local people than by the small number of tourists who venture this far from the main road. When the spring and summer flowers emerge it carries with it a feeling of calm and peace. It feels as if it belongs to a different time.

This was not a feeling lost on the man, that morning, who was standing beside a small, pale blue sports' car, half hidden by trees in a quiet corner corner furthest from the road. He paused for a moment beside the open boot and looked around. He was in his early thirties and casually dressed. His face and arms carried the sort of tan acquired by sustained exposure to a warm climate and his build suggested a man familiar with the rigours of regular and sustained exercise. As he paused he seemed to reflect on the scene around him and a shadow slipped across his eyes. He shrugged it away and checked the boot. It was time to leave.

He slammed it shut and climbed into the front seat. He was about to start the car when he paused. He reached in his shirt pocket and withdrew a phone.

'It's me. Yes, yes, I'm fine...Stop worrying. It all went pretty much as I hoped. I gave our Mr. Deitch something to think about.'

The person he was speaking to went on at some length. Eventually the man grew impatient.

'Yes, yes,' he said, 'I have no more desire for our little scheme to be exposed than you have...Yes, I know...It was my last throw in this particular field...Yes, yes. We'll speak in a few days but don't do anything foolish before I see you...' His voice grew momentarily angry. 'It's too late now for you to back out. Besides, you have as much reason as I have for seeing this business through...and it was you who sought me out, remember. It was you who begged me to help you get revenge on these men....We've both seen people suffer as a result of them...These actions are little more than we agreed...' His tone grew softer and more persuasive. He listened patiently for a moment but could not hide his exasperation for long. After a moment he interrupted his colleague. 'Just concentrate on your role in this. You know what you have to do. Are you in Strathan? Yes? Good. Just do as I asked....' His voice grew peremptory. 'I'll have to go before someone arrives to take their dog for a walk. As you'll appreciate, I don't want to be seen. That would be in neither of our interests....Yes, I will. For God's sake, stop worrying, I'm in the clear... Just do as we agreed. Goodbye.'

He closed the phone with evident irritation and muttered some unflattering words as he started the engine. The car slid effortlessly out onto the road and sped away.

Chapter Ten

Not long after, Leigh Conlon became strangely aware that his movements were being monitored. At first it was nothing more than the regular appearance of a small, pale blue sports' car in his rear view mirror. It was never sufficiently close for him to see the driver nor was it there for long enough for him to be certain that it was there by design rather than chance. He dismissed it as a matter of coincidence.

Some days later as he walked from the hotel he felt sure he was being watched. He caught a half glimpse of a figure which seemed to re-appear at different point on his walk to the town centre. He was sure it was the same person and yet he could add no detail to the vague impression he had formed.

Then one evening he returned to his hotel quite late. He had visited a small restaurant where, once again, he felt strangely conscious of eyes watching him. He looked round at the other diners but there was nothing to cause him alarm. It was just the usual gathering of couples and families. He concluded his meal and was pleased to find himself back within the security of his hotel room. Even there, however, he could not shift the feeling of insecurity that had been troubling him for a number of days.

He walked over to the window and eased the curtain back. He looked out into the darkening street. He glanced uneasily towards the traffic lights where the shopping centre began. Street lights illuminated the pavements. A solitary car accelerated quietly away. He saw its headlights brighten the road and watched as it passed below him. He drew back from the window sharply. The driver's head was most markedly glancing up towards him; and he was driving a small, pale blue sports' car.

Conlon checked out the next morning. It was time to move on. He moved to another hotel in a small seaside town just along the coast. After a few days he had almost persuaded himself that all of this was a figment of an overactive imagination. Unfortunately he was acutely aware that he had never been noted for the quality of his imagination and that this explanation was less than reasonable. He remained troubled and irritable. He found himself constantly pondering who might be responsible. He even made a list. It was not a short one. When he started to feel the same eerie sensation, as if every corner, every doorway and every window might be hiding an accusatory pair of eyes, he decided it was time for more radical action.

Conlon owned a detached property on a secluded estate on the edge of Portskail. It was his first substantial purchase, acquired when he was still in his twenties, and at a price he could scarcely afford to pay. He rarely visited it now, spending most of his life flitting from one hotel to another or renting apartments in different cities, but he could never bring himself to sell his first property. It held an uncharacteristic sentimental attachment for him associated with memories of those early days when he was still making his way in shady corners the business world. It was a quiet house, surrounded by trees and lawns, which he used as an occasional retreat and, most importantly, it was known to very few people. He would retire there now for a few weeks. It would give him time to think.

Perhaps he would then return to visit Deitch at Strathan Tower. Deitch sometimes needed to be reminded that he was always there, watching.

The following day, after a lengthy journey, he finally reached Portskail and drew up outside the door. He looked around with some annoyance. The garden was overgrown in places and the lawn was in need of a cut.

'I'll need to speak to the gardener,' he muttered. 'He's been letting things go.'

For a moment his thoughts turned to Strathan and to Robert Wilkie.

He picked up the usual pile of circulars from behind the door and threw them on the kitchen table before visiting the different rooms and pulling back the curtains. He then returned to the kitchen and switched on the central heating. He sat back and thumbed through the pile of letters which had accumulated since his last visit. He cast the majority of them aside to be disposed of later.

There was, however, one neatly addressed envelope that caught his attention. It was written by hand in a small, tidy script. The postmark was local and it had been posted only the day before. The envelope was pale blue. He opened it curiously and removed a single sheet of blue writing paper. It was only then that is heart began to beat faster, his pulse to race and his brow to sweat. He opened the sheet which had a single fold across the centre and laid it out before him. There were several lines of the same neat script. As he read it his body tensed, his eyes shone and his hands clasped the sheet tightly.

The letter was unsigned. It gave no indication of the sender. However, the writer was confident that the reader would not wish the information it contained to be made public. The handwriting showed that. He (or she) was flaunting a clue to his identity. Conlon read and re-read the missive until he could have recited it by heart. Before he slept that night he checked the windows and the doors. He slept with a hammer beneath his bed. Whenever he stirred, disturbed perhaps by the breeze rattling branches against the window, he reached beneath the bed to feel its reassuring presence. He listened as cars changed gear to ascend the road some distance beyond the house to ensure they passed on towards the town. And through every half waking moment his mind scanned backwards through his history to recall the faces of those who might have been the writer of the letter. For the first time in many years Leigh Conlon saw his career as it was viewed by his victims.

The next morning, over breakfast, he wrote down a shorter list of names. There were five. These were people who had paid the harshest penalties for their association with Conlon and Deitch. At the top of the list was the name of John Deitch himself.

Conlon stared at the list and after a few moments he took a pen and scored out the first name.

That left four – Harmison, Barden, Gill and Waterson. He realised there was little more he could do at present and he was sufficiently sure of himself to feel that a few elementary precautions would ensure his safety. He had never feared these people before; there was no reason to fear them now. He would always be stronger than them.

Over the next three days, although his mind reverted to the letter occasionally, it gradually drifted from his mind. There was little there, he now thought, that could cause him alarm. The menacing tone of the letter was just bluster. If the writer had the power to harm him he would have done it already, he told himself. It was a bluff, just as the effigy at the Hall was a bluff. He burnt the letter and discarded the ashes.

He made a quick visit into Portskail four days later. He needed more provisions and felt a desire to get out of the house for a while. Since it was a bright morning with only an occasional shower threatening, he decided to walk the four hundred metres down to the town centre.

The main road was quiet even though the tourist season was well underway. A few cars sped past him. It was only as he passed the filling station and turned along the shore that he was aware of the numerous parked cars all along the front. The shops were bustling and groups of holidaymakers walked slowly along the harbour side. Several boats rose and fell on a gentle swell. Set against the backdrop of trees and mountains and the long narrowing perspective along the loch the scene was made for photographers. Few people walked the length of the harbour without taking advantage of the opportunity.

Just beyond the ferry terminal was a small hotel. There was private parking for residents on the other side of the road. As Conlon approached it he glanced along the grassy sward which lay on either side. Ahead of him the road ended and a small path led on along the loch side next to a caravan park.

Suddenly he stopped. He stared towards the hotel car park. There were five cars parked there at the moment but only one of them was of interest to Leigh. It was a small, blue sports' car and it was parked in the space closest to where he was standing.

For a moment he was unsure what to do. He glanced around. The road was empty. Even the small lanes which led to the shore from other roads were momentarily empty of people. He looked towards the hotel. He could see no-one inside its door or at the windows. He sidled towards the vehicle and glanced inside. It was immaculately clean and it was empty of anything that could offer any clues to the identity of the owner. On the back seat there lay a local newspaper. Beside it there was a single sheet of paper. There was some writing on it.

Conlon looked round again. There was still no-one on the street and only a couple walking away from him along the lane. He could risk a closer look. Besides, if challenged, he could profess an interest in an unusual sports' car like this. It would not seem particularly suspicious. He looked more closely through the window. He could make out the writing now. It was a list of names, written quite large in block capitals. It was laid carefully on the seat as if it was intended to be read by someone peering though a window.

Leigh Conlon stepped back and then stepped back again. The names he had seen on that innocuous piece of blue paper were exactly the same names he had written, when considering who might have sent the letter. He turned and walked a few steps towards the town, his heart racing and his brow wet with perspiration. Then he stopped. He thought for a moment and then he turned resolutely round. He removed a scrap of paper from his pocket and jotted down the registration number. Then he walked across to the hotel and pushed open the door.

He was immediately encapsulated in the warm, quiet world of the hotel lobby. The three small tables, upon which the proprietors had laid newspapers and tourist leaflets, were unoccupied. The reception desk was unattended. He walked across to it. He pressed a small button to summon assistance and then waited, restlessly drumming his fingers on the mahogany surface. He glanced towards the door. He could no longer see the car park.

After a few moments a small man, in late middle age, walked in from the rear of the hotel. He was holding a towel with which he wiped his hands. He passed though a door and re-appeared behind the reception desk. He smiled with the benign joviality of a professional host.

'Can I help you?'

'Yes, yes, I hope so.' Conlon added his own smile to the jovial mix. 'There's a car outside in the car park, a blue sports' model. I'm sure it belongs to someone I used to know. His name has completely escaped me. I assume the owner is staying here? This is the registration number.' He held out the scrap of paper to the proprietor.

'A blue sports' car?' the hotel owner repeated, 'I'm not sure, let me look.' He picked up a small book from the reception desk and looked down it carefully. 'No,' he said, 'we have no record of a vehicle with that number. I always ask my guests to write their vehicle registration for me. The car park quite clearly indicates the name of the hotel and the words 'private parking for hotel guests only' but some people just choose to ignore it. I have some signs that I put under their windscreen wipers now just to express my annoyance but I'm wasting my time. Some people just don't care. I'll just come to the door with you and see for myself if you'll....'

Conlon had already turned away. He walked quickly towards the entrance of the hotel and stepped outside. There were now only four cars in the car park. There was an empty space where the blue car had recently been standing. It had gone.

Conlon did not wait to speak to the hotel owner. He turned towards the town. He quickly checked the main streets of the town. If the blue car was there he intended to find it and to confront the owner. Whatever else he was Leigh Conlon was not a man who was easily intimidated. The only thing that truly disturbed him was the fear that he might one day lose the power to act and to control. If he could find the driver he would stabilise matters very quickly with a few carefully chosen words and - if it proved necessary - with a suitable degree of covert and untraceable brutality.

Unfortunately there was no blue car to be seen. Conlon completed his few chores and made his way home in no good humour. He opened the door and walked through to the kitchen where he dropped everything on the table. He turned round and retrieved a couple of official looking letters from behind the door. His mood was not improved by their content. One was from his solicitor, Jarrett; the second from Inland Revenue.

The conclusion of the first letter caused him particular concern.

'It would appear that someone has been making enquiries into your business dealings. They have been both persistent and thorough. I think it would be advisable for us to speak as soon as possible to discuss matters. Could you telephone to arrange a time and a place? I don't think we should meet at the office.'

Leigh Conlon frowned. His cheeks twitched nervously. He opened his phone and quickly pressed a familiar series of numbers.

'I need to speak to Jarrett,' he snapped. 'Tell him it's Leigh Conlon.' He frowned impatiently. 'I don't care who he's got with him; just tell him.'

A moment later he heard Jarrett's deep, familiar tones. Conlon explained quickly what had occurred. Jarrett listened patiently. Leigh could imagine him complacently nodding his heavy, broad head as he listened. There was nothing that disturbed Jarrett. He was immune from harm. For him this was just business as usual. Eventually Conlon fell silent.

It was a moment before Jarrett spoke. He liked those silences. They suggested gravity and wisdom. 'There can be little doubt that someone is attempting to muddy the waters. Whoever it is believes that if they stir things enough they may make discoveries that will make you vulnerable. I think these actions smack a little of desperation. If they had anything of substance to accuse you with they would have done it already. I don't think you have anything to fear. My advice would be to sit tight and continue with the strategy you've used all along. Your finances, I take it, are in order?'

'They're watertight,' Conlon said, 'I pay tax on everything that I declare and I declare everything with which I have a direct connection. I'm a model citizen.'

'And your other incomes are carefully protected?'

'They are banked or invested overseas and are secure.'

'Then I advise you do nothing; and Leigh,' Jarrett paused, 'I know you're prone to precipitate action, but in this case you really should sit back and do absolutely nothing. This is a futile bluff from someone who has failed so far to link you to anything. My advice is that you wait and see what happens next – if anything does happen. I suspect your accuser will either vanish without further action or will make a rash move which will confirm his or her identity. At that point you should hand matters over to me. We're sufficiently secure to be able to use legal means to win this particular battle – provided you've left no loose ends. You have been careful to leave nothing, haven't you?'

'Yes, of course; I'm careful, you know that.'

'Are you sure of Deitch?'

'Deitch will do nothing,' he said firmly. 'I have him hooked too tightly. He can wriggle but he can't escape. I'll remind him of the vulnerability of his position when I next see him. That should suffice. He's basically a coward.'

'I hope you're right, Leigh,' Jarrett said, 'for both our sakes.'

The conversation concluded, Leigh sat back on a chair. The list of names he had written earlier lay on the table before him. He picked it up. The driver had the same list. Leigh frowned and stood up. He walked across the room and back again, deep in thought. Had the driver contacted these people? What might he have asked of them? What might they have told him? Could he be sure that there was nothing that could expose him? There were four names. Of course, they could prove nothing, he was pretty sure of that. But someone had put those names together. Someone had tied these names to his own. Someone had established a link that it shouldn't have been easy to make.

He looked at the names again. Had they somehow learned of each other? Had they been in contact?

'It does no harm to have insurance,' he muttered under his breath, 'whatever Jarrett says. It's not him they're after. He can sit in his office, fat and complacent, and just draw the money.' He felt an upsurge of contempt and distaste for the solicitor.

He opened his phone again.

'Carlton Brooke,' he snapped. 'Tell him it's an old friend' He laughed unpleasantly. 'I introduced him to his wife. Tell him I have some work to put his way.'

The next day Conlon packed his bags and drove away. He knew how to hide himself away if the need arose. He would not be seen now unless he chose to be seen. No-one would find him. Leigh Conlon would take control.

Chapter Eleven

Emma Varley spent the first part of the evening alone. John had been out from early morning. He left her a hurriedly written note; business, it said, although it was not specific as to the nature of the business. She sat quietly in her apartment and read. Softly, in the background, music played. She liked music nowadays; it was better than being alone. It was after nine before she heard a gentle tapping at her door. John Deitch put his head into the room.

'Could I join you for an hour, Emma?' he asked. This was the nature of their relationship. Proprieties were important.

He entered the room and sat down. He was strangely restless. He stood up and walked across the room to where a dresser housed a bottle of brandy. He poured a drink and returned to sit down. He swirled the liquid in its glass and sipped.

'You have been out for a long time today,' Emma placed her book on a small table beside her chair.

'Yes, yes indeed. I have been quite busy.'

He seemed disinclined to say more but Emma saw that his eyes were bright and restless. They moved quickly. He had difficulty remaining still. Emma knew better than to ask. She sat back and listened to the music – Mozart, an evening favourite. Eventually he spoke. The words emerged in a barely coherent flurry, like a sudden fall of snow in a strong wind.

'I did it,' he said and his eyes brightened unnaturally, 'I went to see him. I spoke to him. It wasn't at all as I expected, no, not at all. He made me feel so cheap and vile but that was alright – yes, that was only to be expected. I hoped he would strike me or swear or anything – something - but he didn't. He invited me in to his home. I said to him, I told him, I tried to explain...'

'Who?' Emma exclaimed. 'For Goodness sake, John, you're making no sense at all. Whom have you visited? Where have you been?'

'I've started,' John said. He laughed and sipped the brandy again. He stood up and walked excitedly across the room. 'I've made my first step. God knows, I was scared. I was really scared. I don't think I've been so anxious since I was a child - but it was alright.'

'What? What was alright? Slow down and explain to me. Sit down.' He sat down beside her and took her hands. 'You were right,' he said. He spoke more calmly now and his eyes did not move from hers. 'You were always right. I've been a coward all my life.'

'I've never said that of you, John. I would never say that.'

He shook his head impatiently. 'No, no, you were quite right. I know what I've been. I have no illusions, not any more.' He took a deep breath and spoke quietly. 'He could not forgive me, of course.

That would be too much to expect, and he wouldn't accept my offer of help. But he listened to me; he listened to me and he was gracious and polite.' He looked up at her and held her hands more tightly. 'I shall help him, you know, and I shall help the others. I have started now and I shall not rest until I have done something to make amends.' He broke off suddenly. 'I can't make things how they would have been, you know, how they might have been had we never met. I wish I could do that but I cannot. But at least I can do something.'

'Whom did you visit?' Emma looked at him anxiously.

'Harmison,' he said. 'I visited Maurice Harmison. He still has a beard, you know, just as he had when we first saw him. He's older of course, quite grey now and worn down and faded like an old rug, but he still looks remarkably the same. We treated him very badly, you know, very badly indeed. When everything collapsed he was left alone to face the consequences. Conlon was in New York; I was in Spain. We thought him so gullible and foolish, Emma. We never considered what the consequences would be for him. He thought he was making an investment in a legitimate business. He signed all the papers, took on the directorship. He trusted us absolutely. He was such an idealist, a perfect target for us. He lost his home, his family and he risked his freedom. It was our fault, Emma, mine and Conlon's.'

'How did you know where to find him?' Emma asked. She was anxious. John looked feverish and excited.

'Jarrett found him for me. He was far from willing I have to tell you, but I wouldn't take no for an answer. He said nothing but trouble would come of it; he said I was stirring up a hornet's nest and that I should let things be – let the past stay in the past, he said - but I insisted on knowing where I could find him.'

'Are you sure that was wise. He will tell Conlon, you know.'

Deitch shook his head impatiently. 'I can't wait for Conlon to grant his approval. It would never be given.'

'Where does Mr.Harmison live?' Emma's voice betrayed her anxiety.

'That was the most surprising thing, Emma. He lives no more than eighty miles from here. I never knew that. All these years I have imagined him living in a city or abroad in some foreign country. I didn't imagine he would have stayed here.'

'And Jarrett found the address for you?' Emma asked quietly.

'Yes.'

'Oh, John, I hope...' Her words faded.

Deitch turned to her, his eyes unnaturally bright. 'Perhaps I shall find the others – Barden and Gill....'

'What about Conlon, though?' Emma asked anxiously. 'He won't be pleased.'

'No, Conlon won't be pleased; but Conlon has no regrets. He just has fears. He's frightened that his actions will be discovered and that one day he will be held to account. When I see him I shall assure him that he is in no danger from me. I have no desire to see him punished. This is about me, my guilt, my shame and my actions. It's about me.'

'He may not see it like that. He may consider it a threat.' Emma looked at him with concern. He looked strange, almost ill; his eyes shone unnaturally and beads of perspiration stood on his brow. His face was flushed red. 'You should speak to the police.'

He shook his head. 'There's no need to involve the police. Leigh Conlon has nothing to fear from me.'

He drained the last of his brandy and walked across to pour another. Emma's anxiety grew. This was not what she desired. It was too quick, too spontaneous and ill thought out. He was about to speak again when she raised her hand.

'Tomorrow,' she said. 'You've had a long day; you are excited and impassioned and I have a rather unfortunate headache. I can't hear any more tonight, not tonight.' He seemed about to protest. 'Please, John,' she pleaded, 'this isn't the right time. It will do no harm to wait until tomorrow.'

She ushered John towards the door. 'We'll speak tomorrow. I need time to think.'

'I shall not change my mind, I assure you,' he called back through the door. He laughed excitedly. 'I've waited far too long already.'

Once alone, Emma returned to her chair. She picked up a book and then put it down again. She stood up and walked across to the phone and picked it up. She picked up a card from beside it.

'Oh, what have you done, John?' she murmured. 'What have you done?' She replaced the phone and the card and walked over to the window. The sun had set and the clouds were streaked red and silver. A breeze ran fingers through the tops of the trees. Silence, like a warning, was moving over the house. 'What have you done?'

Chapter Twelve

At this time of year it was often late when Wilkie finished work. It was summer and the requirements of his profession outstripped the time provided for the tasks he had allotted himself. Under those circumstances, especially when the evening was warm and fair and the midges kept at bay by a gentle breeze, he would remain for a few hours and then make his way home along the cliff top.

It was a fine evening and the combination of a hazy warmth, a cloud flecked blue sky and an enticingly gentle breeze persuaded him that the pleasure he would derive from a brisk walk would more than outweigh the effort involved. He had, he reminded himself wryly, no-one to please but himself. His cottage on the harbour front at Strathan would await him whether he cycled or drove the three miles of road or walked the cliff. Besides, he had things on his mind. A brisk walk would give him time to think and he would be rewarded by views of cliffs, rocky bays, tiny sand coves and green headlands framed by distant mountains peaks. Eventually the secret beauty of the tiny village and its weather beaten harbour walls would open like a flower below him.

He paused and listened as a golden plover cried and rose from a peaty moorland pool. Over the sea, black and white specks flew back and forth from the cliff ledges, a hurrying, bustling mass of life. Far out, lines of gannets made an effortless and stately progress as they banked and turned over the waves.

He looked at his watch. 'Seven o'clock.'

The sun barely set at this time of the year. It slipped its head beneath the horizon and grabbed a few short hours glowing sleep and then emerged, ready for the new day. A seal's head emerged from the water and watched him curiously. Far out a yacht moved slowly. Suddenly he stirred himself. 'It won't do. No, it really won't do. I have to talk to her.'

As he neared the village the houses came into sharper focus and the black, lichen clad, harbour walls glistened. A few boats lay still by the quayside. He stopped.

'What the....' he muttered.

Someone was walking along the quayside and out along the harbour. Even at that distance he could see it was a woman, an old woman, rather weak and unsteady. She stopped momentarily where some roughly hewn steps gave access to the top of the harbour wall. She seemed to think for a moment and then clambered carefully up the uneven steps and stood upright on the wall. She seemed to look slowly to left and right and then to stare out towards the distant horizon. Then she turned and walked along the rugged stone surface until she reached the end. There she stopped, on the very edge, looking down into the water.

Wilkie took it all in at a glance. She was a tall, slender woman, obviously frail and elderly, yet decisive in her movements and firm and resolute in her manner. She stood very upright on the top of the wall. She wore an outdoor coat over which she had flung a short, dark, hooded cloak.

'Mrs. Waterson!' Wilkie murmured. 'What are you doing out there, my dear, in your state of health?'

He reached some grassy steps which led down to the village and hurried down to the quayside. There he clambered up stone steps onto the wall. Mrs. Waterson did not move. Wilkie coughed. The old lady slowly turned and the hood fell back from around her head to reveal a narrow face, a head of grey hair and two soft, blue eyes. She looked towards Wilkie but gave no indication of having seen him until she had slowly turned her head back towards the sea.

'What are you doing up here, Mrs. Waterson?' Wilkie spoke gently, as if to a child. 'You might fall.'

Mrs. Waterson answered without turning her head. 'I have little to fear,' she said, 'in my present condition. I can take whatever risks I please, don't you think?'

'Yes, but Agnes, what would she think?'

Mrs.Waterson didn't answer. 'Come here, Wilkie, see what I've found.'

Wilkie approached her carefully. He saw that her toes were over the edge of the wall.

'Come back from there, Mrs. Waterson. Do!' he murmured anxiously. 'It makes me nervous.'

Mrs. Waterson raised her hand and pointed out towards the outer wall where the surf broke gently. 'Can you see him?'

He saw a sleek brown body, glistening eyes and a long, broad tail. An otter rolled in the water. After a moment it turned and vanished with barely a sound and emerged by the buttressing of the harbour wall.

He's breaking limpets off the rock, I think,' Mrs. Waterson said. 'I've been watching him for several minutes. There's another but I think it has moved out beyond the harbour and towards the deep pools near the shore. Do you think they are a pair, Wilkie? I would like to think so. Everybody should have a partner in life, don't you think? I....' She stopped as an unwelcomed thought entered her mind. She looked at Wilkie and her face softened into a gentle smile. 'Of course,' she said, 'of course; perhaps I shouldn't have...' She looked up. 'No matter,' she said resolutely. 'We have put it behind us, I think.'

Wilkie blushed but he didn't answer. 'I was hoping to talk to Agnes. I have news for her.'

'Oh yes, yes, of course. Yes, I shall follow you in a few moments. Now go. I am perfectly alright as you can see. I shan't fall and I don't intend to jump just at present.' She laughed softly.

There was a sound from behind them. A young woman was climbing cautiously up the step. She stood for a moment at the top and dusted her hands then walked towards them. The same upright stance, the same firmness of manner, the same soft blue eyes and the same slender build left no doubt as to the relationship of the two women.

'Mother,' she called. A tremor in her voice betrayed her anxiety, 'What are you doing here? You must come home at once. How could you let her climb out here, Wilkie?'

Mrs. Waterson turned her head and then stepped back from the edge of the wall.

'There were otters here, Agnes.'

'Never mind otters, mother, please. You shouldn't be here. It's not safe for you.'

'Sometimes I wonder who is parent and who is child,' the older woman muttered impatiently. 'It doesn't seem many years since I had to fetch you from this very spot when you disobeyed me and spent an afternoon jumping from the wall and into the sea. Now you treat me like a child. I'm old but I'm most certainly not senile. I shall do as I please.'

'You're ill, mother. You should be at home. You need to rest.'

Mrs. Waterson waved her arm impatiently. 'I shall rest when I'm dead and that will be soon enough. Until then I shall do exactly as I please.' She turned stubbornly away.

'You must come home now.' Agnes crossed her arms and stood resolutely watching.

Wilkie looked from one to the other and smiled. Mrs. Waterson turned to him sharply.

'What are you smirking at, Robert Wilkie? I seem to recall it was your idea that my daughter should leap from this wall. It was your example and her wilfulness. You were impossible children, very stubborn and heedless.'

Wilkie's smile broadened.

'I think there can be little doubt about where I inherited my wilfulness from,' Agnes said. 'You are impossible, mother.'

'I have earned the right to be difficult. It's one of the few benefits of age. I shall stay here for another five minutes and then I shall return home. You must go back with Wilkie. He wishes to talk to us. No doubt he has some information about all these recent occurrences at the Hall. Now go, go.'

There was nothing else to do. Agnes and Wilkie turned away and walked along the narrow road past the harbour. As they passed Wilkie's cottage they looked back. Mrs. Waterson slowly raised her arms above her head and threw her head back as if drawing the scene into her soul. She remained thus for a moment on the very edge of the harbour. Then she relaxed and her arms fell slowly to her sides. She turned slowly to walk back along the edge of the wall, above the water, her arms outspread to balance herself. Her cloak hung down like dark wings.

'She does it on purpose,' Agnes muttered, 'just to worry me.'

Wilkie could not resist a smile. 'You two are so very alike,' he said.

'We are most certainly not,' Agnes retorted sharply, brushing her hair abruptly from her eyes.

They paused briefly at the end of the harbour where the road turned uphill towards the white house.

'Forgive me, Agnes, but I have to ask if you know who is responsible for the disturbances at the hall?'

Agnes turned to him, her eyes bright and angry. 'Of course I don't. How can you ask me such a thing, Wilkie, you of all people?'

'I know, I know, but you can act impulsively at times – you know you can.' Agnes blushed and frowned as an unwelcomed thought passed like a cloud. Wilkie saw her change of countenance at once. 'I didn't mean that, I...'

Agnes took his hand quickly and earnestly. 'I know you didn't, Wilkie I know you wouldn't think ill of me or punish me for my stupidity...but I can't help...' She raised her hands in despair at the futility of her words. She turned away and looked across the harbour to the distant sea. 'If I met the intruders at the hall I'd offer them a hearty handshake,' she said stubbornly. 'I'm immensely grateful that they're making life unpleasant for those ghastly men.'

'I hear things,' Wilkie murmured. 'Deitch...Conlon...Things are getting out of hand. I don't know what these people hoped to achieve but they may stir up more than they bargained for. I'm worried, Agnes. I don't want you or your mother drawn into this. It's dangerous. We know only too well what sort of a man Leigh Conlon is.'

'I'm just pleased that someone will not allow him to forget what he has done – to others if not to us.' Agnes said stubbornly. She looked at him and her eyes flashed. She turned away petulantly. 'I don't want him to sleep easily in his bed; I want him to see us in his dreams. I want him to be plagued by nightmares.'

She stared out towards the long breakwater. Gulls gathered along it and at the end a number of cormorants perched, wings outstretched, drying in the breeze.

'Conlon has no conscience and I expect he sleeps easily enough. Maybe Deitch is different, who knows. He never seems truly happy.' Wilkie reached towards her but seemed to think better of it and drew back his hand. 'I don't like the way things are turning.'

'Well, none of it has anything to do with me, I can assure you.'

'I know.' He stepped forward so that she was obliged to see him and to listen. 'But someone has chosen to involve themselves in these affairs. It puts us all at risk. Conlon is certain to suspect our involvement.'

'You mean my involvement,' Agnes smiled. 'He can hardly suspect my mother and he knows nothing about you and...' She paused for a moment, '...about your friendship with our family.'

'Who could it be, Agnes?'

Agnes shrugged. 'Perhaps you should question Mrs. Davidson. Perhaps she and Andrew have been digging your garden at the dead of night.'

Wilkie laughed softly. 'You have a cruel tongue, Agnes Waterson. 'But I really am concerned for your safety and for your mother's.'

'I know.' She took him by the hand suddenly and drew him closer. 'But I see an opportunity, Wilkie. Even if Conlon is beyond our influence I suspect John Deitch is not. From what you've said it would appear that these incidents have caused him considerable distress. Can't we use that to our advantage?'

'No, Agnes, you must promise me. Who knows what these people want? And Conlon – you know only too well what he is capable of. Promise me you won't get involved. Think of your mother.'

Agnes was silent for a moment. 'I must think of mother,' she said, 'you're right. I can have no time for anything else at the moment.'

She continued to hold his hand. For a moment they stood still. 'Conlon can't be allowed to get away with what he did, though,' she said firmly. Their eyes met. 'We must have justice one day. You've always been there for me, Wilkie, don't let me down now.'

Wilkie looked into her eyes. 'I shall never do that; but you must trust me, Agnes.'

Her eyes faltered and she released his hand.

Mrs. Waterson had reached the road and was making her way towards them. Agnes raised her hand and waved and smiled. 'Look what they've done to my poor mother!'

Wilkie looked along the quayside. Mrs. Waterson had been so strong. She had always seemed so unchangeable, as permanent as the sea and the cliffs and the mountains. She was like the rocks upon which the waves beat. No adversity could destroy her. Whilst she had her home and family she was inviolable. Now she seemed so frail and broken, so fragile, a butterfly in the wind. In a short time, a very short time, between the closing of an eye and its opening, she would be no more.

'We can't let him get away with it,' said Agnes and there was anguish in her voice that hurt him more than any physical pain. 'It isn't only a matter of justice. It's to do with right and wrong, good and evil. It's about order. He's flaunting all the negative and hateful things that make life so unbearable. We have to put it right. Do you see, Wilkie?'

Wilkie watched Mrs. Waterson make her way slowly towards them. She looked weak and tired. 'I won't let you down,' he said, 'but we must find another way.'

'You must stay for dinner, Wilkie,' Mrs. Waterson called to him.

Agnes nodded. 'You must,' she said, 'mother so enjoys your company,' She squeezed his arm, 'as do I, but say little to her about these recent events at the hall.'

'I still find it strange to sit down to a meal with your mother,' Wilkie murmured 'I feel as if I should be sitting in the kitchen. Even as children we were never allowed to eat in the main dining room. It was sandwiches in the garden or the nursery, I recall.'

'Things change,' Agnes sighed. A shadow passed over her.

'Not everything,' Wilkie said. He smiled and their eyes met. Agnes looked away.

It was late that evening when Wilkie left the White House and made his way home. His footsteps echoed in the silence and the gathering darkness.

He did not notice the solitary figure leaning against the harbour wall and watched as he fumbled with the front door and let himself inside. He carried a camera and turned and studied the red glow of the sky beyond the harbour as if to avoid being seen. He leaned on the rough wall as if to frame a final picture then drew himself up and walked away. He strolled past Wilkie's house, pausing momentarily to glance towards the closed curtains and the dim light beyond, and then made his way towards the end of the village where he paused outside the White House. He stood for a moment and stared at the lights in the upstairs rooms until they were switched off and the house slept. Then he moved quietly away.

Wilkie, fatigued after a day's work, a long walk along the cliff and an evening in the warmth of the White House, saw nothing. He slipped into an untroubled sleep from which he did not awake until morning.

Chapter Thirteen

Wilkie planned to spend the following evening alone. The sun slanted through the tiny window at the front of his cottage and bands of flickering light illuminated the bare wall. Catching a crystal that hung from a pendant it flung a rainbow of colour in the corner above a small alcove. It was Friday. The weekend lay ahead.

'I'm going for a good, long walk tomorrow,' he told himself. 'I need some fresh air and some exercise. He patted his stomach. 'I mustn't let myself go.'

He frowned as a dark thought flitted like a ghost. Time was flying through him marking him with inevitable signs of increasing age. He shook his head as if to drive away the image. 'There's no point in getting miserable – no point at all.'

He had just settled back when he heard a gentle knock at the door. He muttered a few words under his breath and walked to the door. It was not a long journey. The door of the room in which he was seated was no more than four steps away and the front door barely a step beyond that. A narrow entrance hall led directly to stairs which rose without deviation to a small landing and two further rooms.

'Mrs. Waterson? What brings you here at this time of the evening? Does Agnes know you are out?'

She stood in the doorway, tall and pale, her cheeks hollow and her eyes sunk in dark shadows. She wore a dark cloak around her shoulders.

'I am not a child, Robert Wilkie. I don't need the permission of my daughter to take a stroll on a sunny summer's evening. Now, are you going to invite me in or shall we remain here at the doorstep?'

Wilkie grinned and shuffled back to allow her to enter. He ushered her into the living room and quickly cleared papers from the sofa. Mrs. Waterson glanced disapprovingly at the table by the window with its clutter of books and letters. She looked at the bare walls and the small dresser. There were few ornaments. On the mantel, above the open fireplace, was a framed photograph of a young woman. She was perhaps seventeen or eighteen years of age. She walked over to it and picked it up. Wilkie blushed deeply.

'Agnes,' Mrs. Waterson murmured. 'She was a beautiful young woman, wasn't she, but wayward, very wayward. It wouldn't have worked, you know, you and her – not then.'

She replaced it and turned back to Wilkie who had recovered from his discomposure. She seated herself on the sofa.

'Do sit with me, Wilkie, I have something to ask you. If it's impertinent of me I hope you'll excuse me. I'm growing older and I'm growing weaker. I don't have many good days left and I plan to use them wisely.'

'If there's anything you need of me, Mrs. Waterson, you know I'll be happy to oblige.'

Mrs. Waterson looked at him and her eyes brightened momentarily. 'I know,' she said. 'I know.' She held his hands in hers. 'I hope you'll continue to watch over my foolish daughter when I'm no longer here. I worry about her, you know. It will take many years for her to recover from that brute of a husband.'

Wilkie murmured words to convey how surely she could rely on him. Mrs. Waterson waved her hand impatiently.

'Now,' she said, 'to the matter which brings me here this evening; I have an ambition, Wilkie, before I die, to visit a number of places which are significant to me. I don't want to trouble Agnes. She would become mawkish and sentimental and tell me I was too weak or too ill or some such nonsense. She would try to dissuade me.

'I would like to go to the beach at Sandway, Wilkie. I want to remove my shoes and socks and walk in the edge of the sea. Will you take me there, Wilkie?' She turned and looked directly at him. 'If it's an inconvenience you must say so. I should perfectly understand. You may have much better things to do than drive a sentimental old woman around the countryside in search of memories.'

Wilkie laughed. 'I should be delighted to take you. When would you like to go?'

'Tomorrow,' Mrs. Waterson said decidedly. 'There is no time to waste, Wilkie, don't you think.'

'Then tomorrow it is, Mrs. Waterson. Shall I collect you around ten thirty?'

'That would be very good of you, Wilkie.' She took his hands again and squeezed them. 'My family have always been able to rely on you. You are a good man, Robert Wilkie.'

Wilkie was momentarily troubled. 'Are you sure this isn't a moment you wish to share with Agnes? These are precious family memories.'

Mrs. Waterson shook her head. 'Agnes and I shall have our times together. Besides, there are matters I need to discuss with you. Agnes will understand. I shall be very diplomatic. Now, I must be going. Pass me my walking stick, Wilkie. I detest the thing but it's an unfortunate necessity nowadays.' As she stood up, she moved her feet unsteadily as if to maintain her balance. 'There's no need for that look of concern, Wilkie. I am quite well. I merely stood up rather quickly. I sometimes forget that I'm ill. It is most annoying to be reminded.'

'Wait a moment, Mrs. Waterson,' Wilkie said. He grabbed a coat. 'I'll walk back with you. I need a little air. The walk will do me good.'

'That would be very kind of you. I would enjoy your company.' Mrs. Waterson looked around the room again. She shook her head. 'You shouldn't be alone here, Wilkie,' she said softly. 'A man like you needs…' She paused. 'You must do something about it.'

She turned and opened the front door and stepped out into the evening light.

Chapter Fourteen

The morning dawned much as the previous day had ended. There was a cool breeze raising a swell on the sea which broke against the harbour walls and cast low waves over the slipway. The tide was past full and as it withdrew the breeze would drop and the clouds which at present masked the sun would break and fade. It would be another pleasant day.

Wilkie collected Mrs. Waterson at 10.30 as they had agreed. She was waiting at the door as he pulled up and carried a small rucksack. Wilkie smiled. It would contain a light lunch of sandwiches - cottage cheese and cucumber probably - and a flask. The flask would contain hot water and milk. There would be two tea bags, earl grey. Mrs. Waterson had reluctantly made this sacrifice to modernity some few years ago. She had never managed yet to stir a tea bag in water without a look of distaste.

'You are very prompt, Wilkie. I appreciate that. I have never been able to take to a man who could not arrive on time for an appointment. It shows very poor manners, don't you think?'

'It looks a fine day, Mrs. Waterson,' he ventured, 'but it would hardly dare be otherwise.'

Mrs. Waterson looked at him sharply. 'You have always been an impudent man, Robert Wilkie, but I shall forgive you and overlook your impertinence.'

Ill health had rendered her body weak but if there was a fragility about her body there was no such weakness of mind. Mrs. Waterson was as imperious and strong as she had always been.

Wilkie helped her into the car. He looked round for a moment.

'Agnes is upstairs in her bedroom and I do believe she's cross with both of us. She doesn't think I should be going on such a - what did she call it? – such a foolish jaunt. She is worried for me. I understand. But I must be allowed to live out my life as I wish, don't you think?'

'It would be a brave person who tried to stop you. Only someone just as stubborn would even try.'

As he turned the car in the drive he saw Agnes watching them from an upstairs window. Behind the soft lace Wilkie saw the familiar stubborn look fade and give way to anxiety. She waved her hand slowly and her mother waved back.

'She's a good girl,' Mrs. Waterson said quietly. 'I love her dearly.'

'As do I,' Wilkie thought, 'as do I.' Feelings he had long repressed flickered momentarily into life and caused a familiar pain to seer through him. He had imagined those feelings buried and beyond reach. He knew at that moment he was mistaken. He was not a man whose feelings, once aroused, could be so easily dismissed.

The car pulled out of the drive and turned away from the village. They headed through low, craggy undulations towards the road north. As they paused at the junction Mrs. Waterson suddenly cried out.

'Oh look, Wilkie! Look!' Above the crags a golden eagle soared on outstretched wings. Feathers pointed out like fingers and the wings gently curved and flexed in an effortless glide towards the mountains. 'Richard and I used to call the golden eagle our very own bird, you know. They are always associated in my mind with the happiest of days. I think it is an omen, Wilkie. Do you believe in such things?'

'I think it's telling us to have a really pleasant day, Mrs. Waterson. Of that I am quite sure.'

Memories rolled one upon another and poured out in conversation which lasted most of the journey to the bay. Each village, each mountain peak, each waterfall tumbling down towards the road, seemed to carry with it a recollection of the past.

'We had a house in London for a while,' she said, 'when Richard left the army but it was always a relief to come home. It was like removing a suit of armour and replacing it with a light dress. I felt as if I had wings.'

'You must have had some happy times there, nonetheless,' Wilkie said. The car slowed and turned at the junction which led down to Sandway..

'Oh yes, indeed we did. I was never one to sink into depression. I enjoyed the theatre and the parks. I enjoyed any number of social occasions. We had good friends, kind people. Then Marcus was born.' She looked momentarily troubled. 'I hope I shall see Marcus again before the end,' she said. 'I wait for him every day, you know.' She looked out of the window. 'Oh look, Wilkie, this is the view I remember so well.'

The narrow lane had swung to left and right before rounding a small hill to look down upon the wide sweep of sea and a narrow, sandy bay. A small campsite lay at the southern edge and there were five or six small houses spread along the road like a guard of honour. A number of small dunes separated the parking area from the beach.

'Please stop, Wilkie. I want to look at it from here.'

Wilkie pulled into a passing place and drove forward onto the grass. Mrs. Waterson clambered out and stood by the car, drawing deeply on the cool air and gazing down towards the shore.

'There is nowhere in the world that has such a mix of colours,' she said. Her eyes shone and the light breeze blew back her hood to reveal her thin greying hair and hollow cheeks. 'Look, Wilkie, look at the azure of that sea, the brilliance of the surf, the vivid green of the shore, the soft sand and the grey dune grasses – there's nowhere else in the world like it; oh, I so love this place. Breathe the air, Wilkie. I'm quite convinced one can smell the sea from here – not just the shore but the deep ocean. Don't you think so?'

At that moment Wilkie felt the scene now before him, like the cliffs and the mountains, like distant memories, draw from the deepest waters.

They drove down to the car park and walked across grass and flowers towards a short path which led between the dunes to the pale sand of the shore.

'Look at the flowers, Wilkie, - vetches, campion, squil, - and look, oh look at the orchids, Wilkie. It is all just as I remember it.'

Wilkie held her arm as she leaned forward and bent her knees to reach down towards the flowers. She brushed them with her hand and then stood upright. Wilkie was shocked to notice how thin her arms were and how light she had become. She was like a wisp of straw ready to be broken in the lightest of breezes. He felt a sudden sorrow. Her life was so fragile and her hold on it so weak. He imagined how it would be when she was gone. 'Agnes,' he thought, and a wave of affection and pain surged.

'Now, I must walk on the beach, Wilkie. Take my arm as we walk through the dunes. My footing is a little uncertain nowadays, even with a stick. Once we are on the sand I shall walk barefoot and I shall bore you with reminiscences. Come, Wilkie, you must walk with me in the surf.'

Mrs. Waterson laughed again, reliving a long distant memory. 'Major Waterson proposed to me here,' she said. 'He was such a romantic fool. He held my hands and he knelt down right in the water. He refused to stand up until he had finished speaking. The water soaked right through. We sat on the grass amongst the flowers. There's another tiny bay just a few hundred yards along the shore. That's the last place we must visit, Wilkie. We shall have our picnic lunch there and then we shall return to the car. You've been very good to me, Wilkie. I shan't forget it.'

When they reached the shore they sat on the warm grass among the flowers.

'When you meet the woman you wish to marry you should bring her here, Wilkie.' She leaned back and rested on her thin arms. The breeze rippled silk sleeves.

'I don't know that I shall ever marry now,' Wilkie's hand brushed the grasses beside him and he looked down at the tiny, hidden bay. A solitary couple walked past. Gulls rose from the beach.

'Of course you must marry,' Mrs. Waterson said sharply. 'You're not the sort of person who should live alone. Besides, I have decided you should marry and I always get my way.'

Wilkie leaned back and laughed. 'You didn't always feel like that.'

'That was different. You and Agnes were not suited to each other at all at that time and you were far too young.'

'Could it have been any worse than what actually happened? Believe me, Mrs. Waterson, I bear you no ill will for your decision. I understood then and I understand now. I merely wish we'd been free to make our own choices and our own mistakes.'

Mrs. Waterson looked away. She gazed over the flowers and grass towards the sky and the clouds. 'I've grown too old for the modern world, Wilkie. I'm too set in my ways and my ways are set in the distant past. I believe in the proprieties. I like the simplicity of courtship, marriage and children. I've been left behind by modern times. No doubt many things have happened for the better but I would not exchange my own life for that of today.'

She fell silent. After a few minutes she spoke again, 'Now, Wilkie, it is time we made our way back. I don't want to take up all of your day and you have been most generous with your time. There is just one further thing I wish to speak to you about. I must ask you a most impertinent question.' She turned to him and her grey eyes fixed him with an earnest stare. 'Do you mind?'

'You'll have to be prepared for an impertinent response,' Wilkie laughed.

'That seems most reasonable,' Mrs. Waterson replied. 'Now, Wilkie, I must ask if your feelings towards Agnes are unchanged.'

Wilkie stared at the ground. It was a moment before he spoke. 'My feelings for Agnes have never changed; nor will they ever change,' he said. He looked up and smiled softly. 'However, my expectations are very different. We are friends and friends we shall remain. We can never return to how we were. Agnes would not want it and nor would I.'

'Thank you, Wilkie. Were I able to step back into the past I would make different choices. It is a hateful characteristic of life that one can never erase an error. I'm sorry. I shouldn't have intervened in the manner I did.'

'You have nothing to regret.'

Mrs. Waterson looked at him for a moment. He looked away, confused. 'Now,' she said, 'we must get back to the car. Give me your arm, Wilkie; I managed to get down onto the grass unaided but I think it is a little beyond my strength to reverse the process.'

The journey back was filled with more reminiscences. This was where she came with Agnes as a child; here they collected bilberries; here they sold the finest honey. Red deer crossed the road here on their way to the loch side. As they turned towards Port Strathan she spoke of her previous home and John Deitch.

'I don't bear him any ill will, you know. Perhaps I ought to but I don't. He is a weak, foolish man. Once I knew we had to leave the Hall it mattered little to me who moved into it. In some ways it was a relief to relinquish the responsibility. Of course, I would not have relinquished it willingly. It was my duty to remain there as long as I was able. Yes, it was my duty. Once the sale became inevitable I felt relieved – relieved and at the same time dreadfully guilty.'

She laughed. 'Let Mr. John Deitch have the hall,' she said, 'I am happy in my little house on the hill, very happy. I have only two desires now. I want to see Marcus again and...' She paused then continued softly, '...and I want to see my daughter smile again as she used to do.

'I would have felt differently had it been Leigh Conlon who moved into the hall,' she continued after a moment. 'To have seen him on a regular basis driving in and out of those gates would have been quite intolerable. John Deitch is merely a pawn, a victim like the rest of us. I pity him but I cannot hate him. You must teach Agnes not to hate. Ah, here we are, home again and there is Agnes waiting for us.'

The car pulled up outside the front door of the white house. Agnes helped her mother from the car.

'I have spent a most wonderful few hours at Sandway,' Mrs. Waterson smiled. 'I am tired now and shall rest but I would not have missed today for the world. I have bored Wilkie with my reminiscences and he has showed no resentment. He has been a perfect companion.' She held out a hand to Wilkie whilst Agnes held the other. Together they helped her into the house. As they crossed the threshold their eyes met briefly. Mrs. Waterson was right; Agnes didn't laugh as she used to do. It was a long time since he had seen her laugh with the careless joy that had driven him to such raptures in their youth. The year she had spent with Carlton Brooke had drawn away all the spontaneity and humour that had been so characteristic of her. It saddened Wilkie to see her and it angered him to think of those wasted years. She had never truly loved Carlton and Carlton knew it; his resentment poisoned their relationship and he became cruel. If she wanted to fly he would clip her wings; if she wanted to laugh he would make her cry; if she wanted to hope he would make her despair. She had emerged from the marriage like a bird with a broken wing. She didn't think she would ever fly again.

'I shan't invite you to join us, Wilkie. I think I need to lie down for an hour or two,' Mrs. Waterson said, 'and I'm sure you have other things to occupy your afternoon. Thank you once again. You have been a good friend.'

Wilkie's mind was in turmoil. He could not settle. Within half an hour he was striding down the harbour front towards the cliff. The morning's conversation had stirred feelings that he had long suppressed. He was aware now how weak his resolve had been and how easily all his good intentions could be overturned. He needed to walk and to regain control; otherwise there was no hope for him. He told himself over and over that the events of the last few years had left an irreparable gulf between them. Agnes had never shown any sign of wanting anything more than their unconditional friendship. No, there was no point in tormenting himself.

Unfortunately, emotions such as his, once roused, were not easily subdued. For the first time in a number of years he was tormented by hope.

Chapter Fifteen

There lies a particularly remote croft in the far northwest, situated several miles from the nearest significant road and accessed by a narrow track whose sole purpose is to allow visitors or occupants to reach it. The house is small but well maintained and has a small dormer window and a stone conservatory overlooking a sloping grassy pasturage. This falls away towards the cliffs overlooking the sea. There is a telescope on a tripod in the window facing the sea no doubt to observe the birds, whales or vessels that pass occasionally. The croft has a small but carefully tended garden with fruit bushes and some meagre vegetables in a well tended bed and several flower tubs. Narrow, carefully placed fences enclose some areas set aside for the maintenance of a small number of sheep and cows, although the fields are empty now. Beyond these, all attempts at cultivation and stock rearing fail against the bleak rocky outcrops and extensive moorland used by a nearby farmer for the summer grazing of a few sheep.

The occupant of this lonely croft was sitting in the conservatory. He was evidently drowsing because the book he had been holding had fallen onto his lap. A cup of tea which lay on a small table beside him was cold. Thin strands of grey hair had fallen forward and hung in wisps across his face. He wore an untidy, grey beard of a style reminiscent of earlier decades. A small radio stood on the floor beside him. Its volume was turned low as if to provide sounds which would fill the silence of the lonely croft and conjure a semblance of human company. There was no-one else in the house. There had never been anyone else.

Outside the windows it was dusk. The sun was sinking fast and only a ruddy glow cast a last lingering blush on the clouds. A few solitary stars flickered into distant life. Then darkness crept over the waters and the land and the night closed in.

Still he slept; and still more stars gathered until the tumbling clouds rolled from the distant horizon and closed them out. The wind increased. The slates on the roof rattled. The wooden beams creaked. The rain began to fall, tapping gently at the window as if to awaken him from his sleep. He did not stir so the wind and the rain, impatient now, beat more heavily against the panes and shook the lonely building.

All night the wind and rain worked but to no avail. When daylight began to break weakly, lightening the grey cover of cloud, they gradually gave up all hope and slipped away. The day was still. But no matter how still the day it could never be as still as the man in the conservatory of that lonely croft. He had been sitting thus for two days and two nights now. He would not wake again.

At ten o'clock that morning a red postal van drove along the track. The postman emerged and passed beside the conservatory on his way to the door. He knocked on the window. He knocked again and again. He could have knocked forever. He hurried back to his van and then along the lane until he could find a phone signal and called the police. Half an hour later a car arrived. They broke the door and forced an entry, covering their faces to escape the smell of death and decay that had been building up as if in expectation of their arrival.

An hour later, Aaron Marks drove slowly along the track and pulled up in front of the house. He looked around.

'Who found him?'

The police officer indicated the postman who was seated in the car, a second policeman beside him.

'What do we know about the dead man?'

'He was called Maurice Harmison,' the policeman informed him, 'a bit of a recluse from what I gather, kept himself to himself. 'He's been here about ten years. He spent most of his time improving the place and working in the garden and on his patch of land. He wasn't seen out and about much. I'm a local man so I get to know these things. Sergeant Bill McCrae.'

A doctor, masked and anonymous, was leaning over the body. He stood up.

'He's been dead for two days,' he said. 'The poor sod died out here alone and nobody knew.'

'Have you any idea yet as to how he died?'

'See for yourself.'

A small box of tablets lay on the floor beside him, hidden from sight by the legs of the chair. Its contents had gone. Aaron carefully picked it up and looked at it. He picked up the cup and tilted it to view its contents.

'There were enough tablets there to do the job,' the doctor said. 'It looks like he'd been saving them up. He took them with a cup of tea and then sat back and read his book whilst he waited for them to take effect.'

Aaron picked up the book and glanced at it. Then he walked around the room. He tried the door.

'Your policemen were a bit premature when they knocked down the front door,' the doctor said. 'This one was already open.'

Aaron turned to Bill McRae standing at the door. 'Is there any sign of a note?'

Bill shook his head.

Aaron walked back through to the living room. It was tidy and well maintained but rather bare. The furniture was not new but it was tasteful and clean. The books on a single shelf were not numerous but they were a well judged balance of classical and modern literature, local flora and fauna and history. The room was comfortable and warm. A burnt out peat fire was in the hearth. He had noticed peat stacked against an outbuilding. There were only three photographs; one showed a happy couple with a child; another showed an elderly couple and the third a tiny child lying on a blue cushion and laughing. On a table beside the window were two glasses and a wine bottle. One chair was pushed back but the other was set squarely by the table. Aaron opened a drawer on a dresser and glanced though some papers. He held one in particular and looked at it closely. He picked up a handful of photographs and skipped through them, family shots from years ago. Once again he paused at a particular print and looked at it. He took the two photographs and sealed them carefully in a bag.

'There's no television and there's no computer,' he murmured, 'just that small radio. I can't see any newspapers either. He seems to have cut himself off from the outside world.' He turned sharply round and summoned the constable from the door. 'Bill, can you and your colleague seal this place off for me. I don't want anyone else in here until I've checked a few things out – not that it's likely we'll be overwhelmed by visitors. I may want to get a forensic team down here later today.'

He wandered to the kitchen and then through each of the other rooms. Eventually he returned to the conservatory and the well tended garden.

'Where are his nearest neighbours?'

'There's a farm two miles away,' Bill told him. 'If you go back to the road and turn right it's the first place you meet. There are a few more crofts along the road to the left and there's another over the hilltop from here. Another track leads down to it from the road.'

'Can you find out if he had any friends or acquaintances hereabout? Somebody must have known something about him. You can't live in a place like this and be completely unknown. See if anyone noticed any visitors. Ask if he had any regular callers, any family coming to stay, you know the sort of thing. Someone will have seen something. There are a few photos and a handful of letters, mainly bank statements and hospital appointments, but very little else.'

An ambulance pulled up outside. The doctor opened the doors of the conservatory as a man and a woman entered.

'Can we remove the body?'

Aaron nodded. 'It's the room I want to check.'

It was no more than ten minutes before the ambulance doors were closed and the vehicle moved slowly down the track. The doctor fastened the clip on his bag and moved towards the door.

'There'll be a post mortem, of course, and an inquest, but for what it's worth it's as clear a case of suicide as I've ever seen. Living on his own like this must have got to him. Some people find the life up here difficult, especially during the long winters. It looks like he was completely alone here too, no family. It's sad, very sad.'

Aaron nodded. He thought again of the two glasses and open bottle of wine. Perhaps he was waiting for a visitor who never arrived. Or perhaps he had a visitor shortly before his suicide. 'If he did have a visitor I wonder what they spoke about?' he mused. Perhaps the visitor brought bad news.

He turned from the conservatory to look around the kitchen and the living room again. Then he looked into the two tiny bedrooms. The one used by the dead man was as barely furnished as the rest of the house. The other was used to store sundry household items, a vacuum cleaner, brushes, outdoor clothing. There was no guest bedroom. He hadn't expected visitors. Aaron tried to reconstruct something of the life that had flickered briefly here before being extinguished so sadly. It wasn't enough to simply turn away, to close the door and forget, not for Aaron. There was something terribly tragic not just about the death but about the life that had preceded it. There were so few photographs, so few memories. At some point in the past this man had chosen or been forced to sever all ties with his previous life.

He returned to the drawer and to the photographs. The dead man had been married; he had one, two children – a boy and a girl. There were photographs of them in parks and gardens, at the seaside, at school. There were no photographs of the children beyond the age of eight or nine, not one. He was in his late thirties in the photos. It was intriguing that there were only two photographs which was not of a family apparently lost to him many years before. They were the photographs Aaron had carefully sealed away. He looked at them again now. They showed the man at a formal dinner of some sort. He was amongst a small group of businessmen raising wine glasses and beaming at the camera from perspiring faces. On one one of them, just behind him, pressing a friendly hand on his shoulder, was the smiling figure of Leigh Conlon.

'I don't like coincidences,' he murmured. 'I don't like them at all.'

Aaron put the photographs back. He picked up the papers. There was little of interest, just the routine documentary accompaniment of normal life. There was just one document different from the others. It was a letter from someone in the probation service wishing him good luck and happiness in his new life. It was typed and hand signed many years earlier. It sounded personal and sincere. There was nothing else. There were no names of family members, no letters, no certificates of birth or death, no birthday cards, no Christmas cards, no memories. New life indeed, Aaron thought; there was little or nothing of the old one here.

He looked at the table and the bottle and glasses. 'It wouldn't do any harm to check them for finger prints, I don't suppose,' he said to himself, 'though I doubt I'll find anything.' He would call the probation officer too although the likelihood was that the officer would have moved on or retired or even died.

There were several things about this that unsettled him. In particular it was the name of Leigh Conlon coming so close after his interview with the businessman. Then there was the extra wine glass and the absent guest.

'Ok, Bill,' he said as he closed the conservatory door, 'I'll leave it in your capable hands. I'm going to have some colleagues take a closer look but at the moment it looks to be just what we thought – a rather pitiful and sad suicide. I'll just have a quick word with your postman and then he can get away home.'

Chapter Sixteen

Half an hour later, Aaron climbed in his car and headed down the track. As he turned on to the road at the end of the track he saw a woman, probably in her mid seventies, walking her dog, a sharp eyed black and white collie. He pulled up and held out his identification card.

'Do you walk down here most days?'

She nodded. She had the energetic look of someone many years younger.

'Do you know the man in the croft at the end of the track here?'

'Yes, I know him,' she said, 'but in twenty years or more we've never spoken more than a handful of words. He's a very quiet, private sort of person. It's unusual round here. We have to depend on each other so we tend to know each other at least well enough to hold a conversation.'

'Hang on a minute, I'll get out of the car,' Aaron said. 'I can't talk through the window like this. Did he have any visitors that you know of? Did you ever see cars going down the track?'

'Has something happened to him? I saw the postman go down but he didn't come back up. Then I saw the police car.'

Aaron smiled. 'Did you happen to notice my car arrive?'

She nodded again. 'From my window I can see the corner of the track where it turns down towards the croft. When I'm in the kitchen or the garden I can see anyone heading down there. Not that there's been much to see in all these years – the occasional delivery van, the postman, the doctor once or twice but nothing much more than that. Then suddenly there's a regular flurry! First there was a car last week then another car three days ago and now all this activity today.'

'Is there anywhere we can talk?'

The woman looked pleased. 'I've just baked a fruit loaf and I can soon put a cup of tea on. My house is just beyond the corner behind that tangled group of spruce trees.'

'Hop in,' Aaron smiled. 'For a cup of tea and a slice of fruit loaf you can have a lift.' He knelt down and stroked the collie. 'Both of you,' he added. 'Fortunately my springer spaniel is having a day at home. He'll be chasing a ball up and down the beach about now. I'm Aaron Marks,' he added, 'Detective Inspector.'

'Mary Darnley, pleased to meet you.'

The cottage was set back from the road behind a canopy of trees and surrounded by a small garden. Aaron walked through to the kitchen. She was right; from that room, across a stretch of moorland, it was possible to see a small stretch of the track. From the front she could see the road. If she was in the kitchen she would be more than likely to see anyone heading towards the croft or away from it.

'Mr. Darnley died six years ago. It gets a bit lonely out here sometimes but I have a number of friends and I keep busy. That reminds me – do you know, Mr. Harmison actually sent me a condolences card and a small bunch of flowers. It was very kind of him, don't you think? It was completely unexpected. He hardly knew me.'

Aaron nodded. 'Indeed it was.' He bit into a piece of fruit loaf. 'This is really excellent,' he said, 'You must give me the recipe. I'll make some for my wife. She's called Andrea. Do you spend a lot of time in the kitchen?'

'Looking out of the window, do you mean? I'm not nosey – just interested,' she laughed, 'but you would die of boredom if you waited for anything to go down that track. Twice a week he used to walk up to the road to catch the service bus. He came back three hours later with a few bags of food, Monday and Friday every week without fail. He'd only just got back when that car came down.'

'He'd been shopping just as usual?'

'Oh yes, I didn't see him set out because I had a friend visiting and we were in the sitting room but I most certainly saw him on his way back. I was baking bread. I was standing just beside the window there. He got off the bus and was walking quite slowly down the track. It was not surprising really. He was carrying a back pack and three or four carrier bags. It must have been both heavy and uncomfortable.'

'It seems strange to stock up on food if you are going to kill yourself,' Aaron murmured. 'Had he never owned a car?'

'No, not since he lived here. It's very unusual not to have a car hereabouts. I can't imagine why he would come to such a place without a car. There are only two buses a day along here and no shops nearer than the town.'

'The town?'

'The village is nearer but it has only a small grocery store and a post office. Our local town - it's little more than a large village really - is further but at least you can get whatever you need there. You need to change buses at the junction with the main road and there's a twenty minute wait but it's not a bad journey. I have a small car but I use the bus too. I like the company.'

'Have you travelled on the bus with Mr. Harmison?'

'It would be an exaggeration to say travelled with him. I've been on the same bus several times. I've sat opposite him and even tried to engage in conversation. He was always polite but dreadfully shy, dreadfully reserved. He had a gentle smile, I remember, almost apologetic. There was nothing to dislike about him and a lot to feel sorry for. It was as if he didn't have the courage to speak.'

'Or perhaps he was frightened to speak or found it hard to trust?'

'I hadn't thought of it like that but yes, yes; his eyes were often lowered and only flickered upwards as he smiled or glanced at you momentarily. He had a nice smile. I think he was dreadfully lonely but had no means to remedy it. As I say, I felt a great deal of pity for him. It doesn't surprise me that his life has ended like this.'

'Tell me about the car that you saw three days ago.'

'Oh, it was a common enough sort of vehicle. We see a lot of them hereabouts; four wheeled drive, silver. A lot of local people have them. This road can be quite hazardous in winter and the gritters rarely get out this far until after nine. Personally I stay inside and wait for the thaw. I telephone the shop and get my groceries delivered. Mr. Harmison did the same when the buses weren't running.'

'I don't suppose you could see anything of the driver?'

'Not really. It was a man, of that I'm sure and I don't think he was a particularly young man. He opened the window at one point and threw a cigarette end out. Stupid man! We've had fires around here started by people discarding cigarette ends. He obviously wasn't local. He had a sort of town look about him, if you know what I mean, and he was wearing a shirt and tie. I assume his coat was on the seat. He looked expensive.'

Aaron couldn't help but laugh. 'Mary, I wish all my witnesses were as perceptive as you. You have gleaned more information from a casual glance at the fleeting passage of a vehicle eighty metres away than most people could from five minutes staring at a crime scene. I am most grateful to you.'

Mary blushed. 'If there were twenty cars a day going down there I probably wouldn't have noticed anything. It was unusual, you see, so I paid rather more attention.'

'Did you see him return down the track?'

Mary looked rather sheepish. 'I don't know what you are going to think of me,' she said. 'You'll probably mark me down as a dreadful busybody and someone you would hate to live near. I...well it was sufficiently unusual to see someone visiting Mr. Harmison that I couldn't help but keep a casual watch for him coming back.' She noticed a half smile flicker across Aaron's face and blushed again. 'I didn't stand at the window for the rest of the afternoon, if that's what you are thinking. In fact I was in the garden bringing in some washing when the car came back up the track. He had his windows open, I think, even on the passenger side. I could hear the car radio playing music. I had the distinct impression he was singing along with it but that might have just been a flight of fancy. He turned at the corner and came past my house but he was gone before I could see any more.'

'Bless you, Mary,' Aaron smiled. 'You have been very, very helpful. I would love to have you as a neighbour. I would never fear burglars if you were around.' He winked. It earned him another piece of cake and a refilled cup of tea.

'Could you tell me about the other visitor, from a week ago?'

'It was very early in the previous week – Monday, I think. The postman had just called and I was ready to go out. I had just stepped out of my gate when a car passed me. I saw it turn down towards Mr. Harmison's croft. It was a red estate car. I noticed particularly because of Mr. Mackay from the farm. He has a similar vehicle. But this one was particularly clean, not at all like a farmer's car, so I took particular notice. The driver was a small man about sixty years old, I suppose. He had a strangely intense expression on his face, I recall. I'm not at all sure he even saw me.'

Aaron sat back. He asked some further questions but learnt little more. It was another half hour before he eventually climbed back in his car and headed home. He had a great deal to think about. There was one person he knew who owned a red estate car. He had seen it parked discretely beside Strathan Tower on his first visit. It belonged to John Deitch. Perhaps it was a coincidence. It was better not to jump to conclusions. It was something he would need to check. His thoughts turned to the other car.

'Silver four wheeled drive, driver not particularly young, a town dweller, smoker, shirt and tie – I wonder. I wonder.'

If the first driver had been John Deitch, was it possible that the second car had been driven by Leigh Conlon? He shuddered slightly. If that was the case Jack was right; things were taking a rather unpleasant turn. He would hurry back and speak to Jack at once.

Chapter Seventeen

Agnes held Wilkie gently by the arms and spoke in a hushed voice. It was some days after the outing to Sandway and they were standing by the side of the white house. It was early evening. The kitchen window was only a short distance away through the trees which grew near to the road. She drew him to one side. She did not want her mother to see them and ask questions.

'You are the one constant force in my life, Wilkie. I don't know what I would do without you.' A curl of soft, fair hair fell over her eyes and she brushed it back. 'Will you help me?' She pressed a hand to his lips. 'Say nothing until you hear what I ask.'

She reached inside her coat and removed a small number of plain, brown envelopes and handed them to Wilkie then she turned away as he studied them. On each of them the address was printed in the same square, box-like font and they had all been posted from the regional capital. He opened the first and withdrew a sheet of nondescript white paper. The message, such as it was, was communicated in the same font but large and bold and underlined.

'I KNOW EVERYTHING.'

Wilkie looked towards her and opened the second.

'YOUR MOTHER WILL BURN IN HELL AND SO WILL YOU.'

'My God, Agnes, when did these start to arrive?'

'The first was delivered just after the disturbances at the hall.'

'You didn't tell me.'

'I thought they would stop.'

Wilkie opened the third.

'YOU AND YOUR GARDENER WILL DIE.'

'Someone thinks it was us. We must take these to the police, Agnes.'

Agnes turned back to him and held his arm tightly. 'No, we can't do that, not yet. Think of mother. It would destroy her. It would ruin the few weeks she has left. We can't; we just can't. Promise me, Wilkie.'

He opened the next one and the next – obscene insults, threats, accusations.

'He's deranged; whoever it is is deranged. If I could lay my hands...'

'Look at this one,' Agnes murmured. She produced another envelope.

'I'M COMING TO KILL YOU, SLUT. COUNT THE DAYS.'

The envelope had no postmark. Wilkie looked at her in horror. He reached out and threw an arm round her and drew her close.

'It was pushed through the door, Wilkie. He's here. He's here in the village.'

'I'll find him,' Wilkie said, 'and when I do...' His words failed. He looked away down the lane. 'I cannot stand by and see you get hurt again.' Rooks rose from a distant field. 'I shall find a way,' he said, 'but you must be patient and you must trust me. As for this...,' he gestured at the letters with contempt, 'These are just the sadistic ravings of a bitter mind. He'll do nothing.'

'Are you sure?'

'Quite sure – besides, he'd have to get past me first and that will prove no easy matter.'

When she turned back her eyes were moist and her lips trembled. She brushed aside the emotions with annoyance.

'I can't find any peace, Wilkie. All the old certainties are gone. I don't think I will ever be truly happy again, not like before.'

Agnes turned and ran towards the house. As she reached the door she turned to watch his familiar figure turn the corner by the harbour and vanish from sight. A shadow fell across her face but whether it was the cloud behind which the sun had just fallen or certain dark thoughts that broke over her like waves, was unclear. She opened the door and disappeared inside.

Chapter Eighteen

Neither of them was aware of a movement at the kitchen window or of the anxious face looking out and observing them as they parted. Mrs. Waterson sat down and tried to read the daily newspaper but the pain was quite bad today. She found it hard to concentrate and she had things on her mind. She worried about Agnes. Ever since she had escaped from that unfortunate marriage to Carlton Brooke Agnes had lived at home with her mother. She seemed contented enough and never complained but Mrs. Waterson knew her daughter; she was aware that some unhappiness lingered just below the surface and it distressed her.

'I wish she had never met that damnable man,' she murmured. 'Perhaps if I hadn't been such a dreadful snob, perhaps if I'd allowed matters to take their course, she would be happier now.'

She shook away the thought. Mrs. Waterson's nature was too stern to allow her to linger over past misjudgements. Things had gone the way they had and that was that. It was the future that she must concern herself with. Her own future was now clearly delineated, but Agnes had many years ahead of her. They must not be wasted.

Mrs. Waterson winced as another surge of pain rose within her.

'I must put things right,' she said firmly, 'whilst I can.' As Agnes entered the room she shrugged away the pain and smiled.

Wilkie too had a lot to think about. His mind raced. Could it be Conlon or Deitch who were responsible for the anonymous letters? It didn't see like Conlon's style. Nor could he equate John Deitch with anything quite so sordid and personal. So who could it be? Whoever it was knew about the events at the hall but why had these threats suddenly materialised after those very events? Did someone believe he and Agnes were responsible? His mind returned again and again to Conlon. Conlon had a formidable network of unsavoury accomplices so perhaps...perhaps... He was suddenly and painfully aware that Agnes had him, just him, and no-one else.

It was Sunday evening and Wilkie walked down the tiny public bar of the Fisherman's Retreat Hotel. He was immediately aware of a hum of conversation at the bar. It was clear that events at the hall had captured the interest of a trio of local drinkers.

'Well, it won't be anyone local, of that we can be sure,' he heard the landlord say. He was a good humoured, swarthy ex fisherman who looked permanently uncomfortable in a smart shirt and tie ('for the tourists' he explained, 'I'd best look smart for the tourists. The missus says so and what the missus says...'). 'No-one round here has any particular grudge against the man though I can't say I've taken to him. He's been generous with his money, he uses local craftsmen and he's been here a time or two so I won't speak ill.'

'Mrs. Waterson and Agnes suffered at his hands, though,' one narrow, withered individual contributed. 'Do you think it could have anything to do with them?'

There was a roar of raucous, derisive laughter.

'I can't imagine Mrs. Waterson and Miss Agnes stringing up a blood soaked effigy from a tree!'

'It's a shame Marcus Waterson isn't here.'

'That was a bad business,' the landlord sighed, 'the way he was duped out of all that money. They lost the house and everything. And now he's away on the continent, they say, too ashamed to come home.'

They saw Wilkie approaching the bar.

'What do you think, Wilkie? Can you imagine Agnes Waterson climbing a tree and hanging an effigy from it?'

'I don't think either of those ladies has climbed a tree in many a long year though Agnes would undoubtedly have the spirit.'

There was a burst of laughter.

'She was a lively young lady and that's a fact,' the landlord agreed. 'There wasn't anything you boys dared do that she wouldn't do as well. I remember her diving off the harbour wall after you, Wilkie, and wandering deeper into the caves on the hill than any others dared.'

'Aye and a lot of trouble she landed me in as well,' Wilkie reminded them. 'Somehow it was always my fault.'

'Here's to Agnes,' the slender man said, raising his glass and drinking, 'and to Mrs. Waterson. God bless them both.'

'Aye,' his broad companion agreed, 'things will never be quite the same now they've left the hall.'

There was a moment of silence.

'It can't be a local,' the landlord repeated. 'There's no reason.'

Wilkie raised his glass and drank deeply. He didn't speak.

'Has there been any news of Marcus Waterson?' the landlord asked.

Wilkie shook his head.

'Is he still somewhere in Europe?'

'I believe so.'

'What's he doing now?'

'Something to do with tourism and hotels, - high end clientele I believe. I think he's doing quite well.'

'Do you think he'll come back some day?'

'He'll need to make it soon,' Wilkie said. 'Time is running out. Have you got a newspaper?'

He took the paper and sat in a quiet corner. He had to think. For an hour he sat with the paper unopened in front of him. It all began in the walled garden but why there? Why the graves? Why the theatrical effigy? Who could it be? He thought about the items buried in the mounds – the ring, the lock of hair, - loss, tragedy, betrayal... Who had suffered such a loss?

He barely moved. His thoughts shifted to Agnes and the anonymous writer. His fist clenched and his eyes blazed. He muttered something under his breath. The drinkers at the bar glanced at him and turned enquiringly to the landlord. He shrugged.

'Something on his mind,' he ventured. 'Better leave him be.'

Another half hour passed before Wilkie moved then he laid the paper down on the table. 'It can only be him,' he said suddenly. He stood up. 'There's no-one else could have done it, no-one. And if it's him then he must be stopped...' He drained the last of his drink and turned to leave. 'But if it is him....then why now...? It all comes back to Conlon...somehow...' He paced towards the bar. 'It's got to be done,' he muttered towards the group at the bar. 'Someone's got to do it. It might as well be me.' He put the glass down heavily on the oak bar and left the hotel without a backward look.

'What was that about?' one of them asked as the door closed behind him.

'Search me,' the landlord said, 'but it looks like Wilkie has a lot on his mind.'

Wilkie headed directly home. Once inside he rummaged through a drawer, throwing the contents aside until he found what he was looking for. It was a creased, worn business card. It contained an address. He smiled, grimly triumphant.

'Now we'll see,' he muttered, 'It's time to pay a visit.'

There were other people in the bar that night, a family who were staying at the hotel, a couple out for an evening meal and a man who sat on his own in a corner of the bar. When Wilkie entered the room he seemed to withdraw even deeper into the shadows. He turned sideways and kept his head low. When Wilkie left he waited a few minutes and then gathered his camera, which was lying on the seat beside him, and slipped unnoticed from the bar. Once outside he turned and hurried to the small car park which lay behind the row of cottages and beside a small childrens' play area. His was the only car remaining. He climbed hurriedly in and drove away and as he turned onto the road beyond the village he sighed with something like relief.

Chapter Nineteen

The photographer drove across the main road and headed east into a barren tract of moorland and forestry, his eyes resolutely focused on the road ahead. The landscape was depressingly dull but he saw little of it. His mind was busy, preoccupied with the events of recent days.

'A fool's errand,' he muttered, 'and nearly caught.'

The road gained height and passed through blank and sullen lines of grey conifers, hunched and brooding and lying over the hillsides like a shroud.

'I should never have got involved,' he said, forgetting for a moment that it was he who instigated the conspiracy. 'You're a fool, John Gill, a bloody fool. How could you hope to defeat the likes of Leigh Conlon?'

Occasionally there were breaks as the landscape broke clear of the forests. Rocky crags rose through heather and peat. He could see the mountains now, distant, a troubling presence, ghosts sleeping beyond the moor.

'Let them sleep,' he thought morosely. 'Why awaken ghosts? What's the point? Your father wouldn't expect this of you,' his monologue continued. 'He'd say, 'Get on with your life, John, and forget about revenge and justice. Leave the past where it is.' That's what he'd say and he'd be right. Besides, he's dead and gone so what's the point, eh? What's the point? I was nearly caught tonight. What if he's asked questions? What then?'

The road began a gradual, winding descent. It fell once more into the brooding darkness of commercial forestry only emerging as he approached the lights of a small collection of houses huddled around a bridge and river. He turned the car slowly into a small car park outside Trask Bridge Hotel and turned off the lights.

'I want no more to do with it,' he told himself. 'I'll tell him. Tomorrow I'm going home. We should never have started. I've had enough.'

Trask Bridge was the sole and singular speck of civilisation in this barren tract of country. The hotel was just off the road, strangely turreted with projecting granite towers. Birch woodland gathered beyond it and there were lawns to its side. A sun lounge with extensive glass windows looked out over the lawns towards the river which passed beneath a wide arched Victorian bridge before vanishing behind a cluster of disparate houses. It was a perfect place to hide, far from prying eyes, a safe place to plot and plan.

'It's alright for him,' he muttered as he opened the car door. 'He's got nothing to lose. I've got a job, a family...He keeps himself safe up here and he sends me to wander round the village. He says I'm to watch and wait...but what for? What for, eh? I'm damned if I know. Wait to be caught is what I think...'

He clambered from the car and strode angrily towards the hotel entrance. He ran up the stairs, two at a time. On the first floor he turned down a short corridor to a room at the end, overlooking the river. He knocked sharply and entered without waiting for a response.

Half an hour later the proprietor of the establishment passed the door. She heard voices inside but being acutely aware of the protocols associated with her occupation she thought it best not to linger. However, the voices were quite loud and impassioned and she could not help but catch snatches of their conversation as she walked (slowly) towards the stairs.

'I've taken enough risks. I'll take no more,' she heard one person say sharply. 'I should never have listened to you. I'm going back to the continent. I should never have left.' The voice sounded angry and fearful. 'We should leave it to the investigators we hired. Perhaps they'll find something in the business accounts.'

She recognised the voice which replied. It was the voice of the refined young man who had booked the room for four weeks but now seemed disinclined to leave. Only that morning he had booked until the end of the following month. He was well dressed and had an educated accent.

'Just the sort of person we like,' she thought.

'That's a hopeless business,' he said. His voice was gloomy and without hope. 'His accounts are locked tight. It would take a decade to find a path through his dealings.'

'Then there's nothing more we can do. We have to get on with our lives.'

'Nothing more we can do?' The young man spoke more quietly now but his words were expressed with such icy determination she could not help but hear them. 'I will not stop until this matter is resolved. With you or without you I'll continue until he's exposed for what he is.'

She could find no further excuse to remain so close to the door and moved down the stairs.

Later she saw the refined young man lead his visitor through the hotel lobby. She looked at the second man curiously. He shared a similar tan but was slighter and had a haunted, hunted look about him. The two men shook hands amicably and in a manner that suggested a friendship which would endure brief disagreements. She felt relieved that there was no discord and that her young gentleman had no cause to leave the hotel.

'You will let me know how matters develop?'

'Of course.'

'I'm sorry...I...family, you know... I have to think of them... I...'

'I understand.'

'Will you return to Strathan soon?'

'I shall return as soon as I can, very soon now I think. But first I shall apply a little more pressure to our adversary.'

'Be careful.'

The outer door opened and closed. A draught of cold air fought momentarily against the warmth of the hotel lobby but was quickly repulsed. The proprietor watched as the young man approached. He smiled as he passed her on his way to the stairs.

'Is everything alright, Mr. Waterson?' she asked.

'Yes, yes indeed. Everything is as good as it can be,' he smiled. 'Goodnight.'

'Goodnight.'

Chapter Twenty

'Maurice Harmison, John Deitch, Leigh Conlon,' Jack said. 'There was an investigation a number of years back where those names occurred together. Harmison was arrested for a property scam involving villas in Spain. Within a period of six months he sold twenty properties on a new development which didn't even exist. It was one of my city colleagues, long retired now, who pursued the case. It was very well organised. Harmison said he had been approached by a businessman who introduced himself as Leigh Conlon. Harmison was recently redundant and facing an insecure future. He was one of those bearded, ex–hippie, idealist types. He was easily convinced to join in a business venture which seemed designed to solve all his worries. He mortgaged his property to the hilt, drew out his savings, persuaded his wife and her parents to support him and invested the lot. Everything seemed above board. He had seen the details of the properties; he'd been invited to Spain to look at the development for himself. He was introduced to a man called John Deitch who was in charge of the practicalities. The money was transferred by solicitors into a bank account in the name of the business. Harmison sat back and waited for the profits to roll in. He paid himself a modest salary in expectation of a share in dividends at the end of the year.'

'I assume the profits never came,' Aaron said. 'Perhaps he should have seen it coming. But desperate people are the most easily fooled. They want to believe in schemes that are too good to be true.'

'Harmison was a fool,' Jack agreed, 'but he was a drowning man grasping a straw and an idealist too. He won't be the last person to be fooled by promises of easy wealth. Things turned very sour indeed. Communication with Deitch and Conlon ceased entirely. His salary, meagre as it was, ceased to be paid. He couldn't make any contact. They didn't answer his emails; the phones were cut off; the office addresses turned out to be bogus. People demanded updates on their investments. Some wanted their money back. It was then that he discovered the bank account had been emptied and closed and his anxiety turned to panic. Deitch and Conlon had vanished from the scene and so had the money. When the walls crumbled it transpired that Deitch and Conlon had been on different continents all the time and had perfect alibis. The people who had introduced themselves as Deitch and Conlon bore no resemblance to them. The solicitor vanished. Harmison was beached.'

'And since Deitch and Conlon had no records of significance our colleagues assumed that two con men had impersonated them and that Harmison was either a victim or an accomplice.'

'There was a general feeling that he was a foolish victim of an elaborate fraud but there was also evidence that he had handled some of the money and had drawn a salary. He was also on the point of departure to foreign climes when he was arrested. He was prosecuted and received a short sentence but the cost in other ways was severe. He lost his home, his family, every penny he had and his reputation. He spent some time receiving psychiatric support on his release and after a few years working offshore on oil rigs he bought the croft where he died.'

'You think Deitch and Conlon were behind the scam?'

Jack nodded. 'The money was carefully laundered through legitimate companies of course but yes, I have no doubt. I imagine their legitimate businesses saw their profits and investments rise considerably over the next year or so but no-one was inclined to check. The case was closed.'

Jack and Aaron were sitting in the inner office of the police station in Portskail. Outside the window they could hear vehicles moving slowly along the road between parked cars. They were on the first floor. From where they sat they could see out over the rooftops to where the sea loch stretched inland for ten miles where it narrowed and was lost beneath grey and purple peaks. The sun was falling slowly towards the south west but was still high in the sky. Yachts and small inshore craft moved restlessly on the water. Gulls soared over the roofs.

'I assume there'll be other such frauds for us to find if we begin to search,' Aaron said.

'I found two other names with tenuous associations with our friends, - Gill and Barden - but detailed evidence is hard to uncover. Gill died abroad last year. Barden could be anywhere. I'm sure that we would find others were we to devote our lives to the search,' Jack agreed, 'but I must decline the opportunity to participate. Pursuing this sort of fraud is well beyond my skills and even further beyond my patience. Even my colleagues have been stretched to the limits by my persistent enquiries. I've contacted the appropriate national squad but they sounded distinctly disinterested. They have bigger prey to hunt and insufficient staffing to pursue historical cases that may or may not exist.'

'Then what are we to do?' Aaron asked. 'I don't feel inclined to let matters rest just yet.'

'I think you should visit Deitch and enquire whether he visited Harmison. He is the weaker of the two men. If it was him, he visited Harmison alone and a week or ten days before Conlon. Perhaps the first visit prompted the second visit – who knows? It will do no harm to stir things up, muddy the waters so to speak. I also think it would be worth meeting the Watersons. Perhaps we can learn something of their dealings with Conlon and Deitch. I find it difficult to believe that Conlon acquired Strathan Tower without some devious practices. Beyond that there is little we can do unless, of course, something else happens. We can keep things ticking over here for a few days. Let's see what we can discover before the end of the week. After that, I think we must move on to other things.'

The next morning Aaron set out to make his two visits. He pulled up outside the White House in the late morning. He found Mrs. Waterson alone. Agnes had driven into Portskail to collect some medicines.

'My life seems to consist of taking various medicines designed to fight against the inevitability of nature,' she smiled. 'In the spaces between the routine they impose I continue to live my life. There is little to be said for growing old. One may become wiser but it would be less than wise not to wish for a few more moments of youthful folly. I would willingly sacrifice my wisdom, I think.'

Aaron introduced himself.

'Do come in, Detective Inspector. I have been expecting you ever since this sordid business at the hall began. Shall we sit in the kitchen? It's a lovely sunny room and looks out over the garden. We shall also see Agnes when she returns.'

'When did you first hear about the recent events at the hall?' Aaron asked once they were seated by the oak table.

'Oh, Wilkie or Agnes or even both of them together – I forget. I heard them speaking about some close circuit television in the garden. It seemed quite preposterous. They told me about the effigy in the tree but not until several days after it was discovered. They think it would worry me. You don't suspect me, I hope. I'm rather beyond such shenanigans. I rather wish I could still climb trees but alas, I cannot.'

'I'm looking for a little background information on Mr. Deitch and Mr. Conlon. I thought your perspective might be of interest. I also wondered if there was anyone you thought might hold a particular grudge.' Mrs. Waterson sat down heavily on the kitchen chair. Aaron looked at her in concern. 'It's a matter of very little importance and no urgency,' he said. 'I can return another day or not at all.'

Mrs. Waterson shook her head. 'No,' she said, 'No, it is better to speak at once. You may not get a second chance.' She laughed weakly. 'I shall be perfectly comfortable in a moment.' Her face was creased with pain. 'I hate taking tablets, you know. They make one so dreadfully drowsy. Soon I shall have no choice, I'm afraid, but for now I must fight back. Now, help me to my feet. I shall walk up and down for a moment and then I'll be ready to speak.'

Aaron lifted her gently and walked around the kitchen with her, supporting her. After a few minutes she seemed to regain something of her strength and walked more easily. Then she sat down and motioned to Aaron to sit.

'Now, you asked who might hold a grudge against either of these gentlemen. I think it would be most reasonable to place my name on your list. Mr. Deitch is a silly man and I have little time for him. He lives in the hall where I was born and where my family have lived for generations but I bear him no ill will. I feel sorry for him. He is like a fly in a spider's web; he had a chance to break free, no doubt, but when the opportunity arose he appears to have turned round and thrown himself back into the filaments. He is too weak, you see.

'Mr. Conlon is different. There are matters for which I can never forgive him. He drove my husband to his death. My husband was a good businessman but there was a flaw in his character. He chose to see the best in the people he encountered. He did not realise that truly evil people like Mr. Conlon existed. He paid dearly for his weakness but I didn't blame him. It's better to trust and be deceived, don't you think, than never to trust? Marcus was the same.'

'Your son had dealings with Conlon?' asked Aaron. 'I knew he had faced some difficult times but....'

'You are very diplomatic, Detective Inspector, but, my goodness, you have been doing your homework,' Mrs. Waterson smiled weakly. 'Yes, my son Marcus is not here where he ought to be. I rarely know precisely where he is. I would dearly like to see him again but letters and emails from different European cities must suffice. Do you know, Mr. Marks, I even have a Facebook Page? Don't you think that is very modern of me? I consider myself fortunate that we can communicate by such means. It's better than nothing, I suppose.'

'Does he know that you're ill?' Aaron asked.

'Of course not, I would be most displeased were anyone to tell him such a thing. He will return when he feels able. Perhaps it will be before the end; who can tell?'

'Where is he now?'

'The last communication from him was a few weeks ago. He posted a photograph of himself in Southern Spain. He has been producing some freelance writings for travel magazines and he has some business in the tourism and leisure sector in several Mediterranean countries. For a time he worked with a university friend but he has his own businesses now. He has been doing very well. I am very proud of him.'

'What about your daughter, Agnes?'

Mrs. Waterson flinched and looked away. 'She is very dear to me,' Mrs. Waterson murmured. 'I could not have managed without her.' She looked sharply at Aaron. 'You have a kind face,' she said.

'Wilkie spoke highly of you and I have great faith in his judgement. I shall follow my husband's example and trust you.'

She paused for a moment.

'My daughter made a very poor marriage,' she said softly, 'and I blame myself for it. Mr. Carlton Brooke was introduced to us by a foolish and gullible friend. He was personable, successful and seemed a most suitable young man. I was happy to see things progress as they did and I placed no obstacle in their path. What I did not know was that Mr. Carlton Brooke had been carefully placed in our company by Mr. Conlon. By the time this became apparent it was already too late. My daughter and Mr. Brooke were married. I shall not describe to you the consequences of this match. He was a brute and a bully. The marriage did not last and Agnes returned home. I could never forgive Mr. Conlon for what he did to my family. If I am truly honest with you, inspector, I would happily see the man dead. I would rejoice.'

Aaron nodded. 'I understand,' he said. 'I thank you for your honesty and trust. I shall not use that information without your permission.'

'Thank you, I would appreciate that.' Mrs. Waterson glanced through the window. 'Oh look, here's Agnes now. Do you want to ask her any questions?'

Aaron shook his head. 'You've been more than generous with your time. I've only one further question. Have you seen any unfamiliar figure in the village other than obvious tourists?'

Mrs. Waterson shook her head. The door opened and Agnes entered carrying a small package and a shopping basket. Aaron was immediately struck by the softness of her eyes as she saw him and smiled. He caught a brief glimpse of sadness and melancholy that her sudden smile had not quite disguised. That smile was a wave breaking on the shore. It hinted at the deep ocean beyond. He felt strangely sorry for her.

'This is Detective Inspector Marks,' her mother explained. 'We have been having a most interesting conversation.'

For the briefest of moments Agnes had the look of a guilty child caught in an act of petty theft. Aaron smiled. He held out a hand. He liked these people.

'I was about to leave,' he said. 'I've taken up enough of your time. I must visit Mr. Deitch and then I shall return to Portskail. There's just one further question I need to ask. Do either of you know a man called Maurice Harmison?'

Agnes shook her head. Mrs. Waterson thought for a moment before she too said she had not.

'You seemed to hesitate,' Aaron prompted her. 'Is there anything, anything at all that is familiar about that name?'

Mrs. Waterson shook her head again. 'I have a vague recollection of a man who visited my husband some time before his death. I remember it particularly because it was quite unusual and rather strange. He knocked at the door of the hall quite late in the evening. He was very agitated, I recall. My husband took him into the study and spoke to him for a few minutes and then he left. I thought the name was Harrison but....well...Harrison - Harmison...I could have been mistaken I suppose.'

'Do you know what they spoke about?'

'I remember my husband was restless for the rest of the evening. He tried to hide it but I'm sure he was worried by what he had heard. He passed it off as a matter of business and of no concern but I remember feeling quite uncomfortable about it and rather cross that he would tell me no more. But why do you ask?'

'Mr. Harmison was found dead. He had taken his own life. It would appear he was acquainted with Mr. Conlon.'

'Do you think his suicide may have some connection to Conlon or Deitch?' Agnes interrupted him.

'I can't say at present. We're making some enquiries.'

Agnes turned and stared through the window. 'I hate that man,' she exclaimed. 'I hate him. He has ruined so many lives. I wish he was dead. He killed my father; he ruined my family. He drove my brother....'

'Agnes!' Mrs. Waterson interrupted her sharply. 'We do not talk of these things. If there is nothing we can do to change events we must not waste our lives trying. Conlon may rot for all I care and Deitch can have the dubious pleasure of living with himself. Now see the Inspector out, Agnes dear, and then come and sit with me.'

Fifteen minutes later Aaron pulled up outside Strathan Tower.

Chapter Twenty One

'Harmison is dead. How can that be?' John Deitch repeated the words over and over to himself. 'How can that be?'

Aaron Marks had just left and John Deitch was left alone. He paced the room in a state of some agitation then gathered together his coat and hat, hurriedly donned outdoor boots and headed down to the shore. The wind was blowing strongly now and the waves were throwing wisps of foam back over their heads as they rolled and broke in long silver lines. Far out he could see a dark Atlantic depression moving towards the land. The good weather was about to break.

He had spoken to Harmison only a couple of weeks ago. He didn't seem like a man about to end his life. He seemed resigned, - not happy, perhaps – but almost contented. He said he had pieced together the shards of his life and had found something to sustain him in his little croft with the moorland and the sea for company. They sat together in the small conservatory at the end of the house. Harmison looked out of the window a great deal, he recalled. He brushed aside all apologies and expressions of regret. He spoke of the sea and the mountains, of his vegetable garden and the animals and birds that haunted the shore. He did not want to hear of anything else. No matter how John tried to talk of the past he turned the conversation back – back to the sea, the gulls and gannets, the walk along the cliffs to a distant blowhole, the storms, the mists, anything except the past. He acknowledged the apology; he refused the compensation.

'I have no need of money,' he said. 'I need very little. I have all I want.' He repeated it patiently. 'There is nothing you can offer me, nothing I require.'

John left after half an hour. He had done what he could. He had made the gesture and taken the first step. He was confident that he had made things better. Yet now, less than two weeks later, in so short a time, Harmison was dead. How could that be? He recalled their conversation; he rehearsed it again and again. There was nothing he had said, nothing he had done that could have prompted such an action, nothing. Yet Harmison was dead and he felt cheated. He wanted to make amends; he wanted to do something good. Now his plan was spoiled.

His mind returned to the interview with Aaron Marks and he went over it again.

'Are you familiar with the name Maurice Harmison.'

'No, I've never heard the name before.'

That was foolish; of course he had heard of him. Harmison had accused them – him and Conlon – of defrauding him. You wouldn't forget something like that, would you?

'Actually, wait a minute. Harmison? Yes, I do remember the name. He was caught up in a fraud case several years back. He tried to blame us, Conlon and me. We were able to show it had nothing to do with us, fortunately. We were on different continents. Didn't he spend some time in prison? Why do you ask?'

'Did you visit him recently?'

'No, I don't know where he lives. Why would I visit him?' His heart raced. Had Harmison contacted the police after his visit? What possible motive could he have? His pulse raced as he strove to regain control.

'That was my next question.'

'I told you, I haven't visited him? What has he said?'

'He wasn't in a position to say a great deal.'

'Why was that?'

'He's dead.'

Just like that – two little words and they struck like a lightning bolt. Deitch felt his face flush and his eyes glisten and stare. His pulse roared and he steadied himself against the table. Everything he had hoped for disintegrated around him like shattered glass and now, instead of telling the truth to Aaron Marks, he scurried behind a feeble wall of lies just like he always did.

Why did he not simply admit he felt sorry for Harmison? He should have been honest just as Emma had said. He should have said, 'I've always felt sorry for Harmison. I've always wanted to help him. I have more money now than I shall ever need and I wanted to do something good to make up for the evil he suffered in the past.' He didn't need to admit his own part in it or the role Conlon played.

But he knew well enough why he could never be honest. Such an answer may have led to further questions and further enquiries he was not prepared to face such scrutiny, not yet.

'How did he die?'

'Suicide, apparently; he took an overdose.'

'Jesus.'

'A car like yours was seen approaching Mr. Harmison's house,' Aaron said.

Deitch shrugged. 'There are a lot of cars like mine.'

'We were given a description of the driver. He sounded remarkably like you.'

He shrugged again – perhaps squirmed was a better word. He felt hot and his eyes felt uncomfortably heavy in their sockets. He tried hard not to show any emotion but it was difficult to disguise his feelings under Aaron's penetrating and relentless stare.

'I suppose there must be other people who resemble me,' he said weakly. He should have known better. No-one could have seen him that clearly. Aaron was just pressing him, goading him, testing him out. He was irritated now to think he might have given himself away.

'Apparently there was another visitor a couple of days before he died,' Aaron remarked casually as he was about to leave. 'He drove a silver four wheeled drive vehicle. You don't know anyone who drives a vehicle like that, do you?'

Deitch staggered as if he'd been struck a heavy blow.

'Are you alright?'

'Yes, yes, I missed my footing on the staircase.'

My God – Conlon! Conlon had visited Harmison and now Harmison was dead. Could Conlon have driven him to suicide? Of course he could. Conlon was capable of any evil.

'A silver four wheeled drive?' Aaron repeated. Deitch was conscious again of those penetrating, grey eyes.

'No,' he said, 'no-one.'

It was a ridiculous answer. The man who farmed the land adjoining his estate had one; the doctor had one. They were as common as horse flies in summer. So what did it matter if Conlon drove one? It meant nothing – until he lied about it.

He opened the gate which led onto the track above the beach and clambered down onto the shingle and sand. Bedrock spread out towards the sea, fissured here and there by rock pools where crabs lingered and beadlet anemones clung in cracks in the barnacled rock. Between the rocks lay long stretches of sand.

'Emma,' he murmured. Suddenly he wanted to call her name aloud. 'Emma.' But Emma was in her studio, far away in the village. He was alone.

At the end of the beach he stood still for a moment. There was nowhere else to go unless he clambered out towards low cliffs which skirted around a headland towards a distant farm. He turned towards the sea instead and walked out across the sand and bedrock towards the waves. When he reached the furthest point, where the waves lapped at his feet, he stopped. He breathed deeply and felt the wind across his face. Already clouds were gathering around the sun. Soon its light would be dimmed and the sky would be grey. It would rain.

A line of gannets glided past, weaving left and right as if avoiding invisible barriers. One, closer in, paused momentarily above the waves then stalled and dived. It emerged for a moment on the surface of the sea. Then, with a heavy beating of wings, it rose again and moved on, scanning the surface and perhaps the depths for food.

For a moment John saw the wrinkled surface as the bird saw it and imagined he gazed deep in the oily depths. He heard the deep beat of the dark waters and felt their slow, eternal motion. His shoulders relaxed. He breathed more softly.

'Poor Harmison,' he murmured. 'I intended no harm – only good.'

He looked up and down the shore. A solitary figure stood near a small headland where the coast turned to the northwest. He seemed to be taking photographs of the sea. He turned towards John and took a shot along the coast towards the hall and its grounds. As he saw John he raised a hand and waved.

Deitch turned away, preoccupied with his own concerns.

There was one thing he could do immediately. He needed to know the truth, for good or ill and only one person could furnish him with that – Conlon. He returned to the hall and hurried up to the drawing room. He took a phone from the drawer and rang Conlon's mobile. The number was not recognised. John knew the signs well enough. Leigh had destroyed the sim card and probably the phone too. He had moved on.

'Damn,' he muttered.

An unwelcomed thought entered his mind. If Conlon had visited Harmison it was because he knew John Deitch had also visited him.

Jarrett must have told him about their conversation, just as Emma feared. His stomach lurched. He knew Leigh Conlon well enough to know what this meant. He was no longer trusted. He was a threat. Maybe Conlon would step back now and let the whole edifice fall in. It would not fall in on Leigh Conlon, though. Oh no, it would fall on John Deitch.

His heart beat rapidly, his head pounded. 'I've got to think,' he said, but for some minutes clear thought was impossible. He poured a drink and sat down. 'I need to speak to Jarrett,' he suddenly thought. 'Jarrett will know how to contact Conlon. I can get a message through. I can tell him he has nothing to fear from me. I'll reassure him and buy some time until I see him.'

He tried the phone again and Jarrett's deep voice answered. He was reassuring. Conlon was thinking of going abroad for a while. No, Conlon had said nothing; there was nothing to be concerned about. Everything was under control. Don't do anything. Don't do anything at all. In particular don't try to make contact with anyone else. Sit tight; he would get Conlon to phone him. Yes, he would tell Conlon. Yes, yes, Conlon knew he could trust him. Calm down, relax. There was nothing to be concerned about.

Jarrett put down the phone and drummed his fingers heavily on the office desk. He thought for a moment and then opened his desk drawer. He removed a mobile phone and flicked it open.

'Conlon, it's Jarrett here. We've got to talk. I think we've got a problem. Deitch is crumbling.' He paused. 'There's something else. The person who has been prying into our business – I think I know who it is….' He whispered a name.

There was silence for a moment before Conlon spoke.

'Okay. I'll deal with it.'

'Don't do anything rash.'

Leigh Conlon clicked the phone shut.

Chapter Twenty Two

Emma Varley knew better than to request an explanation for the strange mood John displayed that evening. He would speak when he chose to. His visit to the isolated croft followed so closely by Conlon's visit and Harmison's death had obviously disturbed him greatly. She could not blame him for Harmison's death but she could not doubt his precipitate action had contributed to it, at least indirectly. Conlon's motivation was unclear but it was undoubtedly less benign. She suspected that there was something else preying on his mind. She waited patiently, glancing towards him occasionally as he paced the room or looked through the window or read half heartedly some item of news from his paper. Eventually he spoke.

'Conlon phoned,' he said.

'Oh?' Emma raised her head and put down her book. John's voice was slow and unemotional.

'He spoke about Harmison. He knew I had been to visit him. He didn't even ask why; he wasn't interested. Perhaps he already knew or perhaps he didn't really care. He reminded me – as if I didn't already know – that my visit was only a short time before Harmison killed himself. Of course he chose not to mention his own visit. He wondered if it was a wise thing for me to do. It would be better not stir up trouble for myself, he told me.' John smiled bitterly. 'If anyone started looking into matters too deeply I might find myself in all sorts of difficulties, he said. He was thinking of going abroad, he told me. He didn't know where. He might even decide to live abroad for a few years.' John laughed aloud now. 'He knew I would understand what he meant. I would face the consequences alone; there would be nothing to link matters to him. He advised me – as a friend, note - he emphasised that particularly - to enjoy my money and my life and to speak of these matters to no-one.'

'He is a ghastly, cruel man,' Emma said hotly. 'How did you ever meet such a monster?'

'John looked at her. His eyes flickered with momentary doubt before a film of indifference slipped over them, obscuring the light. His voice was dry and cold. 'It's not a pretty tale, I must warn you. It will test our friendship. Is it a risk worth taking, I wonder?'

'Ultimately you can have no choice if our friendship is to grow. But what you say and when you say it are matters for you alone. It has always been for you to decide. If you wish to speak then I shall listen. I shall not judge. I know you too well to have my opinion altered no matter how sordid and unpleasant the truth may be.'

John sat down and took a deep breath; then he began his narrative.

'You know I pride myself on being a self made man. I've bored people for many years with my stories about how I began work at fifteen, developed a successful business, saved and invested, bought property, made a profit, bought more property, invested wisely – you've heard it many times. Yes, I am a self made man. That much is true. I like to pretend that no-one else could have made me. The truth is darker; I doubt anyone else would have made me. I would have been a poor return for the effort involved.' He laughed another cold, dry laugh. 'It's certainly true that I started from a very low rung on the occupational ladder, although the exact nature of my rise to wealth is known only to Conlon.

'I began my working life at the age of fifteen. I was born and brought up in a village a few miles from Portskail, you know. At fifteen I came to a clear decision that education was not for me. I left school at the end of a Friday in March and never returned. It was several months before my parents became aware of it and by then it was too late. They were horrified, of course, but I was rather wilful and very selfish and after a few weeks of complaining, cajoling, advising and threatening they gave it up as a bad job. When I look back I sometimes wonder why they never seemed to notice that their son was leaving the house at eight each morning, wearing jeans, an old tee shirt and a pair of old and shapeless trainers and didn't arrive home until well after five, generally looking more dishevelled and unkempt than a day at school normally warranted. They never seemed to notice that my school bag never accompanied me. Nor did it seem to cross their minds that I never seemed to lack for money. I think they were inclined to view my progress through adolescence with their fingers permanently crossed. If I was keeping out of trouble it was better not to disturb our domestic tranquillity by asking questions to which they would not like the answers. They were probably right.

'I'd actually got a job in Portskail. I was working with an old school friend and was cleaning windows in the wealthier areas of the town. My partner worked the town centre and the new housing developments which were springing up at that time. My clients - solicitors, doctors, financiers and business men with second homes, - had larger houses and more windows. I believed I could earn more from fewer calls. My friend was obviously wiser. He knew that the wealthier the clients were the meaner they became.

'Being of an observant and calculating nature, even at that age, it didn't take me long to realise that I could also earn a small second income from what I was uniquely placed to observe within the homes of my clientele. It is impossible to imagine the deceit, the corruption and the sordid comings and goings that were hidden behind some of those walls. Anyway, these people had reputations to protect; they didn't want their nasty, greedy little secrets getting out. By carefully noting their comings and goings and identifying unusual or questionable patterns of behaviour I was able to plan my rounds to maximise my opportunities for closer scrutiny. A little trial and error enabled me to settle my ladder quietly at the right window at just the right moment. All that was required them was to allow the occupants to see that they had been observed. In one way or another financial gain followed.

'Sometimes it was a simple matter. I would be met on the drive by someone sporting a handful of cash and a wry smile. 'I can rely on your discretion, I hope?'

'Sometimes they needed a little prompting so I would arrive in the early evening when the whole family were at home. I told them I was collecting the money I was owed. The evenings were better for me, I said. My eyes, of course, conveyed a quite different message. They understood. It was rare that this ploy didn't yield the required results.

'Oh, yes indeed. I was the soul of discretion, especially with an extra £40 or £50 in my pocket. I continued to be the soul of discretion and my weekly income was supplemented by a healthy tip.

'I was very thrifty with my money. Even as a young man I had ambition. I planned for the future. Whilst my friend got a flat, went out to the pub and spent his money on pleasure I stayed at home and saved. It wasn't long before I had sufficient capital to purchase my first property. It was a cheap terraced house which I bought for a small amount at the lowest point in a housing slump. I turned it into a couple of flats and then I sat back and watched my investment grow. Making money was just so easy.

'I should have stopped then. I was in my early twenties. Money was starting to come in. It wouldn't be many years before I would buy another house and then another. I could have diversified. But the window cleaning was so lucrative. The problem was a simple one – greed. I had the opportunity now to assume the mantle of a respected and bona fide business man with exemplary credentials. I should have stopped. In later years it was a thought rarely absent from my mind. Had I stopped at that point I would never have met Leigh Conlon and my life would have been very different.

Unfortunately at that precise moment I found another victim amongst my customers.

'This particular victim proved quite intractable. I saw him in the process of exchanging some bejewelled items for hard cash with a dubious looking character in a cheap suit. There had been a couple of burglaries reported in the local newspaper over previous weeks so I imagined myself on fairly solid ground. I also thought I could risk demanding a rather higher fee for my services than normal. I was wrong on both counts.

'My target ignored all my preliminary approaches. He even laughed, although there was something icy about that laugh which a wiser man would have retreated from. It was only when I was driven to recklessness that my victim reacted.

'Pay up now or tomorrow morning I'll go to the police,' I said. I was bragging and I was foolishly confident. 'I mean it. Don't think I don't. Either you give me two hundred now or the police will be here in the morning.'

'The man smiled at me. It was like a knife blade being sharpened. He spoke slowly and dispassionately but the smile never faded nor did his eyes flinch. He looked at me like a smiling cat might watch a mouse, a mouse that was posturing and bragging of its strength and superiority. Why, the cat only needed to reach out one paw, extend a tiny claw, and rip him apart.

'I admire your enterprise, I really do, but the police will find nothing here. I am an honest businessman. I have a car lot in the city, I have a skip hire business; I have a small portfolio of properties and some substantial investments in stocks and shares. I have a reputation. You have absolutely nothing with which to threaten me. Here,' he reached into a pocket, 'take this for your trouble. I do so admire an entrepreneurial spirit.' He tucked a fifty pound note in my chest pocket.

'Suddenly the smile which had never left his face vanished. His hand moved from my pocket to my collar and his grip tightened. I was pretty scared at that moment, I can tell you. I'm no fighter. He pulled me so close I could feel the warm breath on my cheeks. I remember his eyes. They were hard and vicious; they were predatory.

'Take it.' The narrow lips parted and the words escaped in a soft, menacing hiss. 'Take it and back away. This is the only chance you will get.'

'I was not of a heroic temperament. When the grip relaxed and I found myself free I stepped back and then back again. Then, from a safe distance, I turned and threatened him.

'I've got a photograph,' I yelled.

It was a lie of course and he knew it. I stepped back again to ensure sufficient time to take to my heels should the man in the doorway venture out. ''Let's see what the police make of that, shall we? And the price is three hundred now.'

'The smile had returned to the face at the door. Without speaking he shook his head slowly and then turned round and went inside. The door closed behind him. I was left alone, seething with resentment from the indignity and the disrespect.

'I turned away and walked down the drive which led between trees towards the road. I reached the gated entrance when I heard rapid footsteps behind me and heavy breathing. I turned just as the man from the house reached me. He took me by the throat and pinioned me with my feet off the ground against the stone gatepost. My loss of composure was instantaneous, my loss of breath followed shortly. I tried to struggle but it was hopeless. Although he was only a few years older he was of a greater bulk and had the advantage of both surprise and a nature composed of a significant amount of brutality.

'He pressed a flushed and perspiring face close to mine and spoke in short bursts.

'I could rip out your throat…and dispose of your body…and no-one would ever know where you'd gone…. Do you understand me? Do you understand?

'I understood although it was far from easy to make that understanding clear. My attacker flung me down like a cat might momentarily free a mouse before returning to the attack. He pressed his foot across my throat until I thought I would die.

'Now get up,' he snarled and released his foot. As I regained my feet I was instantly felled by a substantial blow to the head. There followed a brutal kick to the ribs which drew the last breath of air from my lungs and left me gasping and groaning.

'That's for making me run,' the man hissed. I remember the words precisely, 'and getting mud on my clothes. Now get up.'

'I clambered to my feet rather warily, as you can imagine. I still couldn't stand upright due to the ferocity of the blow and I gasped for air as if it were something tangible that I couldn't quite reach.

'Come on,' he said. 'I'm not standing out here all night. We've been lucky. There are no neighbours about and, so far, no cars. We won't be lucky forever.'

'At that moment I was uncertain whether I would have described my situation as lucky. I certainly had little desire to follow the stranger to his house. I found myself wishing a car might pass by or a neighbour, disturbed by the noise, might emerge and venture onto the street. I contemplated shouting for help but thought better of it.

'Hurry up,' the man said. He turned to walk back to the house. 'Don't worry; if I was going to kill you, you'd be dead already. I want to talk business.'

'I followed him towards the house.

'The man I had so mistakenly attempted to blackmail was, of course, Leigh Conlon. Leigh, for reasons that he never disclosed, saw in me a malleable and useful individual who could be exploited to good advantage and who could be nurtured to assume a supportive (and far more exposed) role in the more nefarious of his enterprises.'

John Deitch paused and looked anxiously towards Emma. She was looking down as if in thought. After a moment she looked up.

'You must rid yourself of that man forever,' she said quietly. 'I shall offer what help I can but you must do it. You'll never be free unless you do. You must speak to Aaron Marks. It's time this was over.'

Chapter Twenty Three

The sun was breaking fitfully through soft clouds as Agnes left the White House. It was just after lunch. Her mother had suffered a particularly bad night but she was sleeping now, the nurse was with her and the crisis had passed. The doctor and the nurse had wanted her admitted to hospital but her mother was adamant she would remain in her house, surrounded by her own things, and she would lie in her own bed. Agnes had pleaded too but more half heartedly. She understood her mother's wishes.

Mrs. Waterson was rather better now and the nurse advised Agnes to escape for a few hours. Agnes looked at her mother's thin body beneath the bed clothes and at her hollow cheeks. Tears rose in the corners of her eyes. She wiped them away quickly. The nurse looked at her with concern.

'You look drained,' she said. 'You need to spend a few hours alone to recoup, get your energy back and recover your spirits. If you can't sleep you should at least go out. Your mother will be well looked after. You'll be no use at all in your present state. I'll remain with her and if she wakes up I'll explain that I made you go out. She'll understand. It will be several hours; she's heavily sedated now.'

Agnes shook her head. It would feel like betrayal. The nurse looked at her sharply. 'Your mother would be most displeased to think you wouldn't heed my advice,' she said.

'Thank you,' she said softly. 'I think I'll take a walk along the stream towards the hills. I'll be back by five o'clock.'

'I'll be here until late evening,' the nurse said gently. 'I don't expect your mother to wake before then so enjoy your walk. You have a phone; if there is any reason I shall call or text you and you can hurry back.'

Agnes quickly took her leave. She paused briefly as she walked along the harbour side and passed Wilkie's cottage. It was Sunday, Wilkie may be at home. He would, perhaps, join her to walk to one of their favourite places. She took a step towards the door and paused beside it. She took a deep breath and rapped with her knuckles. She waited and then tapped again. There was no reply. She turned disconsolately away and walked towards the cliff path.

Low clouds covered much of the sky now and there was an onshore wind which hurried the waves onto the rocks and drove spray against the cliffs. It caught her hair and blew strands across her cheek and mouth. She pushed it back and walked on, her thoughts as heavy as the clouds and as impenetrable. Her emotions were a turmoil of fears, regrets and dull longings, the latter of which were by far the most poignant. Her mother had been acting strangely recently. She knew she had not long to live and she seemed in a hurry to share with her daughter all those memories which would one day belong to her alone.

'I shall leave you little else, my dear,' she said, lying on the couch by the fireside, her daughter's hands held firmly between her own, 'the house, of course, and some bonds. You will share those with Marcus. I am sure he will return one day soon.' Her mother paused and looked earnestly into her eyes. 'I would like to leave you something else, my dear, were it in my power. I would like to leave you happiness and security. I have made mistakes, Agnes. I have done things, spoken words I should not have spoken. If I could undo....' She patted Agnes' hands and closed her eyes for a moment. Her head fell back against a cushion. Then, from a strange depth far behind her closed eyes, she spoke again, quietly. 'It is in your own hands, my darling. He requires no more than a word from you. He is as constant as the hills...Wilkie.... If you...were to...I would be...overjoyed....' She fell into a light sleep.

The words burnt like a small flickering flame, barely visible, so easily extinguished, but her memories and her thoughts fanned it gently until it took a secure hold. Soon it burnt in her darkness like a beacon. It would not go away. She grew impatient with herself and strode on up the cliff path, beyond the tiny bay and towards the highest part of the cliff.

'It's impossible,' she muttered.

She turned inland and crossed the narrow lane before following a succession of sheep paths through heather and grass. The path rose slowly and then more steeply and the heather gave way gradually to grey rock. A few minutes later she could hear the soft trickling of water, liquid jewels tumbling over mossy rock. It was a tiny stream crossing her path. As she traversed the rocks the sound faded and there was another noise ahead of her. It grew steadily more persistent. The trickling brook had been left behind and ahead was the larger stream and her destination. She paused eventually at the top of a steep rise below which a lively stream tumbled restlessly through a narrow gorge.

She turned and looked back towards the sea. The village was invisible from here but she could imagine it, hugging the narrow stretch of shore and carrying within it all those old associations which made it real to her. It was more like another character in the drama of her life than a collection of buildings crafted together from wood, stone, mortar and glass.

A few hundred metres further on she would be at her secret place, where a deep pool lay over white rocks at the foot of a series of tumbling, shallow falls. Above it there was a smooth, flat rock, a long, angled, slippery rock worn smooth through the ages and over which the water slid towards the pool. As a young child, with her father and mother, she had watched fish slither down that rock; as she grew older, encouraged by her brother, Marcus, she slid anxiously down it herself to be immersed in the luscious cold of the pool. Later she brought Wilkie there. She remembered how anxious she felt, rather as if she were introducing one special friend to another.

A few more minutes brought her to the stream, bubbling like laughter over a pale bed, and to her deep pool. She felt her spirits rise. They rose but they could not soar, not as they used to do. Her mother was dying; her recent life had been a misery of pain and loss. Her feelings now carried a weight of sadness which held them down, pinned to the earth, and would not let them fly. But she was happy, in a fashion, to be there. The most complex and knotty of problems somehow unravelled in the presence of that stream, that pool and the simple clarity of the water.

Above her the mountain loomed, immovable and impenetrable. Rocky buttresses rose on its north and western sides but from here the rocky ground rose past gentle crags towards the summit ridge from which the true splendour of the mountain could be seen.

She slipped her shoes and socks off and dangled her legs in the water. Tiny fish fled like silver echoes into the shadows. Above her the sun broke momentarily though the clouds.

She hummed a song softly to herself; it was an old folk tune she had learned as a child, a simple song of love and death. Its melancholy tune and simple lyrics suited her reflective mood. This was her special place. People rarely came up here. As a child she had kept it a strict secret. In all those years she had only shared it with two people beyond her family. One was her best friend at primary school, a girl who had long since left for the south, and the other was Wilkie.

For a time it had been their special place, their secret rendezvous and the place around which their imaginations, their sensibilities and eventually their affections had grown and flourished. If she closed her eyes she could still remember those years. If she concentrated hard she could recall the times they had spent there. But no matter how hard she concentrated she could never force into life the emotions she felt all those years ago. They could not be coerced. If they arose, it would be as if carried on the crest of a wave, when she least expected them and when she was least prepared. The touch of the water, the smell of the grass and the earth, a momentary touch of the sun on bare flesh would resurrect in her the feelings she had as a child and later as a young woman. It was agonisingly beautiful.

She had been sitting by the pool for some time before she heard below her the tread of boots on rock. She turned to see John Deitch making slow, painful progress along the edge of the stream beside the waterfalls. He did not see her until he had almost reached the pool and looked instantly embarrassed and confused. She turned her back to him and moved her legs in the water. She felt a surge of anger at his intrusion into this place. Was there nowhere safe from his grasping meanness?

He paused for a moment, as if uncertain whether to speak or not. At last he decided he could not pass without some words. His route lay past her and could not be avoided.

'Good afternoon, Miss Waterson. I wasn't expecting to see anyone here today.'

Agnes forced herself to turn towards him. 'Nor I,' she said, 'or I shouldn't have ventured out.'

'May I ask after your mother's health?'

'She is very ill, Mr. Deitch, but I thank you for your concern. The last few years have been difficult for her and I'm afraid they've taken their toll. She had a particularly bad night but is resting now.'

'I am very sorry to hear that. If there is anything I can do....'

'Oh no, no indeed, Mr. Deitch, it is far too late for any of us to do anything. The damage that has been done can't be undone. My mother has weeks, perhaps days left to her.'

'Good afternoon, Miss Waterson.'

He turned to walk away then stopped and turned.

'For what it's worth, Miss Waterson, I'm truly sorry for any part I've played in causing such distress. Sometimes one is…sometimes one cannot extricate oneself from….' He paused, mumbling, incoherent. 'One cannot escape the past…I am sorry, truly sorry. I wish…'

Agnes turned her head sharply. 'This sounds like a weak man's excuse for inaction,' she said quickly. She was suddenly conscious of how much she sounded like her mother.

'Good afternoon, Miss Waterson.'

'Mr. Deitch.'

Agnes found it difficult to suppress her anger. Her afternoon had been spoilt. How could she remain there now? The water had been polluted, the mountain soiled. She tried to recapture her mood but it had vanished like a ripple, a bubble, a wisp of air. It would not return. She slowly picked up her shoes and socks and clambered to her feet. She heard a sound from above her and turned impatiently expecting to see John Deitch retracing his steps.

It was not John Deitch. It was Wilkie and he was clambering down towards her. She could not suppress the blush of pleasure that hurried to her cheeks and sent small flames to her eyes.

'Agnes,' he called and his face too brightened with pleasure at their unexpected meeting. 'I've been to the mountain top and along the north ridge. I must tell your mother that I have seen the eagles again. They were soaring in the distance over the cliffs.' He paused and looked at her. 'It is so nice to see you here.'

Agnes smiled and turned away. She felt a momentary flush of confusion as his words resonated with her recent feelings.

'John Deitch passed me a moment ago. Did you see him?' she asked without turning. She stared down towards the distant sea. White lines of foam raised wrinkles on an ageless surface and rolled in to die upon the shore. She too had been cast upon the barren shore.

'I followed the stream down. He probably ascended further over, following a direct line to the ridge.'

'He asked about mother; I'm afraid I was none too polite to him.'

'It must have come as a surprise to find him up here.'

She nodded. 'It was not a pleasant surprise; to see anyone here feels like an intrusion. His presence was a violation. This is a very special place to me.'

'And to me,' Wilkie said. 'Your mother spoke of the places that were special to her, especially the beach and shore at Sandway. It was easy for me to understand what she said. I have felt the same. This will always be the place to which I shall return as I grow older.'

Still she did not turn. She could not. Her eyes followed the path of the stream until it vanished between heathery slopes into its rocky gorge. She heard the distant song of a skylark and pointed.

'Look, Wilkie, the skylark is singing.'

High above, as if perched on an invisible treetop, the skylark hovered and sang and sang. She turned to him.

'Will you walk back down with me, Wilkie? I've been away too long. I must return to mother. She's been ill, very ill.'

Wilkie had cast his pack from his back and was sitting by the pool.

'Please,' he said, 'just five minutes. Sit here with me. Then we shall walk back down together just as we used to do.'

She sat beside him. They did not speak. Wilkie cast a stone into the pool and watched the ripples circle out to the rocks. The sun emerged again and the air felt suddenly warmer. Waves of water, waves of light, waves of warmth – but there were other waves too, moving out from a stone of a different sort, cast in a deeper pool, and those ripples would not cease.

They did not look at each other. Moments passed but they did not move. Only when the sun slipped behind a cloud and a chill breeze rolled around them did Wilkie seem to awaken from his reverie. He spoke slowly and earnestly and his eyes rested on the deep pool.

'I have been harbouring some secret hopes of late. I must speak of them now or I never shall. I don't want to risk our friendship or cause you embarrassment and I shall never speak of the matter again if that's what you wish.' He paused for a moment but she did not speak. He reached out a hand tentatively and took hers. 'My feelings for you are unchanged; they have never changed and they will never change. Is there…could there be…any hope for us?'

She didn't speak; she rested her head on his shoulder and held his hand tightly. It was all the answer he required. He smiled and his smile widened until he felt it encompass the pool, the mountain and the sky.

The walk back down to the cliff and the village seemed to be undertaken on a cushion of air. They spoke and laughed and it seemed that there was no emotion that he had felt that had not been shared by her. As they approached the village their pace slowed.

'Shall we speak of this to your mother?' he asked doubtfully.

Agnes laughed. It was a carefree, joyful laugh. It was a sound he hadn't heard for a long time.

'My mother has been conspiring and plotting this for some time,' she laughed. 'She's the one person to whom it will come as no surprise. She will be delighted.'

They reached the door of the White House and walked quietly in. The nurse heard them from the stairs and hurried down to them. Her expression was grave. The colour drained from Agnes' face.

'She hasn't awoken,' the nurse said quietly, 'not yet. Her breathing is spasmodic and laboured. I have called the doctor. It may be best to prepare yourself, my dear.'

Without speaking Agnes hurried up the stairs to her mother's room. Wilkie looked at the nurse. She nodded.

'Follow her,' she said. 'She needs you. I'm not without hope but this crisis may not pass.'

Chapter Twenty Four

They spent the night at her bedside. They spoke in low tones but there was little to say that seemed appropriate to the time or place. The hours passed slowly and the minutes were tolled by the sound of shallow and irregular breathing. There were moments when the breathing slowed to such an extent they both leaned forward and waited for fear it was her last. But each time the next breath came and gradually as the night wore on it became deeper and more peaceful. The crisis was passing.

The doctor remained with them. He administered a sedative and waited. When her breathing settled he packed his bag.

'Mrs. Waterson will not give up on life that easily,' he smiled. 'I have never known anyone so stubborn.'

'She has things to do which she refuses to leave undone, I think,' Wilkie said quietly.

'Agnes, you may safely go to your bed,' the doctor said. 'She will sleep until morning. I'll return then.'

Agnes shook her head. I shall stay here,' she said. 'I can sleep quite adequately in my chair.'

The doctor didn't argue.

'They're as stubborn as each other,' he grumbled to Wilkie as he opened the front door. 'Will you stay?'

Wilkie nodded.

The morning found them all asleep. The sun, an early riser at that season, was penetrating the curtain even on this dull, damp morning. Mrs. Waterson stirred first. She opened her eyes and gradually allowed them to focus on the scene around her. She felt strangely comfortable and without pain. Agnes and Wilkie were asleep at her bedside. Wilkie had his arm around her shoulder and her head rested on his chest.

'I have been dreaming,' she said. Her voice felt oddly weak. She rather wanted to laugh at the strange sound she made. 'It would seem that my dream has turned out to be real.'

Wilkie and Agnes stirred and yawned. Agnes leaned forward and held her mother's hand.

'I was beginning to think I would have to speak to her for you, Robert Wilkie. You have taken a dreadful amount of time. I assume you have agreed to view Wilkie as a lover and not merely a friend.' She turned her eyes towards Agnes. 'I would be most displeased if you had not.'

Agnes smiled and nodded. 'You are quite incorrigible, mother,' she said, 'but on this occasion I forgive you. The outcome, as you can see, is agreeable to both of us and to you.'

'I am happy for you. You will, no doubt, argue as much as most and will fall out more than many and you will spoil her, Robert Wilkie, and allow her to have her own way far more than is good for her, but you will be happy. Of that I'm quite sure. Now, you must leave me. I shall sleep for a little while and then I shall have some breakfast; a little scrambled egg, I think.'

They retired to the living room.

'I shall never cease to admire your mother,' Wilkie shook his head and laughed gently. 'She will die on her own terms or not at all.'

Agnes yawned and sat back, her head resting on the cushioned back of an elegant floral sofa. 'I must try to contact Marcus today,' she said. 'It's time he swallowed his pride and returned home. Can you stay for a while?'

Wilkie looked at his watch. 'I should phone the hall,' he said, 'as soon as I'm sure Ruth is in the kitchen. She can pass a message to Mr. Deitch.'

It was still quite early so they sat together for a while, close and warm. Agnes drowsed. Wilkie, his arm arched around her shoulder, listened to her soft breathing and felt the poignancy of love and the tragedy of death roll in alternating waves to fall on the same shore. He was inexpressibly happy and indescribably sad, feelings which fused in melancholy as he looked at Agnes, asleep beside him. Only when she stirred and smiled did he unwillingly draw himself unwillingly away and head towards his home and from there to the walled garden and the hall.

Agnes busied herself around the house. She listened closely for any sounds of movement, any call, any cry but her mother slept peacefully until late morning. Agnes was disturbed only by a phone call and by the return of the doctor who watched his patient carefully for some time and then departed. He promised to return in the early afternoon when Mrs. Waterson might be awake. He shook his head.

'She is a most remarkable woman,' he said, 'most remarkable.'

The telephone call was less pleasing. It was John Deitch. He didn't wish to disturb her, he explained. He merely wondered if Mrs. Waterson's condition had improved. Agnes told him curtly that it had. He was pleased, most pleased. He had been thinking about them for much of the night. Emma Varley asked that he convey her best wishes. Her prayers were with them both.

Agnes was annoyed to find herself responding more politely to his enquiries than she wished. His deference, his tone of voice and the sincerity of his words drew the poison from her replies. She thanked him for his concern and hung up the phone.

'Dreadful man,' she muttered half heartedly. She was irritated. How could she have allowed her manner towards him to soften by even the slightest degree? 'He's a hideous, ghastly man,' she said more fiercely.

Mrs. Waterson was as good as her word. She awoke in the early afternoon and at once ate a small amount of scrambled egg. Her spirits too seemed improved and she berated herself for spending so long in her bed.

'Imagine what your father would have thought,' she said crossly. 'Here I am, lying in bed at two o'clock in the afternoon eating my breakfast. It is almost decadent. Your father rose at six o'clock every day of his life and breakfasted at seven. I shall attempt to get out of this bed shortly and shall spend what remains of the afternoon downstairs. I have some correspondence to attend to.'

'You most certainly will not,' Agnes cried. 'You have had a very bad turn and must remain in your bed today. The doctor will return shortly. He will say the same….'

'…and I shall say the same to him, my dear, just as I shall to our nurse. I am old enough to know my own mind and to recognise the limitations of my own body. Now, pass me my gown and that dreadful walking stick. I think I shall come downstairs at once before you decide to lock me in my room like a naughty child….'

Thus it was that the nurse and the doctor found her and there she remained, despite their admonishments. They left the house with much muttering and shaking of heads interspersed with resigned laughter. The nurse would return later but the doctor, having checked her supply of medication, withdrew to his surgery and the requirements of his practice.

At five o'clock there came another knock at the door. A tidy, smiling eyed young woman stood there. She held a large bouquet of flowers.

'Mrs. Waterson?' she asked.

Agnes shook her head. 'My mother is inside.' She indicated the interior of the house. She took the flowers. 'They are freshly picked from the walled garden at the hall,' the young woman explained. 'Mr. Deitch was very insistent. He had Mr. Wilkie pick them himself. He thought they might bring some pleasure to Mrs. Waterson.'

'Do you work at the hall? I haven't seen…'

'Oh no, I'm recently acquainted with Emma Varley, that's all. Mr. Deitch phoned to ask if I could deliver them for him.'

She turned to leave and Agnes closed the door.

'Who was at the door, my dear?' her mother called.

'Mr. Deitch has sent some flowers.'

'Oh, how very kind of him, do let me see them. Oh, how beautiful they are and my favourite flowers and favourite fragrances too. How very thoughtful although I sense Robert Wilkie's hand in the selection. We used to place these flowers in the drawing room of the hall, you know. How very thoughtful of Mr. Deitch. We must thank him, my dear.'

For the second time that day Agnes felt that she was in danger of allowing her feelings towards Mr. Deitch to soften somewhat. She steeled herself against the temptation.

'Dreadful, selfish man!' she muttered but her words were weak and half hearted. 'Yes,' she said more loudly, 'I believe we must convey our thanks.'

Back at Strathan Tower John Deitch stood beside the telephone. He hesitated for a moment and then picked up the receiver. He looked at a card which he held between his fingers and tapped in the numbers he read from it. He heard the dialling tone but before anyone had time to answer he placed the receiver back down.

'Perhaps tomorrow,' he said.

Jack Munro heard the telephone ring but the line was dead when he reached it. Since he had already traversed the room and had become aware of the stiffness in his back and the tightness of his legs he decided to make a call of his own.

'Aaron? I'm glad I caught you. I'm going out. I'll take D.C. Sim with me. It's important to exercise him regularly or he might become obese. He's only been here a short time and I can see the signs.' He nodded towards a slim young man in a grey suit who occupied a desk in the corner of the room. The young man smiled and gathered his coat. 'I had a phone call from that old friend who specialised in fraud cases some years back – I still find it hard to imagine anyone specialising in a thankless task like that, and living in a city and in the south – but that's how it was. He retired, of course, came home. Anyway, he gave me the location of a name associated with the deadly duo, Deitch and Conlon. Barden is the name. Apparently this particular gentleman owns a village store in Dalnvaig. It's in a rather nice spot and the journey there takes in some fine scenery so I'm going to treat young Sim to an afternoon out.

'Yes, Aaron, you are quite correct, magnanimous is the only word. Yes, I'm sure he'll be appreciative. I'll remind him frequently of his obligation.' He looked across at the young man by the door, 'Now, have you got your handkerchief? Have you been to the toilet? I'm not stopping once we set off.' He turned back to the phone as they young man stumbled over several reposts and applied none of them. 'Besides, if I stay in this office any longer I'm going to develop bed sores and repetitive strain injuries. I need fresh air and daylight. Yes, yes, we'll make sure we enjoy ourselves.' He held the phone away. 'Aaron says, be sure to enjoy yourself.'

The young man grinned and assured him that he would.

'The man we're going to see is another victim of a probable Deitch and Conlon scam,' Jack explained to the young Detective Constable as they drove away from Portskail, heading south. 'He was left holding all the debts and precious little else when the scheme collapsed. Apparently it was some share deal involving gold. This particular gentleman, a Mr. Barden, was fortunate in some respects. He avoided a prison sentence and merely lost his money and his home. The names Deitch and Conlon were mentioned again but Conlon was somewhere else at the time – probably on a flight to the moon – and Deitch was, I believe, quite unaware of the extent his partner's subterfuge. It was shortly after this particular case that the Deitch - Conlon partnership folded and John Deitch retired to a life of ill-deserved legitimacy. Mr. Barden worked in forestry for a number of years, raised a small amount of capital and bought a small, village shop. Now, Sim, why do you think we need to speak to him?'

The young man looked nervously ahead.

'Perhaps he knows something that will help us press a case against Conlon?' he ventured.

Jack nodded. 'Perhaps,' he said, 'but he has been interviewed quite thoroughly before, don't you think? Why should we discover something that our esteemed colleagues, with vastly superior resources and expertise, failed to uncover?'

The young man reddened slightly and thought again.

'They were pursuing a fraud case,' he suggested, 'and were unravelling the details of a scam that involved a number of victims.' He paused. 'We are investigating Deitch and Conlon; that's rather different.'

Jack beamed. 'You have the making of a detective, young Sim,' he said. 'You are already, even after such a short time, showing signs of learning from your mentors. Is there any other reason for our visit?'

The young man shook his head. He could think of none. Jack sighed.

'And yet, there's so much yet to learn,' he shook his head slowly. 'Conlon probably visited Mr. Harmison; certainly Deitch did. Conlon is probably concerned that matters he thought long buried are being excavated, so to speak; Aaron believes Deitch has different motivations but he too will be anxious. I trust Aaron's judgement, Sim, just as one day I shall trust yours. It's quite likely that one or both of those fine gentlemen will already be aware of Mr. Barden's location. I would like to reach him first. At the very least that should cause our targets some anxiety. It may provoke some hasty action which will be to our benefit. It may drive the wedge between Deitch and Conlon even deeper, perhaps even to breaking point. Of course, it may do no such thing. That is our curse.' He smiled brightly. 'But at least we shall have enjoyed a nice drive through beautiful countryside. Just look at those mountain ridges. When I was a younger man I traversed that ridge. It is full of airy scrambles, rock towers and steps. I remember it as if it were just last week.'

The journey continued between small green fields, past long, narrow lochs reflecting at one moment only the grey sky and the next moment transformed and enlivened as the sun broke through and painted silent echoes of the mountains on a watery canvas. They turned to drive westwards and descended towards a narrow sea loch and the small village which lay beside it. There was a small cluster of houses gathered along the road and a village store. They pulled up in a parking space beside the store.

'Well, Mr. Barden, let's see what a real detective can uncover. Come on, Sim, it's time to learn from a master.'

They entered the small shop which seemed remarkably busy for such a small community. The establishment, which from the outside bore all the characteristics of a conventional food store seemed, once within, to expand to encompass a newsagent and hardware store as well as displaying a range of items that the local community must, at some time or another, have identified as essential for their survival. The narrow aisles were stocked with so many items they all but overflowed. It was impossible for two people, regardless of size, to pass each other along those aisles so the management had carefully arranged passing places at convenient points where two could cross, rather in the manner of cars on the local roads. There was a buzz of conversation.

Jack drummed his fingers on the counter. A bright faced, young woman looked up. He smiled and waved a warrant card.

'Is Mr. Barden here? He asked. She nodded towards the back room but made no move. 'Go and tell him Detective Chief Inspector

Jack Monro and a colleague are here, would you, my dear? I'll mind the till.'

She returned a few moments later. 'He's says to go straight through. He's in the back room.'

They were met at the door by a small, round faced man in late middle age who greeted them anxiously and led them inside.

'This must be my week for visitors,' he said, 'I expect you're here about the same matter. I've been expecting you for fifteen years.'

Chapter Twenty Five

Beyond the window gulls called loudly. Conlon sat on a chair in the hotel room where he had been staying for the last few days and considered his situation. He knew that it would be all but impossible to unravel the protective web he had woven around himself. It would take an unlikely combination of persistence, time and single mindedness not to mention a considerable financial outlay. The web was sufficient to protect him from all but the most ruthless of investigations. Anyone who began the task would need to be pretty certain that the outcome would be worthy of the effort. Besides, he told himself, when they reached the heart of the web they would find Deitch - and only Deitch could lead them to him.

He stood up and looked in the cheap gilt mirror on the wall. An aging face stared back, the hair dyed black, the skin tanned. He was not displeased by what he saw. It was a resolute face with a firm jaw and eyes that expressed no uncertainty. It was a face that conveyed assurance, strength and power.

'No-one can reach me,' he told his reflection in the mirror.

He brushed aside any uncertainty. A few precautionary steps might be needed, nothing more. It would only take a few words, a few veiled threats, to settle Deitch. Conlon would remind him of his vulnerability. He would explain yet again that he risked losing everything and that at the very least he would lose his fortune and spend a number of years in prison. 'Who knows,' he would say, 'you're growing older, John, you'll probably die in prison.' He would advise him to keep quiet; there would no danger if he kept quiet.

Conlon imagined how he would smile icily as he reminded Deitch that the world was still a big enough place to get lost in. Conlon could change identity as quickly as a normal man could change a shirt. Deitch knew that. Deitch would face the consequences alone.

He opened his phone and pressed the familiar numbers; then he stopped. He remembered what Jarrett had said. Someone was enquiring into his affairs. The name which was rumoured was a surprising one. His was not the sort of mind that would penetrate to the heart of the web but if Deitch was placed under pressure by such a revelation who could tell what he might reveal.

'Not yet,' he said to his reflection. 'Think it through carefully first. There must be no mistakes.'

He sat down on the bed in his hotel room. It was not his usual style of hotel. The room was functional, plain, boring, sparsely furnished and painted white. Conlon was unconcerned. It was adequate for his purposes and for the few days he might spend there and it was far enough away from Strathan and Portskail. No-one would link him to this place. No-one would follow him. There was a television and an internet connection. He needed nothing more.

It was morning, not much after eight o'clock. Outside on the street of the seaside town he could hear sporadic laughter and voices. It was high season. He looked out of the window down onto a grey promenade which ran beside a long stretch of sandy beach and a grey sea. It had the appearance of a town that had been born in the Victorian era and had lingered there, resisting every effort to change it until, realising that it was sinking into a mire of decay, had suddenly panicked and introduced the trappings of modernity into every available space. There were flower beds and areas of greenery, gardens, sculptures and benches; there were also gaudy lights and random, cheap entertainments with the word 'Fun' impressed optimistically on their windows, doors and walls.

Leigh Conlon looked at it without enthusiasm. A number of people were already meandering aimlessly around. It was not a pleasant day. There was a cold wind and the sky was uniformly, dully grey. It was depressing, boring weather. There were people on the beach, even in the sea. Some people would go to any length to persuade themselves they were having fun. He sneered and shook his head.

'Victims,' he said, 'not worth thinking about.'

He thought about Harmison though and he thought about Barden and Gill. Robert Gill had died abroad - somewhere in Asia he had heard. He could forget about him. Now Harmison was gone. That was a stroke of luck. That left Barden and - he thought again about John Deitch and frowned.

'It would do no harm to remind Deitch of the danger,' he murmured.

He picked up the phone and called John Deitch. Then he spoke to Jarrett. Jarrett was evasive; it took repeated efforts to get him to the phone and his replies were short and distracted. He sounded like a man whose mind was on other things. He just repeated the same advice.

'Lie low and do nothing. We need to tidy things up, check everything. Then we need to see how things develop, if they develop at all. We mustn't act hastily. It will all blow over. Do nothing.'

Jarrett seemed unwilling to help. The business with Harmison had been a big mistake, he said but fortunately their luck had held; if anything were to happen to Barden, though, or if Conlon was seen anywhere near him, even the most inept of police officers would start to put two and two together.

Conlon interrupted him impatiently.

'Harmison was a stroke of good luck, nothing more. Who would have thought the old fool would go and kill himself? Barden has a new life and far too much to lose. He'll keep quiet if I warn him off. I can cause him far more distress than he can cause me.'

Jarrett interrupted him again. He was angry now and he sounded scared. 'Don't go near Barden. In fact, don't do anything at all. Stay where you are for a few days. There may be no need to act at all. Wait until next week at least. We need time.'

It was a strange thing to say. Why did they need time? What did they need time for? Conlon was unsettled. Perhaps it was Jarrett who was buying time, not him. What was he planning? Was Jarrett turning against him too? He knew Jarrett well enough; if the ship was sinking Jarrett would be the first rat overboard. He would be swimming to shore before the first wave hit the deck.

He paced the room for a time and then turned and picked up his coat. Perhaps it was a mistake going so far away after all; maybe he should have stayed nearby - but that was Jarrett's idea too. Perhaps Jarrett wanted him out of the way. The more he thought about it the more certain he became. Jarrett was preparing to bail. He was watching and waiting to see if Deitch turned or Barden spoke out or…he thought again of that other name. Surely Jarrett wasn't scared of him. Perhaps he knew more than he had revealed. Conlon put the coat down again.

'It's time I took control,' he told himself.

He stopped in front of the mirror. Firm, unflinching eyes looked back. Those were not the eyes of a man who was easily diverted from his purpose. Things might look as if they were spiralling away from him. It might take an effort and not inconsiderable skill to bring it all back under control. But he would do it. The corners of his lips curled into something that resembled a smile. He felt exhilarated. The game was on.

He left his coat and took the lift down to reception. He checked the newspaper to see what shows were on and then he spoke to the girl at the desk. He would not require a breakfast the next morning, he told her, smiling benignly. He would be out late at the theatre and perhaps take in a drink or two afterwards. He mentioned a particularly crowded bar in the town centre. He would sleep in for a while in the morning. After that he had a business meeting – a conference call – so he would prefer not to be disturbed. He would require an evening meal as usual. He waited until after dinner before he departed, silently and unnoticed, from the hotel.

Conlon laughed aloud as he reached his car. He felt a surge of excitement. It was like one of those rides at a theme park but better, better. First he would ensure Barden said nothing; then, in a few days, he would visit Deitch and hover over him like a vengeful spirit. He would stay at the hall for a while just so Deitch knew he was being watched. Then he would settle his one final adversary. He knew now how he would do it.

'Everyone has a weak spot,' he sneered as he drove out of the town and joined the motorway heading north. 'I know where your weak spot is. I know it very well indeed, Mr. Marcus Waterson. This time I shall finish you for good just as I finished your dear papa. You will never come back this time.' His laughter persisted as his car sped through countryside which he barely noticed.

He crossed the border as night began to fall and he continued north. The stars emerged and the moon illuminated charcoal clouds and still he sped onwards. He stopped only once to buy petrol.

When he reached Dalnvaig it was still dark and the moon had set. It would be an hour or two before the sun rose over those dark peaks which lay to the east and south of the village. He parked carefully in a narrow lane at the side of the village store and turned out the headlights. He sat for a moment and rehearsed his words. Barden would be asleep. His would be a rather rude awakening, not at all what he might be expecting. But then, what do you expect at this time of the morning? It's not likely to be good news, is it?

He knocked heavily on the door and rang the bell. This was going to be fun.

Chapter Twenty Six

When Wilkie returned home from the hall he called at the White House. It was as if each moment spent apart from Agnes was a burden and he carried it most unwillingly. He spent the days enjoyably enough; he enjoyed his work and easily became engrossed in it. He liked the feel of the earth in his hands and leaves and petals in his fingers. This time of year was a constant battle for an unachievable perfection. Some flowers bloomed and others faded with unsettling rapidity. Branches spread like a virus, foliage threw outspread arms and blooms leaned forward over the pathways under the burden of their own weight. It all had to be maintained, cut back and kept in check, a perfect balance of colour, shade and light. He felt like a lion tamer with a chair and whip.

Occasionally he stopped and rested and at such moments he became aware of barely suppressed, dark thoughts. Mrs. Waterson was growing steadily weaker. She did not leave the house now and was often confined to her bed. At such moments he wanted to cast aside his cherished work to sit with Agnes in the house or walk with her in the garden or along the lane and offer what comfort he could.

This day was no different. His tasks were completed and Wilkie stowed the implements of his work in their correct places in the greenhouses and sheds. Then he locked up, called at the house to check for any instructions for the next day, spoke briefly to Ruth and hurried to his car. He found a small, white card tucked under his windscreen wiper.

'I am in the walled garden,' the note said.

Wilkie turned and looked towards the Waterson Gate. It lay wide open. Wilkie knew he had closed it carefully when he finished work. He glanced towards the hall. There was no-one at the windows or door so he strolled through the gate and along the narrow aisle of flowers towards the rose beds in the centre. There was a seat in a small alcove in the south eastern part of the garden, set deeply within a yew hedge and hidden by a heavy growth of bushes and shrubs. He headed directly towards it.

As he approached the yew hedge the bench came into view. A man was sitting there. He was leaning forward with his elbows on his knees. His face was obscured by his hands. He wore suit trousers and polished, black shoes and an immaculately pressed white shirt beneath a light overcoat which hung over his shoulders and spread across the seat.

He heard Wilkie's feet on the gravel but he did not raise his head until the gardener was almost beside him. Wilkie was about to speak when the man slowly raised his head.

'Hello, Wilkie,' he said quietly and a soft smile played across his lips.

Wilkie nodded. 'It's very good to see you here, Marcus, very good indeed. There's little time to waste. You must visit your mother and Agnes today.'

Marcus nodded. 'Perhaps you are right,' he said.

'Your mother speaks of you often. She never doubted you would return. I'm glad you've overcome your pride. I had some fears that you might not.'

'Pride?' the other man asked quietly. 'Is that what it was? Yes, perhaps you're right; pride, shame, embarrassment. They have little meaning in such circumstances, don't you think?'

'There have been strange happenings at the hall,' Wilkie said. 'I've been very fearful for your mother and Agnes. Do you know of them?'

Marcus smiled gently. 'There are matters I need to discuss with you, Wilkie, important matters. I need someone I can trust.' He looked around. 'Is there somewhere more private where we can speak? I feel uncomfortable sitting like an intruder in a place that was once home.'

Wilkie indicated the office between the greenhouses. 'We can reach it without being seen,' he said.

Between the peat, the rows of potted plants, the wheelbarrows and the empty seed trays they sat and drank tea from chipped mugs.

'Is she so bad?'

Wilkie nodded. 'But she's as stubborn as a mule. She won't go until she's ready. Stubbornness is a feature you all share.

Nonetheless you should swallow your pride and see her today. It would be cruel beyond words to hesitate.'

Marcus turned towards a row of geraniums in pots. He brushed the leaves with his hand and carried the musky scent distractedly to his nose.

'You must prepare them to see me.'

'You can wait in my cottage whilst I call at the house.'

They were silent for a moment.

'I'm glad you've been here for my family, Wilkie.'

'You should have been here yourself, Marcus, but they always understood your reasons. '

'I know.' Marcus smiled. 'But I've returned rather wealthier than I left, just as I promised. I've worked hard and I've had my share of good fortune.' There was another silence. 'It was me, Wilkie, me and another victim of Conlon, who were responsible for disturbing your garden. I met him in Spain. He's returned there now and I can't blame him. He was frightened.'

Wilkie smiled ruefully. 'I suspected it was you,' he said, 'though I knew nothing of your accomplice. It's fortunate you stopped when you did. The detectives who investigated matters are no fools.'

'If you stir the sediment firmly enough strange things rise to the surface. It was our hope that Conlon or Deitch would be driven to some precipitate action. Deitch is a weak link and Conlon knows it. I wanted them to know they were not safe, that they could never be truly safe. I wanted to sow seeds of doubt in their minds. Fear and doubt are strong weapons, Wilkie, and I've used them against my enemies. Conlon is becoming anxious; he may start to make mistakes. The police are adding an extra pressure of their own. It may not take much more. I've also enlisted the help of several friends and some professional accountants to delve in to their financial dealings. It is likely to be a futile pursuit since their tracks are very well covered but it may stir the sediment further.'

'Have you ensured that echoes of your activity have reached back to Conlon?'

'Yes, through Jarrett, his solicitor.'

'I hope you haven't stirred up rather more than you planned. Conlon is a dangerous man. If he feels threatened who knows how he might respond? I'm concerned for Agnes and your mother. He may imagine they're implicated. If he fears them he may act against them.'

'Barden has been watching my family. I wouldn't let anything happen to them.'

'Ah, the photographer...'

'Yes. He was frightened you had seen him and thought him a threat. It was the last straw. He's gone.'

'Does Conlon suspect that you're behind it?'

'He may have his suspicions by now.'

'Then we must take steps to bring matters to a conclusion.'

'Yes, but how?'

'I don't know. We need time to think, Marcus, and to plan. What do you know of our two detectives?'

'I've made it my business to know the principal characters in this drama, Wilkie. Jack Munro and Aaron Marks are a formidable team. I've barely started to lay clues before them and they have already made a number of important connections. I'll make myself known to them soon. We'll need them if we are to ensure Conlon faces justice. I believe in justice, Wilkie, just as my father did. A society which has values and ideals must fight for them, don't you think?'

A soft breeze was playing through sweet peas and honeysuckle and the roses nodded almost imperceptibly.

'You sound like Agnes.'

Marcus relaxed and laughed. 'I lack her strength of character, I suspect, but I've been thinking about this for a long time. I think I shall stand for parliament one of these days. Some of those people at Westminster need to be reminded about what really matters.'

Marcus looked out of the window and across the garden. 'Everything is just as I remember it,' he said. 'The flower beds are looking particularly well this year and the roses are magnificent. Their scent took me back immediately to scenes of our childhood – you, me, Agnes. It seems a lifetime ago.'

'I thought you might become a private detective?' Wilkie's smile was ironic.

'I don't think I'm cut out for that sort of work, do you? A blue sports' car is hardly ideal for covert observations. I was very nearly caught in Portskail. Still, it served its purpose.'

'You must let me help you. I made a promise. I intend to keep it. Conlon must pay for what he's done.'

'Thank you, Wilkie.'

Marcus took the key to Wilkie's cottage and departed.

'I'll walk to Strathan over the cliffs.'

'Where's your car?'

'It's well hidden. I'll collect it later.'

'You can take my car.'

'No, I'll enjoy the walk. I've thought about it many times whilst I've been away.'

As he made his way towards the village he anticipated with joy and sadness the reunion with his mother. He also thought of Deitch and Conlon and of justice. He was certain they would drive Conlon to recklessness and that, with the assistance of the police, he would see them pay for their crimes.

Marcus was wrong. He misjudged the nature of the two men entirely. He viewed them through the prism of his own morality. He did not understand how much it would take to drive John Deitch to confess his crimes, to admit his failures, to expose himself to scorn and contempt and to spend several years in prison. John Deitch was a weak, insecure man but he had a great deal to lose and little to gain. More worryingly Marcus did not realise that Leigh Conlon, once cornered like a wild animal, would not cower and submit to his fate. He would become unpredictable and dangerous. Conlon's nature was that of a cold, heartless predator.

As he drove down the lane to the village, Wilkie was under no such illusion. He was scared. He'd seen enough of Conlon to know that, driven to such an extreme, he would be capable of anything, anything at all.

Chapter Twenty Seven

Leigh Conlon left the village store in something of a hurry. He wiped every surface with which even his gloved hands had been in contact then he opened the outside door and peered carefully out. The lane was deserted and windows were curtained and closed. He crept from the doorway and hurried across to his car. The click of the lock sounded ridiculously loud, like a bullet shot or a night time alarm shocking the silence. He started the engine and reversed as slowly and as quietly as he could out onto the road. There was no-one to be seen. Good; perhaps it would be alright after all. He accelerated slowly, quietly in darkness until he had passed the last street light. Only then did he switch on his headlights and accelerate away. Despite the cool and calculated manner in which he performed these tasks, he was sweating profusely and his hands were shaking. It had taken a considerable effort to get this far without his legs buckling under him.

He never imagined Barden would react like that – timid, docile Barden, foolish, greedy Barden. From the first moment, when the door opened a crack to reveal his face, he was emboldened, cavalier and arrogant. He had laughed. Conlon shuddered as he recalled his words.

'They're on to you, Conlon. They'll put you away and I'll be there to watch.'

He wanted to put many miles between himself and Dalnvaig as quickly as possible. He dreaded another car coming towards him or the headlights of a car appearing in his rear view mirror. He saw nobody for twelve miles and then joined another road which headed south east. Another thirty miles of darkness and solitude passed before he met another road and turned south. It was only then, as he passed through the first small town, that he encountered another vehicle. Its driver, on his way to work probably, paid him no attention. He drove on.

This was the worst of nightmares. It wasn't meant to be like this. Barden was docile, timid, a fool. It was he, Conlon, who had control. How had it gone so wrong?

Barden ignored his threats. He was loud and angry.

'They're on to you. I've had visitors; the police have been here asking questions, other people too! They're going to put you away, Conlon, and I'll be there to watch.'

Barden had walked towards him and pushed him, actually pushed him towards the door, fingers prodding his chest impertinently.

'Wait till I tell them you turned up here with your ridiculous threats!'

Conlon shuddered slightly as he recalled the look in Barden's eyes. They had been exhilarated and excited. Worse still, they had no look of fear. Conlon tried to focus on the road. He flinched physically as he shook aside the thoughts and images.

Slowly the grey day was drawing an unwilling light from the early sun and the moorland through which he had been driving gave way to a wider valley and fields where steaming cattle grazed. In the distance, mountains raised cautionary heads to advise of their presence and to warn that the traveller had a long way to go before reaching his urban destination.

A few miles more and he turned onto the main trunk road south and accelerated. He was beginning to feel safer now. No-one would pin this on him. He was in the clear. He just had to cover what was left of his tracks. It had been a close call, though.

Barden had brushed aside his threats. 'You dare threaten me?' he snapped, his mouth widening in a sneering grin. 'Let's go outside. Let's shout so loud we waken my neighbours. I want them to see you here. I want witnesses.'

He meant it too. He pushed forward again and again. Conlon felt something that resembled fear. That sensation unnerved him. He was panicking. He stopped and held Barden still and at arms length. He was Leigh Conlon; he didn't fear people like Barden; he used them. He sucked them dry and cast their empty skins aside. They were nothing.

'You'll tell no-one,' he hissed. 'I won't allow it.'

A man who was in greater control of his emotions at that moment would have realised that Conlon was in a dangerous state, but Barden was caught in a rush of adrenalin that carried him heedlessly forward. He just did not see that Conlon was now at his most vicious. He didn't note the dilated eyes, the perspiration and the cold, quiet voice. He didn't see the tension in shoulder and arms nor did he take heed of the unblinking, threatening eyes.

'I'll tell them all. I'll tell everyone. I'm not scared of you.'

A dual carriageway and increasing traffic drew Conlon's attention back to the road. He crossed the firth and by-passed one large town in a matter of minutes. Then the road rose again towards more mountains. In a couple of hours he would reach the motorway and after another hour the conurbation of the Central Belt. His car would be swallowed up in the grime of city traffic.

Why did Barden shout out like that? If he had simply remained quiet, if he had cowered, fallen back on his chair like the trembling, pathetic creature he remembered, he would still be alive. It was his own fault. Barden had raised his voice and shouted. He had pushed Conlon heavily against the door and then tried to reach for the handle to open it. He must have known that Conlon would defend himself. It was self defence; anyone could see that. The first blow had felled Barden and drawn blood from his nose and lips. The second and third had sent him sprawling across the room. He should have stopped; he knew he should have stopped but he was angry now and humiliated. He hit him again and again and then stood back as Barden convulsed and dragged at his throat. Soon he lay still, gasping and groaning on the floor. Slowly he ceased moving and then breathing. His eyes remained hideously open. The light that lived within them slipped away. He was dead.

There was no time for regret or fear. Conlon had to act and act quickly. He had left footprints in the widening pool of blood on the floor. He had blood on his gloves and a few splashes on his coat. He looked around. There was nothing else to connect him to the scene. As far as anyone was concerned he was still in the seaside town asleep in his room after a night out. There was no evidence to suggest he was anywhere else. He just had to think and plan carefully. He rinsed his shoes thoroughly in the sink and then rinsed the sink. He stepped quietly out of the door, closed it behind him and returned to his car. He collected a wheel brace from the boot and with it prized open the door through which he had entered and which he had just carefully locked. He was sweating and anxious but he remained icily calm. It would not do to panic now; nor would he work with undue haste even though every sound he made seemed to resonate through the darkness with unnatural and alarming clarity. This had to look like a foiled burglary. He would sponge out the small specks of blood on his coat and have it dry cleaned as soon as he reached the town. The gloves he would pack in a plastic carrier bag. He would leave it deep in an overflowing bin in a small parking place near a tourist spot. It would be in a landfill site without anyone noticing. His guilty bag would be just one among many.

He drove on through the mid morning traffic of the conurbation. In another couple hours he would reach the seaside town. He would make one, obscure petrol stop and then make timely return to the hotel around lunchtime. If he was lucky he would sneak quietly to his room and emerge as if after a lengthy sleep and a morning of work. If not, he would simply comment on the pleasure of a morning walk after a late night. No-one would think anything of it. He was just one person amongst thousands. He liked it like that. In the countryside people noticed you; not here. Here you could become invisible, a shadow amongst shadows. He would settle down and slowly forget, forget.

Later that day, after leaving his coat at the cleaners and making arrangements to exchange his car for a newer model – one could never be too careful – he sat down in the hotel lounge and awaited dinner. He was surprised to find himself unusually hungry until he remembered that he hadn't eaten since the previous night. He also felt strangely calm.

He held a newspaper open on his lap but his thoughts were elsewhere. It was time to think and to plan, to reconsider his situation and to plot out the actions that would be necessary to ensure his safety. Then he would move away to the continent. He would never be seen again. He considered the potential threats which remained.

'The police, Deitch and Marcus Waterson,' he thought. He chose to disregard the police. These were just local detectives with too much time and too little crime. They hadn't the expertise. Besides,' he smiled, 'they've got something else to busy themselves with now.' He thought of the distant village and its tiny store and imagined the shock that had greeted some pasty faced shop assistant that morning. It was pleasant to look back and reflect on it from the comfort and security of the town. He felt strong, unassailable.

An image of Jarrett flashed momentarily through his mind and his face hardened into a cruel frown. 'Jarrett is a fool,' he muttered, 'Deitch won't weaken or crumble. He has too much to lose and he's a coward. He always has been.'

A flicker of doubt burnt momentarily. Deitch had caught compassion in the last few years. It was a dangerous disease. People acted rashly when the fever took hold.

'It's time I made a visit to apply an antibiotic,' he thought menacingly, 'or perhaps...'

His mind turned to Marcus Waterson. Marcus would provide an interesting challenge; He was a worthy opponent but he lacked a ruthless streak. He had limits. Conlon suffered from no such limitations.

He felt strangely exhilarated, unusually excited. 'First I'll see to Deitch,' he murmured, 'and then Waterson. Then I shall retire to the sun.'

He picked up the paper and opened it and began to read. He leaned back in the comfortable arm chair and looked up.

'It's a dreadful state of affairs,' he said to an elderly gentleman who had taken an arm chair close by. 'The papers carry nothing but bad news nowadays. The world is not the place it was.'

The old man murmured an agreement. Conlon heard the words 'terrorists', 'murder', 'robbery,' 'not safe in our homes'. He nodded fierce agreement.

'And the police can do nothing.' A cold smile played across his lips. 'It makes you wonder where it all went wrong.'

Chapter Twenty Eight

The village store at Dalnvaig was closed. The lane beside it was sealed off at the road end by a police cordon. A solitary constable stood beside it and glanced up and down the street. A small number of local people stood on the opposite side of the road, their backs to the tiny car park and sandy bay, watching. They remained largely silent, occasionally whispering to each other in the subdued tones of parishioners in a church. One of them, prompted by others, walked across the road and questioned the policeman. He walked back with a look of self importance. The policeman told him very little that they had not heard already. Mr. Barden was dead. He had been found in the back kitchen of his home by the young girl who worked in the shop; the door had been broken open.

'Murdered,' was whispered from one to another, 'someone broke in to steal from the shop. He must have discovered them and they murdered him.' They were shocked. Things like this didn't happen in Dalnvaig.

'It'll be drugs,' someone said.

Aaron emerged from the doorway which led into the lane beside the shop. He inspected the door closely and then knelt down and looked closely at the broken tarmac and loose gravel. He stood up and walked across to the gathered group.

'Did anyone hear anything unusual during the early hours of the morning?'

There was a shaking of heads. Even the couple who lived across the alleyway had heard nothing. Their bedroom was on the other side of the house, you see.

'Has anyone noticed anything unusual in the last few days? Have you seen anyone paying unusual attention to the shop, for example?' The heads shook with comical synchronicity.

'Two detectives were here a few days ago,' one elderly woman commented.

Aaron smiled. 'That would have been my colleagues DC Sim and DCI Munro,' he said. 'Was there anyone else?'

No-one had noticed anything or anyone, just the usual tourists. It was most disappointing. Aaron thanked them and turned back to the shop.

A small boy was standing at the edge of the group. He didn't want to speak in front of all the adults but as Aaron walked away he ran out beside him.

'I saw something,' he whispered. Aaron knelt down beside him and smiled. He was eight, maybe nine years old, a smart looking lad with wide, blue eyes and a look of intense seriousness. 'There was a blue sports' car parked there the day before', he said. 'I like sports' cars. It was really neat.'

'What can you tell me about it,' Aaron asked.

The boy told him the make and model. 'I had a look inside,' he said, 'but it was empty.'

'Did you see the driver?'

'I waited for ages.' The boy sounded disappointed. 'Then I went home.' His face brightened. 'I saw it going away, though.'

'Did you see the driver?'

The boy concentrated. His brow furrowed. 'It was a man,' he said, 'but not a very old man. He was a man a bit like you.'

'Was he about my age?'

The boy nodded.

'Was he about my height?'

'He was smaller and thinner. He had smart clothes. He had a hat.'

Aaron smiled.

'Did you see anything else?'

'I wrote down the number,' the boy said. 'It was a special number, but I lost it. M-A-W I think or M-W-A. I can't remember.' He sounded it out phonetically.

Aaron asked the boy's name and address and the boy answered with very adult seriousness and obvious pride. This was an adventure like in one of his books. He would tell his teacher when he went back to school. He might be asked to tell everyone in assembly.

He left the boy to run home with his exciting news. 'Mum, mum! I've been talking to a real detective. I gave him some clues so he can solve a murder. He says he might come to my school. Mum!'

Mum was suitably impressed and had a lot of questions to ask.

Inside the store Sim was talking to a tearful young woman in a small sitting room behind the shop. She was describing how she opened the shop that morning. It was not unusual for Mr. Barden to come into the shop rather later. She had been working there for three years now and he trusted her with many of the day to day tasks. She often opened up in the morning. It was only when nine o'clock came and went that she became concerned. It was about this time that the shop got busier. She went through the back of the store and knocked on the door to Mr. Barden's private rooms. There was no answer so she opened the door quietly and looked in. There was no-one in the living room so she went through to the kitchen. He was lying crumples on the floor, his head twisted upwards at a strange angle. There was blood everywhere. His eyes were open and staring at the wall. He was dead.

She shook as she described the scene and answered the few questions Sim asked her. Then she walked back though to the shop where an older lady was waiting for her. She bent her head and wept as the older lady comforted her.

Jack was in the kitchen with the body when Aaron returned. He nodded gloomily.

'It's difficult to picture this as anything more than a burglary which went horribly wrong,' he said, 'but I doubt that's the case. First Harmison kills himself then we find Barden dead. Leigh Conlon is behind this somewhere.'

'I met a little boy outside who saw a blue sports' car parked outside yesterday,' Aaron told him. 'He even noticed the number plate - MAW or MWA. It could be a personalised plate.'

Jack nodded. 'Marcus Waterson, perhaps? That would be most intriguing. It may offer an answer to a number of questions. I think we need to look at this developing scenario rather more closely.'

It was two hours later before they set off to drive back towards Porskail and another hour before they entered the two storey, granite Victorian building which housed the police station.

'You look like you need a cup of coffee,' Jack said sympathetically to Sim, 'You look tired.'

The detective constable nodded.

'Good lad, you can get one for me and Aaron at the same time. Go to the café across the road. I can't drink that effluent in the machine. You can get us three cream cakes while you're there.'

Sim grinned and the laughed. 'I suppose I'm paying for it too,' he said. Jack tapped his pockets. 'I don't carry money,' he said. 'I'm like the royal family in that respect. It would probably be useful for you to think of me in that way. I'm the office royalty, Sim. If you need money, ask Aaron.'

Aaron laughed and reached in his pocket. He handed over a note. 'We'll wait till you get back before we begin our discussion,' he said. 'It'll give Old King Jack time to regain his strength.'

Sim hurried down the stairs and across the road to Arabella's Tea Room. The owner, a middle aged woman of a greying disposition, who had opened the café a few years previously and was, for reasons they never quite understood, called Annette and not Arabella, served him with smiling indifference. As he turned to cross the road, carefully balancing coffees and cakes, he noticed a small, blue car parked by the roadside. It was a blue sports' car and the number plate began MAW. It was empty. He redoubled his speed and hurried up the stairs.

'Jack, Aaron,' he called, 'the blue sport's car is just down the road.' He stopped in his tracks. A heavily tanned man, of a similar age to Aaron but rather shorter, was sitting at the table with his two colleagues.

Jack looked up with an ironic smile. 'Ah, Sim, there you are. Let me introduce Mr. Marcus Waterson.' He turned back to the visitor while Sim disposed of the items he was carrying. 'We are particularly pleased to see you, Mr. Waterson,' he said. 'You have saved us the effort and inconvenience of having to search for you. You visited Mr. Barden in Dalnvaig, I believe. He's been murdered you know, just last night, beaten to death in his own kitchen, by a burglar perhaps.'

Aaron understood his role at this moment. He said nothing but he watched Marcus Waterson carefully. There could be no doubt about his reaction. His face drained to an ashen whiteness and he lowered his head into his hands. He did not speak because he could not speak. Too many thoughts raged through his mind. Aaron could see it all. Marcus Waterson had played no part in the murder but he imagined he might have indirectly brought it about.

Eventually he spoke. 'You say it was a burglary,' he asked slowly. 'Are you quite sure that is what it was?'

'Quite the contrary,' Jack replied calmly, 'my colleagues and I, being of relatively sound minds, are quite convinced that it was nothing of the sort. Now, Mr. Waterson, perhaps you can explain to us your own part in this business and stop adding to our workload. '

Marcus nodded. 'It's a long story,' he said.

'We have coffee and cakes,' Jack's expression betrayed no emotion. 'Begin.'

Chapter Twenty Nine

Jack and Aaron had a lot to think about but it was late already and home beckoned.

'You've done well today, Sim,' Jack said as they gathered their coats. 'You can go home and bask in the realisation that you are likely to make a good detective. Enjoy the moment. Tell your family. I may not be so kind tomorrow. I need to speak to Aaron for a little longer about serious, grown up matters that needn't concern you until later. Now run along.'

Sim was laughing as he reached for his coat and headed towards the door. He tested a quip by way of response but it faltered on his lips and he left without speaking.

Jack turned to Aaron. 'I think we should fetch that dog of yours and take a walk along the shore. I need to get out of this office and clear my head. Are you in agreement?'

The two men collected an eager Rosie and set off towards the edge of the town where a narrow path crossed a field towards the sea loch. As Rosie ran across the grassy shore beyond the town, gathering mud and heather and applying it in a random fashion across her coat, their minds were gradually refreshed.

'Summarise for me what we have learnt from Mr. Waterson,' Jack said. He picked up the ball and threw it. 'I need to hear it fed back to me.'

'Would you like the full summary or a synopsis of the main points?'

'The latter, I think.'

'In which case, it would seem to me that Mr. Waterson has added very little in the way of useful information. He has a lot of facts and figures about Conlon's legitimate businesses. There's certainly a pattern of increased income over the years subsequent to the scams we've discovered. They're gradual, though, and spread across a number of ventures. There's nothing that couldn't be explained away by an increase in trade, new investment or rationalisation. The evidence of overseas accounts is inconclusive and is hardly a crime. Investments showed occasional spikes but a good solicitor would tear shreds in any attempt to suggest a link to criminal acts. At best the evidence is cumulative and circumstantial.'

'So our obvious course of action is to pass it on to our boring friends in fraud and leave them to pursue it or leave it as they think best,' Jack said. 'They will almost certainly cast a cynical eye over it and adopt the latter strategy. It will be filed under 'dormant pending further information.''

Aaron agreed.

'Continue.'

'He has however stirred matters up quite admirably,' Aaron continued. 'Pursuing Conlon so carefully in a very distinctive vehicle took a great deal of courage and remarkable dexterity. Even according to his own modest description he was almost caught in the hotel car park. The letters and notes were strategic and clearly designed to suggest an impending catastrophe. Yes, that was well played and very clever.

'He was not quite so clever with regard to Barden, however. Do you think he planned this entirely alone? He seemed overly insistent that he had.'

'I doubt it. However, I think we must exonerate him with regard to Harmison and Barden. He could hardly have anticipated such an eventuality. After Deitch and Conlon both reappeared in his life, Harmison must have imagined the whole ghastly history was coming back again. It was a different sort of mistake which left Barden so seriously exposed. He has managed, however, to probe a long stick into this particular hornets' nest and stir it up remarkably well. The question is, of course...'

'The question is what our Mr. Conlon will do next - precisely so. We must also consider our own strategy. We are agreed, I think, that Conlon is responsible for the death of Barden, despite the very obvious evidence to the contrary.'

'It would seem so.'

Rosie circled round their feet. She dropped her ball. When they walked past it, she scooped it up, ran in front of them and presented it afresh. It glistened, wet with saliva.

'It's your turn,' Jack motioned with some distaste. Aaron threw the ball some distance over the grass and wiped his hands. They approached the narrow path which led along the edge of the loch and stopped to look out over the wrinkled surface of the loch. Rosie returned and sat at their feet, breathing hard, her white legs dark with mud. Aaron looked down at her. 'I'm not sure what Rosie would make of us leaping to such conclusions,' he said, 'and I've no doubt she would advise us that it would take a huge stroke of luck to find any evidence to link Conlon to the murder or to anything else, come to that.'

'Yes, I imagine he would have to be driven to make a very untypical error.'

'It's most unlikely, don't you think?'

Jack continued to stare over the loch towards the hills beyond. 'As far as I can see, there's only one point of weakness in Conlon's armoury and that's John Deitch and I am quite sure he's aware of that. He will maintain a stranglehold on Deitch, I think. It would take a lot to break it.'

A huge, brown, heavy headed bird flew above them. It had deep, white flashes on its wing. It moved slowly and eyed them closely before sliding away on an air current with a flick of its tail.

'A great skua,' Jack said, 'another master predator watching for signs of weakness. Is it an omen, I wonder?'

They turned silently back and headed across the field.

'I was thinking about Mr. Deitch and Emma Varley,' Jack said. 'I wonder how powerful her influence might be. What do you think?'

'I don't think she would exert her influence to his detriment,' Aaron said. 'I got the distinct impression that hers is a passive but critical presence. She would not intervene willingly.'

'I wonder how he would respond if he thought he was losing her friendship.'

'Do you think it would be acceptable for us to exploit his feelings for her?'

'I merely speculate,' Jack smiled. 'I merely wonder how he would react if Miss Varley could be persuaded to apply a little pressure – for his own good, of course.'

'I think Emma Varley would do a great deal for Mr. Deitch – but she wouldn't deceive him, no matter how it might benefit him in the longer term.'

'I wonder what Deitch would be willing to sacrifice for Emma Varley?' Jack continued. 'As much as Wilkie would sacrifice for Miss Waterson, do you think? Somehow I doubt it. Deitch is fundamentally a very selfish man.'

'Emma Varley seems to believe he's not without nobler feelings.'

'Hers is a generous nature, perhaps to a fault. He's very much under the influence of Leigh Conlon; it's a yoke he seems incapable of removing. He won't remove it without a great deal of persuasion and several assurances about his safety, now and in the future. I wonder...'

'Conlon is easier to judge in some respects, don't you think?' Aaron said.

'I think we can be fairly clear how Leigh Conlon will react. He's a clever and devious man and very calculating. If provoked sufficiently he reacts very quickly, with the greatest of care and with whatever level of violence is required. It would be a very dangerous course of action for anyone to provoke him in order to prompt a particular response – but not impossible. His predictability is his weakness, I think.' Jack was thinking quickly now. His dark eyes shone and his brow was furrowed. 'It would take a special sort of courage. Nonetheless, it's possible we could devise a means by which we could provoke him - under controlled circumstances.' His turned to Aaron and laughed gently.

'You think we could contrive to produce a controlled explosion, you mean, rather in the manner of bomb disposal experts?'

'Were I to devise a plan it would be something of that sort. Of course, we're speaking hypothetically.'

'People have been known to be killed in controlled explosions.'

'Nonetheless, let me speculate a little further.'

'Go on,' Aaron said.

'I think it will take a great deal of good luck and a high level of co-operation from several people. The simple fact is that we can't get at Conlon unless we first persuade Deitch that he has no alternative but to help us.'

'Do you think that's possible?'

'I think it is highly irregular and well outside our official remit, but possible, yes. I dislike the idea that we can let a murderer slip away without making an effort to catch and convict him – especially a sadistic killer who seems to be laughing at us.'

They were approaching the edge of the town. Other people were venturing out to take their dogs for an evening walk. Rosie ran towards a gentle looking labrador and they greeted each other. A moment later she ran after the two men and stood panting at their heels. She stood still suddenly and barked once, twice, three times. She jumped up excitedly.

'I think Rosie wants us to do whatever we can to catch him,' Aaron said. 'I agree with her.' He threw her ball towards the shore and she raced breathlessly after it.

'The thrill of the chase,' Jack murmured and his eyes brightened. 'Tomorrow we must consider our strategy. It will not be easy.'

Thirty

Marcus Waterson returned home with little time to spare. It was evening and Mrs. Waterson was sitting on a comfortable chair in the living room. She looked up as he entered. Wilkie stood behind him at the door.

'You are rather late,' she said. 'I was expecting you some time ago. You are so like your father. He was just the same, you know.' She looked at him closely. 'Now don't stand there looking so shocked. I know what a fright I look; I don't need to be reminded by my own children. Come here and let me see you more closely. Wilkie has prepared me most carefully for your arrival. I shan't die of shock.'

Marcus walked over to her chair and knelt on the floor beside her. He took her hands and then leaned forward and kissed her cheek gently. There were tears in his eyes which he could not suppress. Mrs. Waterson touched his face.

'You look so like your father, you know. It's as if he was standing here beside me. I'm so glad you have come back, Marcus, so very glad. Wilkie, be so good as to fetch Agnes. I know she is loitering in her room so that Marcus and I can share this moment but I would like her to join us. You must stay too.' She turned to her son as Wilkie left and smiled weakly. Her eyes too were moist. 'I've tried to put things right,' she said, patting his hand. 'Wilkie is a good man, Marcus. He has always been a good man. You were correct all along.' She laughed softly. 'There, I have admitted it. Had your father been here things might have been different.' She looked up and shook her head. 'But it's foolish to look back on matters that cannot be changed. I shall look forward. I may not be here when she marries Wilkie but I know it will happen. I shall not see their children but I know they will have several. They will be dreadfully spoilt. Can I rely on you to be equally happy, Marcus?' Her eyes seemed paler blue and more distant but for a moment they touched him like lingering flames.

'Of course, mother,' he sighed softly. 'I'm home now. I shan't go away again. Who knows, I may even find someone to love, just as Agnes has. If not I shall buy myself a dog – a red setter perhaps. What do you think?'

'I think you're incorrigible, but I have hopes for your happiness. But you must put this business with Conlon behind you now. You can't live in the past. You must leave him to wallow in his own corruption. It's foolish to think you can gain anything by pursuing him.'

'I shall give up entirely in a few days,' he said softly.

Mrs. Waterson pressed his hands tightly. 'Good, good,' she said, 'Now, I shall take a little nap, here in my chair. We shall speak later.

I haven't felt so happy for many years, not since...ah, here is my dear Agnes and Wilkie too. Come closer and hold my hands, my dears, and I shall sleep.'

Marcus and his mother spoke again, later in the evening after Wilkie had gone home for a few hours. She didn't rise from her bed. The morphine made her drowsy, she explained. 'The small distance from my bed to the lounge seems immeasurably large some days,' she sighed. 'I think I shall stay here tomorrow. I have everything I want now. I am perfectly content.'

They spoke of the time he had been abroad and of his journeys and his work. Agnes joined them and they spoke of times past, of days and weeks and years full of memories. Their mother repeated stories of happy times which they had heard many times before but it mattered little. As the evening drew on it became clear that she was speaking largely to herself. She was losing awareness of their presence. Soon she slept.

She did not wake again. The doctor was summoned the next day. He increased the dose of morphine.

'You should stay with her now,' he said. 'There's nothing else we can do.'

It was early in the evening that her breathing once again became slow and laboured. Sometimes it felt as if an age passed between one breath and the next. Each time they thought she had ceased to breathe altogether she drew another rasping breath. Her mouth was opened slightly and her lips were dry. Her face was horribly pale and empty. Agnes moistened her lips and brow gently with a handkerchief. They held her hands.

The final moment came at last. The room was still, their only accompaniment the lazy ticking of a clock and the beating of their own hearts. Her mouth opened, round and wide like a bird; she tried to draw life from the air as she had always done but she could not. Her lips opened again, as if pleading for just one more breath. Then she ceased to try and lay still.

She was dead.

Agnes kissed her mother's hand and her tears flowed uncontrollably. Marcus was numb and cold. He was so stunned by the awful simplicity of the moment that he could not speak or cry or grieve. Her life had slipped so easily away and yet that moment was the most dreadful in his life. He could not imagine ever feeling anything again. He put his arm round Agnes and hugged her tight. She was all the family he had left. He would never let her go.

'I'll go and phone the doctor,' he said softly. 'Do you want me to call Wilkie?'

Agnes nodded through her tears but she could not look away. She held her mother's cold hand and wished beyond reason that she could feel its warmth again; but she could not.

The doctor and nurse arrived and Agnes went down to the lounge where Marcus sat silently in the darkness. Wilkie arrived and folded her into his arms. She seemed so fragile, so weak and vulnerable. He struggled to hold back his own tears as he comforted her. Marcus watched, as if they belonged to a different world. He picked up a book, idly, from the table. It was his mother's. It was opened on her favourite poem. He had heard her read it so many times, as a child, as a teenager, as a young adult. Now he heard her reading it again.

'When you are old and grey and full of sleep,' he read, 'and sitting by the fire, take down this book and dream of the soft look your eyes had once, and of their shadows deep...' It was W.B. Yeats.

His eyes filled with tears. He lay the book down. He could read no more.

Chapter Thirty One

John Deitch did not attend the funeral. He sent flowers from the walled garden which Wilkie collected for him and Mrs. Davidson arranged. Mrs. Waterson had liked flowers. She liked colour and scent. There would be many flowers. Her funeral was traditional and dignified and she was buried with her husband in the tiny graveyard which lay adjacent to the austere church which she had attended regularly throughout her life. The church was full; most of the families in the community were represented. Agnes looked around the church interior through misted eyes. Wilkie was by her side.

'Mother would have been most gratified to see all these people here,' she whispered.

'Mrs. Waterson was held in great regard by everyone who knew her,' he replied quietly.

Marcus could not speak or look around. He stared glassily ahead and struggled to control the violence of his emotions. Her death, coming so soon after their reunion, hit him particularly hard. The minister spoke and said prayers and they sang. The final hymn was particularly difficult for him. It was her favourite. He could hear her humming the tune gently and he pictured her clearly as she walked around the hall in years past. He stood up; he spoke to the gathered congregation. He did not know how. He was barely aware of what he said. His eyes absorbed the plain interior of the church but he could distinguish no-one. He was vaguely aware of the presence of people, of eyes watching him, sympathetic eyes, tearful eyes, curious eyes, but he saw no faces and recognised no-one. He concluded the eulogy and sat down. Even as the service ended and he led the congregation to the door he saw nothing. With Agnes and Wilkie at his side he shook hands with each person and heard their voices. He knew they were speaking words of condolence and comfort but he heard none of them clearly. His mind and heart had shut down under the weight of grief.

The majority of the mourners departed now and those who had been invited moved to the quiet graveyard for the private family burial. They gathered at the grave around which a glorious array of flowers was spread. Marcus saw one particular wreath and bent down to look at the card. It was from the hall. He glanced around. It was only then that he noticed a figure standing alone at a tiny gate that led from the graveyard to a small track that ran beside it. It was John Deitch.

After Emma had left the hall John had paced the drawing room for some time before he made his decision. He could not attend the church or the funeral but he would be present. He had to be. It was only right that he should be there. He would stand beyond the wall, sufficiently far away to cause no offence but close enough to pay his own very personal respects. He would risk the contempt and disgust of the family; he would brave their looks of repugnance and distaste. He deserved nothing less.

He changed into a dark suit and clumsily fastened a tie and drove to the edge of the village where he parked his car beside Emma's studio. From there he walked towards the church. He saw the mourners leaving and Marcus, Agnes and Wilkie at the door. He followed a small path so as to keep out of sight. He waited until the family were gathered at the graveside and then slipped quietly inside the tiny wicket gate

Marcus turned back and did not look towards the wicket gate again until everything was over. Then he turned to Agnes and Wilkie.

'I shall only be a few moments,' he said, 'and then I'll follow you back to the house.' He left them and walked over to the gate. John Deitch had already left and was walking slowly down the path behind the church. Marcus hurried after him.

'Wait!'

John Deitch paused and then turned slowly. Whatever happened now was no more than he deserved. He looked up and waited resignedly for whatever form the assault would take. Marcus stood before him. Their eyes connected but it was a moment before Marcus spoke. He held out a hand.

'Thank you for coming,' he said. 'My mother would have been most gratified.'

John Deitch could hardly believe what he heard. He held out a trembling hand and grasped Marcus's hand firmly. He could not speak.

'My mother spoke of your kindness,' Marcus continued. 'She was touched to receive your flowers and your enquiries after her health. She particularly asked that I should tell you.'

John Deitch nodded. He was suddenly embarrassed. He didn't deserve this. Blows or harsh words would have been easier to accept. He wanted nothing more now than to leave as quickly as he could. He turned away.

'Wait,' Marcus said, 'Please wait for just a moment.' John stopped but did not turn round. 'My mother felt no ill will towards you,' Marcus said quietly. 'She said that in many ways you were an even greater victim than we were. She said that we, at least, were free of that man. You were not.'

'I shall never be free of him,' John murmured hoarsely. 'That is my punishment. I must bear it.'

'May I walk with you a while?'

John nodded. The two men walked along the path and rejoined the road. They spoke slowly and intermittently at first but as they reached the harbour their words became more urgent. Marcus did not turn towards the White House; he took John's arm and they turned towards the harbour. They stopped outside Emma Varley's studio at the edge of the village and spoke rapidly and passionately. Then John Deitch turned away.

'I'm sorry,' he said hoarsely. 'I can't; you ask too much of me.'

His head dropped and he walked disconsolately towards the door. He opened it and went inside. Emma was waiting. She had seen the two men approaching and was watching anxiously from the window. As John entered she held her arms out towards him and his head sank on her shoulder.

Marcus watched them then he too turned disconsolately away and walked slowly towards the house and his guests. He met Wilkie at the door.

'I saw you follow Deitch.'

Marcus shook his head. 'He won't speak out against Conlon. He's terrified of the man. I've done everything I can. I promised mother that I would give up all thoughts of revenge or justice. I made one last attempt but I must keep my promise now. We must persuade Agnes that it's all over. If the police can't prove anything against him we must accept that we've lost.' It's time to move on.'

They turned inside and closed the door. The hum of voices from the lounge grew louder as they entered and joined the small group of close friends and the ritual of the funeral tea and reminiscences.

In the studio, Emma Varley held John close for some moments before she drew herself away and stood upright.

'What did he say?'

'He doesn't blame me,' he said quietly. 'He spoke of me as another victim not as the perpetrator of a crime against them. He was most considerate and most kind. He said Mrs. Waterson had appreciated the flowers and bore no malice towards me.'

'That's good; that's really good. It means the good things you are doing are having some effect. They see the person you are trying to become.'

'Wilkie and Agnes are together, you know. I am most happy for them. I like them both immensely. If things had been different I would have liked to have known them better.'

'That's good,' Emma said quietly. 'They will be happy together, I am sure. Mrs. Waterson would have been pleased. I hope we may all be able to die with the peace she seemed to have acquired at the end.'

John shook his head vigorously and frowned. Deep creases formed as if he was struck by sudden pain. 'I couldn't do what he asked of me. I couldn't do it.'

Emma turned away for a moment and busied herself tidying paints and brushes on a trestle.

'But you must,' she murmured quietly. He did not hear her.

'He promised his mother, as she lay dying, that he would cease his vendetta against Conlon. He told me he had done all he could to destroy him but he had failed. He had given his word and he would honour it.'

'He is a man of integrity,' Emma said. 'As were his mother and his father. They would have been very proud of their children, I have no doubt. I suppose that means you're free. You are no longer in danger of exposure by the Watersons. You can tell Conlon he is safe so that he can continue his life untroubled by any anxiety. Yes, you are free. You must be relieved.'

John Deitch looked at her. She sounded strangely cold. 'Yes, I suppose I am free,' he said. 'I should feel relieved and contented shouldn't? But I don't; I can't. I feel strangely discontented.'

She didn't turn round. 'If you really wish to be free, truly free,' she said softly, 'you have only one course of action available to you. You know what it is.'

'The feeling will pass. I can live as I did before and have no fear. Conlon…'

'Conlon will return. He will always be a presence in your life.'

'It is a price I shall have to pay.'

Emma was still. She did not turn round. She looked suddenly tired and her words emerged as if from a deep well.

'You will carry on just as before, I suppose, and nothing will change. Nothing will ever change. That's the true price you have chosen to pay but it may be more than I am capable of paying.'

Chapter Thirty Two

A few days after the funeral, Leigh Conlon sauntered into the kitchen of Strathan Tower. His hands were in his pockets and he was humming tunelessly to himself. He looked particularly relaxed and in control. Mrs. Davidson was placing chopped vegetables in a pan of boiling water. She jumped slightly as the door closed and the water splashed and hissed on the hob. Leigh smiled in a friendly sort of manner but the look of discomfiture that had appeared on her face and as quickly disappeared had not escaped him. He rather liked it. He stood for a moment and did not speak. He was not inclined to offer words of reassurance or to allow her to regain her composure. It was more fun to say nothing and to watch her squirm. He did not blink. Mrs. Davidson squirmed wonderfully.

'Oh, Mr. Conlon,' she stammered. Her heart was beating rapidly as she struggled for appropriate words. 'You gave me such a start.'

'Perhaps you have a guilty conscience,' Leigh Conlon said.

He waited for a moment before he smiled. He allowed her to absorb his words and to sense their implication and to blush deeply.

Then he smiled. 'Of course you have nothing to feel guilty about,' he laughed. 'You must forgive my little joke. I have a dreadful sense of humour. People are always telling me to be more careful.'

He laughed an empty, cold laugh which failed to thaw the ice behind his eyes. He knew now what he had always suspected. Mrs. Davidson, that mousy, little woman whose neck he could break between thumb and forefinger, knew more about the appearances in the garden than she had disclosed. She was, no doubt, complicit. If she was party to the plot then Wilkie and the Watersons would be too. He felt a momentary annoyance as if someone had drawn a cloud across his own, personal sun and obliged him to feel cold.

'Marcus Waterson,' he muttered under his breath. His eyes darkened for a moment.

'I beg your pardon?' Mrs. Davidson chirped nervously.

Conlon looked up and the same cold smile played around his lips.

'I was just wondering what had happened to Marcus Waterson,' he beamed. His eyes searched her like a snake. 'We were good friends, young Marcus and I, before his unfortunate fall from grace. Ah, the folly of youth! Had he confided in me I could have warned him that schemes of that nature were dangerous. I wonder where I could find him. I would so like to catch up on old times.'

Mrs. Davidson was quickly regaining her composure. She bristled with resentment.

'He would never have done anything wrong if he hadn't been misled by those who pretended to be his friends,' she said. She dusted her hands angrily on a tea towel. 'The poor man spent years abroad, trying to make recompense for his mistakes, as he called them, - if trusting people who should never be trusted is a mistake.' The pan behind her hissed as the water boiled over and spilled onto the hob. 'Oh bother,' she said and turned to lift the pan and turn down the heat. 'I really don't have much time for chit chat, Mr. Conlon, I have to prepare dinner for Mr. Deitch and Emma Varley. They will be back soon. I must get on.'

Leigh Conlon was enjoying himself. He had no intention of ceasing his taunting. 'Yes, he was a very trusting young man. I used to warn him to be careful. Take Carlton Brooke, I introduced him to Marcus, you know, and through Marcus he met Agnes Waterson. In some ways I feel responsible for what happened to poor Miss Waterson, although I comfort myself with the thought that I did my best to warn Marcus of the flaws in that man's character.'

Mrs. Davidson banged a pan heavily on the stove but did not turn around.

'He was an evil, unpleasant, cruel man,' she snapped. 'There were some people who knew just what he was and encouraged him in his evil schemes. Well, he has got his just desserts, that is all I can say. It will never be enough for what he did but it will do, it will do.' She turned round and waved a finger towards a newspaper which lay open on the large table. 'I laughed; I positively laughed aloud when I read it. He picked the wrong person this time. Evidently someone got the better of him.'

Conlon was momentarily diverted from his purpose.

'What do you mean?' he asked. 'What's happened to Brooke?'

'Read it for yourself.' Mrs. Davidson pecked towards the paper again then turned away. 'I said to Mr. Davidson, 'Well, that serves him right. Someone has caught up with him at last and taught him a lesson he won't forget. Good, Good.' These last words were accompanied by two fierce nods as if to emphasise her pleasure. 'Let's hope some other people get what they deserve,' I said to Mr. Davidson and he agreed. 'Mrs. Davidson,' he said to me, 'when I read things like that I begin to believe there may be a just god out there after all.' My husband is a resolute atheist, Mr. Conlon, so it is a measure of his delight that he should say such a thing.' She nodded again and stirred a pan fiercely. 'Mr. Davidson is not a violent man, Mr. Conlon, but I do believe he would have chipped in with a blow or two if the opportunity had arisen. I'm sure I would have found it difficult to resist adding a small contribution of my own.'

Leigh Conlon had ceased to listen. The cold, taunting smile had gone from his face. He picked up the newspaper.

Brooke had been attacked and beaten the previous Saturday night. He had been found down a small alleyway beside a public house he frequented. He had been subjected to what the police called 'a sustained attack'. Brooke still lived in the city, just as he had always done, even when married to Agnes Waterson. He was a man with no imagination, no energy and no purpose other than that provided by Conlon. He was just a charming but brutish con man with an eye for a profit, very useful to Conlon for a time but soon discarded until he was needed again. He was not difficult to locate.

Brooke had provided a description of the man who attacked him; he was tall, perhaps 6'3", heavily built, unshaven, stank of alcohol and tobacco, wore a grey anorak and jeans, possibly dark skinned, he couldn't be sure. It was an attempted robbery. The man had followed him and then forced him into the alleyway. Brooke had fought him off and shouted for help. The man had then beaten him savagely before running away when he heard someone approaching.'

It was all lies, of course. No such figure would have been seen in the pub that night and no-one of that description would have been seen anywhere in the neighbouring streets. If the police had enquired they might have discovered a person of very different appearance there that night, someone bearing a remarkable resemblance to Marcus Waterson, perhaps. Carlton just couldn't help making himself sound like a heroic victim, the poor fool.

Conlon thought quickly. Did Waterson think Carlton Brooke held information that might be useful? He scowled scornfully. If Marcus Waterson thought that he, Leigh Conlon, would allow a weasel like Brooke into any secrets he was a greater fool than he took him for. And if Brooke suggested that he, Conlon, had persuaded him to send menacing notes to Agnes Waterson – well, he would just laugh in his face. It was preposterous, he would laugh. Brooke is the one with a grudge, not me. But it concerned him nonetheless. Was there no corner into which Waterson would not pry? He slammed the newspaper down on the table and turned to leave. As he opened the door he found Wilkie about to enter. He pushed past him without speaking and strode angrily towards the upper floors.

'What's up with him?' Wilkie asked.

'Oh nothing much; it was just something he read.' She looked at Wilkie. 'How's your hand? You never did say how you'd hurt it.'

Wilkie smiled. He lifted a bandaged limb. 'I damaged my knuckles on something a few days ago,' he said, 'when I was in the city. It was silly of me, really. I should be more careful.'

Mrs. Davidson threw back her head and laughed a warbling laugh like a little bird.

Leigh Conlon made himself comfortable in the drawing room. Neither John Deitch nor Emma Varley was in the hall. Apparently Deitch had gone to the studio that morning to collect her. They were going for a day out and a lunch at a hotel further north. He did not enquire further. It was of no significance.

He poured himself a large brandy and opened a fat cigar and eased himself back in his chair to review the situation and to check the papers he had collected on his journey north. He had forgotten Carlton Brooke already.

The death of Barden had hit the nationals for a day and had then been relegated to the obscure depths of inside pages. It was a matter of great significance in the local papers and on local news but it wasn't deemed of sufficient moment to trouble the nation as a whole for more than twenty four hours. Had there not been some terrorist incident in the Middle East, had the Royal family not released another photograph of a royal infant, had there been no significant moves in the premier league transfer market and no trailed speech from a senior politician it may perhaps have sneaked in for a few days more but in the presence of these matters of significance it was relegated to a minor league.

'I wonder if Deitch has heard about the murder? He rarely reads the newspapers these days,' he mused idly as if it had nothing to do with him. 'It is terrible, truly awful that such things can happen nowadays, even in such a quiet backwater,' He laughed, 'not that it matters to me whether he heard about it or not. I was three hundred miles away; I can reassure him on that score at least.'

He folded back the page of one weekly, regional newspaper and looked at it closely. 'Ah, here it is, reduced after a few days to a mere column inches on page four, little more than was awarded to Carlton Brooke. Is that all your life is worth, Barden? Evidently it is.' He sighed. 'You don't really matter at all, do you? You were born in obscurity, you lived in obscurity and you died in obscurity. I have provided your pathetic life with two moments of notoriety and fame, I can console myself with that thought; your criminal activities and suspended prison sentence earned you a few column inches and your death a little more. It is something, I suppose. Your name may linger for a brief second before it is chewed and swallowed in the gaping jaws of time.'

He stretched and yawned. He laid the paper on the table beside him, folded and open at the news article. The cigar lay beside it on a silver ash tray.

He smiled. 'I wax lyrical,' he murmured. 'I have always possessed a poetic mind. I am a philosopher and a creator.' He laughed again and rested his head back on soft cushions. In a few moments he was breathing gently and in a deep, untroubled sleep.

He awoke to hear the light voices of Deitch and Emma Varley as they laughed and chatted on the corridor. The door opened and

Deitch entered preceded by Emma. Their laughter fell away from them like a flame extinguished by a sudden draught. Conlon ignored their darkening looks and sprang to his feet. He picked up the newspaper and held it forward.

'Have you heard about Barden, John?' he asked. 'I imagined you would have seen it in the newspapers or on television. It's terrible, terrible.' The couple at the door were quite sure at that moment that he had gone terribly pale and that his lower lip trembled. 'I still can't quite believe it. While I was down in England, enjoying a short break at the seaside, this terrible event was unfolding. I had no idea – no idea.' He looked at John inquisitively. 'Did you know about it?' he asked.

John took the paper. 'I have little interest in the news nowadays. I rarely open the papers.'

As he read the brief article his hands clenched tightly and his eyes stared. He could not look away from it. Emma read over his shoulder.

'First Harmison's suicide,' Conlon shook his head slowly, 'a terrible tragedy; and then this, Barden beaten to death in his own home by a burglar, probably after nothing more than a few pounds taken by the shop that day. I hurried up here to see you as soon as I could. What a ghastly coincidence.' He shook his head and glanced slyly towards the couple,

Deitch looked up sharply. His eyes met Conlon's unflinching stare, flickered and looked away.

'It makes you realise that none of us are truly safe,' Conlon continued slowly. 'We can never tell what might be waiting for us just around the corner. Barden probably had plans, just like the rest of us. There would have been things he still wanted to do, places he wanted to visit, people whose lives he wanted to continue to be part of. Now it has finished.' He sat back on the chair and sighed. 'Don't you think, Emma,' he said, 'that life can be horribly cruel? It's a lesson to all of us that we should not wait for gratification. If there is something we want to own or something we want to do we should go straight out and grasp the opportunity. It may not come again.' He smiled.

Emma Varley looked at him without flinching. Their eyes met and held fast.

This time it was Conlon who looked away and sighed.

'The world would be a better place if everyone could be like you, Emma,' he smiled, 'but the rewards of virtue have been greatly over rated, don't you think? The meek don't inherit the earth, they have it taken from them by the strong and powerful – by those selfish people you condemn. The virtuous lie rotting in their graves, having sacrificed everything and gained nothing; that, I fear, is the sad truth. People like Deitch and I have learned to live with our frailties and perhaps to make a virtue of them, haven't we John?' His smile was saccharine and his eyes were acid.

He paused for a moment. Deitch didn't respond. 'Ah well,' he said more quickly, 'this has been a most interesting discussion but I fear I must ask you to draw upon that selfless virtue you so prize for a moment. I would particularly like to use the apartment during my stay here. I assume you would be happy to extend me the usual courtesy.'

Their eyes met once again.

'I'm afraid it will not be convenient on this occasion,' Emma said firmly. Her eyes did not waver.

Conlon's lips tightened. He continued to stare at her; but she was more than a match for him. Anger had made her bold. He looked away and smiled.

'Then I shall make myself very comfortable in the tower room,' he drawled, 'and consider that I have won the argument and proved my point.' He turned away before Emma had time to respond. 'Now John,' he said brightly, 'I wonder if I could impose on your time for a few moments of private conversation. I'm sure Emma has things she can busy herself with in her apartment.'

Emma Varley looked indignant and turned to John as if demanding his support. He didn't move; nor did he return her look. He stared at the floor and then slowly raised his eyes to meet those of his adversary. 'Do as he asks, Emma,' he said slowly. 'I shall join you in a while but there are matters that Conlon and I must discuss.'

He looked at her and smiled weakly but she couldn't return the smile. She looked at him with pity; he was a broken man. He had no remaining strength with which to fight a manipulative bully like Conlon. He was lost. He would never have the strength to assert himself. He would never make the stand she had long desired.

She turned and walked slowly from the room. John Deitch listened to her footsteps on the wooden floor as she walked along the corridor. He heard her turn, not up towards her apartment, but down towards the outside door. He didn't hear her car engine or the wheels on the gravel drive but he knew she had gone.

He didn't think she would return.

Chapter Thirty Three

'I know you killed Barden,' Deitch said slowly. 'I don't know how you did it and I don't know why you thought it necessary but I know you killed him just as I know you are in some way responsible for the death of Harmison.'

Conlon held out his arms in protest but said nothing. The effort was half hearted at best.

'I know you only too well,' Deitch continued, 'and I'm under no illusions as to what you're capable of. I just don't understand why they were such a threat to you. Hadn't you done them enough harm?'

Conlon smiled. The cat circled closer to its mouse. 'I can't deny that these unfortunate deaths are of some advantage to me,' he said. His narrow eyes focused on a sharp claw. 'But I really resent your accusations. How could I have been responsible? When Barden died I was several hundred miles away having a short break at the seaside. I have no doubt there are any number of people who could vouch for my presence there. It's fanciful to imagine I could be in two places at once. As for poor Harmison, as you call him, it would be far more likely that your visit contributed to a catastrophic decline in his mental state. He was a very fragile man, you know. He had suffered from depression for a number of years. A visit like that, completely unexpected and unannounced, could easily have pushed him over the edge of reason. I know your intentions were good, John, I understand your desire to help the unfortunate soul but I'm sure it would have been better to leave him alone. He had achieved a degree of happiness. What good could your visit have done?'

Deitch glared angrily for a moment but the unchanging, bland expression on Conlon's face drew the venom from him and rendered him weak and harmless. His head fell forward and he held it in his hands. He had little desire to argue with Conlon and Emma Varley had gone.

Conlon smelt victory and continued. 'Whilst I regret the passing of these two gentlemen we have rather more pressing matters to discuss. Marcus Waterson has been making enquiries into our business dealings. Even Jarrett has lost his nerve. There's nothing he can discover, of course - I'm quite sure of that - but we must be on our guard. I must remind you – although I'm sure it isn't necessary – that nothing can possibly lead back to me. I am iron clad. You are rather more vulnerable; but you're safe only as long as you keep your nerve. You are my firewall and I am yours.'

Deitch did not move. He stared at the floor. His hands flexed and relaxed. He felt hot and very, very tired. He wanted to sleep and never wake again. He felt his body trembling. He could hardly concentrate on Conlon's words. Emma had gone and suddenly the latent feelings of affection he felt for her blossomed and grew. He didn't want to continue his life without her.

'There are matters we must deal with,' Conlon said slowly. 'Waterson, whilst he's no serious threat to us, remains an irritation. If he digs for long enough...' He shrugged.

Deitch heard his words as if they were an echo in a dark cave. 'I thought you said we were safe?' he murmured.

'It's always better to be doubly certain,' Conlon said darkly.

'I assume then that, despite your protestations, you think Waterson could be a threat to my security.' John's voice was strangely empty and calm as if devoid of all emotion or concern. 'That of course would make you rather vulnerable wouldn't it, Leigh? You don't fear Waterson but you concerned about me. You're wondering whether there is anything that I hold that would threaten your own security. You needn't fear me; the information is held only here.' He tapped his forehead. 'I have no reason to release these particular birds. They will remain securely caged.'

Conlon's eyes flickered. There was something strange about Deitch. His indifference and his foolish feelings of guilt were familiar. This was different. He was like a vacuum filling slowly with a dark and brooding despair. That was dangerous.

'Have you spoken to anyone about our dealings?' he asked and his eyes searched Deitch for clues. 'Have you spoken to Emma, for example?'

He had thrown down a wild card but Conlon knew at once that the trick was his. Deitch looked up with sudden fear. Conlon saw once that he had struck a nerve, that Deitch had spoken of their various business dealings and that Emma Varley might be a threat to his safety.

'She knows nothing, nothing. She has no part in this.'

'Of course,' Conlon drawled, 'Of course. I'm sure you can ensure her continued silence. She is very loyal.'

Deitch glanced towards Conlon and his look was dangerous but Conlon, looking away, and did not heed its warning.

'I need to find Waterson,' Conlon was saying. 'If I can locate him I'm sure I can silence him. He has a terrible weakness, you see – he has a family.'

'He's at home with his sister,' He spoke without fear and without emotion but behind his seeming indifference other emotions struggled for supremacy. His fear for Emma made him reckless. 'Mrs. Waterson died, you know. Her funeral was held last week. I spoke to Marcus. We spent some time together. I liked him; more than that, I respected him and, if I'm honest, I envied him. He is becoming the man I always hoped that I might be.'

Conlon was startled. He turned sharply. 'What did you tell him?'

'He asked me to confess everything. He said it was time I freed myself of all of this guilt. He was very honest with me. He didn't deny that I might have to spend some time in prison. He reasoned that at least I would emerge clean and free from all of this.' He spread his hands and indicated the room, the castle, the grounds and everything that made up the illusion of his life. 'He asked if he could return to visit me and bring those two police officers. I declined of course. He tried to persuade me that I should go through every sordid detail with them. He asked me if I could live with this any more. I think I left him with the impression that I could.

'How long has he been back here?'

'He returned home just a day or two before his mother's death. It was very fortunate that he arrived in time to see her before she died.'

'Why didn't you tell me?'

Deitch didn't answer. He continued with his own narrative. 'I think Wilkie had been aware of his presence in the UK for many weeks. Apparently he called to see him first in the walled garden and the two of them walked up to the White House. I believe the reunion was both joyous and tearful. Pretty soon the village was full of the news. Mrs. Davidson could barely repress her joy.' He laughed dryly. 'For a moment, you know, I considered driving over to see him the morning after his arrival but as usual my resolve weakened. You see, Conlon, you have nothing to fear from me; I am an inveterate coward. I shall do nothing to place in jeopardy my freedom or my comfort.'

Conlon stood up and paced the room.

'How much does he know?'

'He seems to know a great deal,' Deitch said languidly, 'but not enough to cause trouble. He may even give up his investigations. He promised his mother, you see. She didn't want any of them to live perpetually in the past. She was a very sensible woman. The past is no place to live, as I well know. You can leave the country now, Leigh, and never return. You have nothing more to fear; as you've often said, you have the means to escape. You can live in comfortable and luxurious retirement anywhere in the world. Go now, Leigh, and stay away. I shall remain as silent as a cloistered nun. I shall say nothing that can implicate you. I want to be free of you.'

He stood up and opened the door. He felt unusually calm and strangely in control. It was Conlon who was uncertain now, Conlon who was anxious, Conlon who was frightened. Deitch liked the feeling. He walked to the top of the steep stone stair and Conlon followed. At the top they paused. Those few steps had given Conlon time to regain his composure. He stopped and turned to face Deitch.

'I think I'll remain a few days longer, John; I'll give your proposal some consideration. I'm very tempted by a life of leisure in a warm climate. I've made my contribution to the economy I think.' He spoke slowly and in his familiar languid and cynical style. He relaxed his stare and smiled.

'You're right, of course. Marcus Waterson knows little that could concern me; the police have their suspicions but can prove nothing. Only you, John, hold any information that could be a threat to me and you'll say nothing.' He cast an arm around his shoulder. 'We're partners; after all, we've been friends for many years. You assure me that Emma Varley knows nothing. Good, good. I shall think about your suggestion. Perhaps you're right; perhaps I should retire from this business. We're not getting any younger, John. We should enjoy our remaining years.'

He turned and walked back along the corridor. 'I am one of Margaret Thatcher's children, you know. I learnt the lesson of her decade. It is not only acceptable to be selfish and greedy, it is a positive virtue. I am a virtuous man, John, a very virtuous man.' He laughed unpleasantly. 'Do unto others before they have a chance to do unto you; that was our motto, John, wasn't it? It served us well.' He laughed again and walked back into the drawing room, still laughing. The door closed behind him.

Chapter Thirty Four

Emma did not come back that night, nor did she return the next day. John watched from the window which overlooked the drive, hoping to see her car but it did not appear. A delivery van arrived and departed. Wilkie appeared with a wheel barrow and worked along the grass edges and tidied the flower beds. A solitary robin accompanied him and foraged in the rich soil where the ground was disturbed. A glossy blackbird too landed on the grass, its head tilted, listening to sounds beneath the earth, tiny, indistinct indications of life. It stabbed suddenly, sharp eyed and ruthless. Emma didn't appear.

He saw little of Conlon who seemed inclined to remain in the drawing room where he had ready access to cigars, brandy and newspapers. They met briefly at mealtimes but said little. Conlon knew that his presence was enough, John too. When he looked up from his meal, Deitch saw Conlon's eyes watching him, cold and empty.

'We're two of a kind, you and I, John,' he said. 'We always have been. We were a perfect team.'

John did not answer.

'Will Emma Varley be joining us for dinner?' Conlon asked.

'Emma Varley has gone. She won't return.'

Conlon sighed and shook his head. 'How very unfortunate,' he said. 'I assume you can continue to rely on her discretion?'

Again he didn't reply. Conlon smiled.

'I've always found it easier to avoid too close a bond with women,' he said. 'They are so unpredictable. Men are far more direct, so much easier to anticipate, less prone to emotional outburts...' Before Deitch had an opportunity to interrupt he continued. 'Take the Watersons, for example. Marcus Waterson is a sensible man; he knows when it is time to give up his enquiries. But Agnes, Agnes...dear me...that young woman is so emotional one could never be truly certain how she would react. As far Emma Varley...'

'Emma is no threat to you or me,' Deitch said darkly. 'Leave her alone, Conlon...'

'Of course, of course... I trust you entirely, John. Emma is, as you say, no risk to us.'

'You would be risking a great deal if you were to threaten her.'

'Now, why would I threaten her, John?' Conlon smiled smoothly. 'I am merely commenting on the different nature of men and women. I find men easier to predict, that's all. I've always found Emma an extremely sensible woman, not prone to rash or revengeful acts. I am sure she will return very soon and your friendship will resume.'

Deitch took the earliest opportunity to leave the dining room and wander through to the study. He sat at his desk and gazed out over the shore to the sea.

Leigh Conlon waited until Deitch had disappeared into the study and then he too left the dining room. He headed directly to Emma's apartment and carefully began to search. If she held any papers or had written anything he must find it. There was nothing in the cupboards or drawers in the lounge, nothing in the desk, nothing on the table or window sill, nothing on the table. He tried the bedroom but again he found nothing. Only when he raised the pillow on her bed did he find a small notebook. He flicked through the pages, stopping to read sections of it at intervals. Emma Varley had been using it as an occasional diary. There were references to his own visits and to Jarrett; her comments were not flattering but it mattered little to Leigh Conlon. Only once did he stop and read more closely. He frowned. That fool Deitch had spoken to her about how they had met. He read further pages more closely. Evidently she was waiting for him to tell her everything. The future of their relationship depended upon it, or so it would appear.

'At their age,' he sneered, 'to be so weak and pathetic.'

It seemed that on a number of occasions Deitch had come close to telling her everything. Worse still she described how she had encouraged him to speak to Marks or Munro. He had teetered on the brink, so to speak, but had ultimately declined, coward that he was. That woman was a menace. He swore unpleasantly under his breath.

The last entry was after the funeral of Mrs. Waterson.

'John spoke to Marcus Waterson today. I saw them walking through the village together from the church. They stopped outside my studio. For a few moments I hoped, I really hoped…but I was to be disappointed again. John simply doesn't have the strength or character to act. He simply will not speak and without confession how can there be redemption? It seems that he will never change. I must consider how long I can continue like this. All my hopes are breaking like shells under the weight of an awful sea. Perhaps there isn't any future for us; I don't know; I just don't know.'

Could he trust Deitch not to crumble under this sort of pressure? Jarrett was unsure and now he was uncertain too. How strong was the hold Emma Varley had over him? He replaced the diary under her pillow and left the room. He could never be truly safe – he knew that now. Deitch was unreliable, Emma Varley was a threat, Marcus Waterson and Agnes, particularly Agnes, were likely to keep pushing – it was human nature.

There was one course of action open to him, of course, but he was hesitant to take it. It was a last desperate throw but it would free him forever. He would need to think carefully and to plan with meticulous detail. It was very risky, especially on top of recent events. Nonetheless, it had a certain appeal, a final and crowning moment on a flawless career. It would certainly be an accomplishment if he could pull it off. His eyes brightened for a moment. Then again, perhaps he should simply wait and watch as Jarrett had recommended or perhaps he should disappear as Deitch had suggested. But if he did that they would always be there, in the background, a constant threat. It was a loose end. If someone took hold of it and pulled with sufficient force who knows what might unravel.

Jack Munro and Aaron Marks arrived the next morning which did not improve Conlon's mood or ease his insecurity. Deitch was nowhere to be found. For a moment he wondered if Deitch had telephoned them and, whilst he remained superficially calm, beneath his expensive, lilac shirt his heart raced a little faster than usual. It became clear after a few minutes, however, that their visit was little more than a fishing expedition. They came to dangle the death of Barden before him in the hope that he would bite. Conlon would not bite. They had nothing and they knew it, just as he knew it. He leaned back on the armchair in the drawing room and smiled a long, colourless smile. It was probably a good thing that John Deitch wasn't present.

'I read about Barden in the newspaper,' he sighed. 'Poor man, it isn't much of an epitaph for a tragic life, is it, a brief headline and then three or four column inches tucked away on an inside page?'

He noted the physical arrangement of the two detectives in the room and laughed inwardly. Jack Munro stood before him and would ask the questions; Aaron Mark was positioned further back and to one side. He would watch and assess and cast the occasional disconcerting query designed to catch him off guard. His eyes glistened momentarily with excitement at the challenge before he cast a veneer of sadness over them.

'And Harmison too died so tragically,' he murmured. 'I should feel resentful towards them after the things they said about Deitch and me, but I can't, I can't. They were victims of a heinous deception.'

The detectives said nothing for a moment. Conlon leaned forward and placed a hand on each knee. 'Well, Gentlemen,' he said, 'to business. How can I help you?'

The questions emerged slowly and precisely.

'Where were you the night Barden died?'

Can you produce anyone to verify this?'

'How did you spend the evening?'

'When did you last see Barden?'

'When did you last see Harmison?'

He parried each question with well rehearsed and exemplary answers. Then came the first intervention from Aaron.

'You know the roads well between the Highlands and England,' he said. 'You're a well travelled man. If you were to drive from Dalnvaig to the resort you were staying at what route would you take?'

It was a clever question. It would be easy for a guilty man to describe a route that differed from the one he took. Conlon was equal to the challenge. He described the route he had actually driven.

'I think that would be the shortest and probably the quickest,' he mused, 'although it would be possible, I suppose, to head south and then turn east after....' He smiled benignly and again his eyes flickered with a momentary exuberance. This the sort of competition he enjoyed. He subdued the smile quickly and resumed with cold sincerity.

'But of course, this is all hypothetical. I haven't been through Dalnvaig for years.'

Jack Munro continued with his questions. He asked about Conlon's business dealings, his association with John Deitch, his acquisition of Strathan Tower. Conlon answered each question precisely and clearly.

'There can't be many petrol stations on the journey you described,' Aaron interrupted again, thoughtfully. 'Anyone driving that far would need to fill up with petrol, I suppose.'

It was a calculated move. It implied he had been pondering the route for some time and had only now returned with his question; very clever.

Conlon yawned and leant back on the chair and drawled a slow reply. 'No, there won't be many.' He smiled. 'This is a very strange kind of speculation,' he laughed. 'You can't possibly imagine I drove all that way, murdered Barden and then drove back again and nobody noticed my absence.' He laughed softly. They were good, these two. He would have to be careful. It was important to remember that they knew nothing, could prove nothing and would never link him to the death. Even the plates on his car were false. It was all bluster and bluff.

Aaron neither smiled nor blinked. Jack remained unmoved.

'Humour me,' Aaron said.

Conlon sighed a deep, sympathetic sigh. It was important now not to name too many or to obviously omit the one petrol station he used. 'I doubt there are any outside the larger villages,' he mused, 'perhaps at....' He named two or three of the larger places. 'Of course once you reach the city they would be numerous if you ventured off the main road. I often use....' He described a petrol station on the approach road to the city centre where he bought fuel when he stayed in the town. 'I don't really know the route that well until you reach the main road.' This was true enough.

Jack continued probing; Aaron watched closely and occasionally intervened.

'Well,' Jack relaxed and smiled at last, 'thank you for your time, Mr. Conlon. You have been most helpful. We won't trouble you any further.'

Aaron didn't move. He seemed to be deep in thought. 'Is something bothering you?' Jack asked.

Aaron shook his head. 'It's nothing, nothing at all,' he said. 'I was just imagining the problems the murderer must have faced. He would have had blood on his hands and his clothes and shoes. I imagine it was easy to wash and clean shoes and then dispose of them later. A coat would be easily sponged and then dry cleaned. Nonetheless there would've been sundry items, gloves perhaps, a cloth or handkerchief which would need to be destroyed or hidden. Where's the best place to dispose of a bag of bloodied items, I wonder.'

Conlon shrugged. You had to admire their skill. They were approaching the final throw. Be careful now.

'If it was me I'd probably bury it in a peat bog or deep in forestry. Maybe I'd hide that one bag amongst a lot of others, possibly in an overflowing roadside bin. It would be impossible to find.'

Oh, that was very clever, very clever indeed. 'I don't envy you the search, though,' Conlon smiled. 'There are miles of bog and forestry and innumerable picnic places, even if the bins have not already been emptied. Besides, it's all highly speculative. There are a number of routes one could take from the village and it's impossible to know where the murderer was heading. He, or even she perhaps, may live just down the street.'

'Indeed, indeed. Ah well, thank you again for your time, Mr. Conlon.'

Jack stood up and opened the door. Conlon accompanied them down the stairs to the front door. They stood a moment beneath the arched portico.

'I see you have a new car,' Jack said.

'Yes, I changed it whilst I was at the seaside. It was a whim. I saw this vehicle and just couldn't resist. You know how it is. They offered me a particularly good deal. Do you like it?'

'Indeed I do but it is significantly above my pay grade, I'm afraid.'

The two detectives walked down the few steps to the gravelled drive. Conlon turned to return inside the house. He was smiling.

'Oh, Mr. Conlon,' Jack turned at the bottom of the steps, 'there's just one thing more. I wouldn't want to leave you under the impression that we believe anything you have just told us. We're quite sure you drove Mr. Harmison to his death and that you were directly responsible for Mr. Barden's death. Foolish as it seems we shall probably send cars to the petrol stations on the route you described. Some poor policemen may even be tasked with exploring the contents of overflowing bins in parking places. I feel sorry for them but we must all make sacrifices, don't you think? I also intend to enquire very closely into your movements that night. My colleagues south of the border will no doubt resent having to locate your car but they'll do it and they'll examine it in the greatest detail. Good afternoon, Mr. Conlon. Tell Mr. Deitch that we shall return to interview him.'

He turned and walked away. Conlon turned back into the hall. He closed the door and a brief smile spread across his face. That was their last desperate bluff. He had half expected it. They wouldn't return. He was safe, except for Deitch.He would have to do something to deal with Deitch.

Aaron and Jack walked a few yards until they were sure Conlon had returned to the hall. Then they stopped. Jack turned.

'We have neither the time nor the manpower, of course,' he said. 'We can make no more than a few token enquiries which will give us nothing. It's time for us to give up or continue with the plan we discussed. At least we have Miss Varley on our side now. I think Conlon pushed that lady just a little too far.'

'It's risky,' Aaron said quietly, 'even if we can persuade Deitch to co-operate.'

'It's far from conventional, I grant you that. I'm not sure our superiors would approve. They certainly wouldn't give it their wholehearted support but it's our last throw and I'm loath to allow a vile creature like Conlon to get the better of us.'

'Which, I suppose,' Aaron added, 'is a particularly good reason to at least try.'

Jack nodded. 'I've never been impressed by the ruthless, professional timidity of my superiors,' he sighed, 'and they, for their part, have never really understood my capacity for taking crime personally. They seem to think - wrongly in my view - that one cannot be detached and also care. I think we make them uncomfortable, Aaron. However, it's important to realise that, win or lose, such a cavalier approach to detective work won't win you many friends. I shall take as much blame as I can, of course, but you will be tarnished by association. Sim will be kept in the dark.'

Aaron smiled. 'It's a good plan though, isn't it?' he laughed.

'It's a splendid plan or it will be if we can get it close to a take-off speed. Shall we proceed and at least try? Let's fetch that dog of yours from the car and walk down to the walled garden. Mr. Deitch won't mind. We should speak again to Emma Varley, I think. Then we should speak to Agnes Waterson and Robert Wilkie and, of course, John Deitch.'

'Everything will ultimately depend upon Deitch.'

'That, I'm afraid is the potential flaw in our design, but we must try.'

Chapter Thirty Five

After some discussion it was agreed that Aaron alone would approach Wilkie, the Watersons and Miss Varley.

'I shall hold myself in reserve,' Jack said, 'ready to join the fray at a moment of your choosing. For the moment I shall merely shoulder the burden of responsibility and plan out new career paths should anything go wrong.'

Aaron telephoned Marcus Waterson and spoke to him briefly.

'I'd like to call and see you tomorrow,' he explained. 'I'd like to speak to Miss Waterson and to Robert Wilkie at the same time if you could arrange for them to be present.'

'Yes, certainly; has something happened?'

'I'll explain tomorrow. I'll be seeing Emma Varley earlier in the day. I'd rather like her to be present if you have no objection.'

'No, none at all; my mother held Emma Varley in high regard. She'll be most welcome. I'm intrigued. What's this all about?'

'Tomorrow, I'll explain everything tomorrow. When is most suitable?'

'Why not come in the evening?'

It was agreed. The phone went dead.

'What on earth could it mean? Do you think he has some news about Conlon or Deitch?' Agnes asked. 'Do you think he has some information which may convict them? I do hope so.'

Marcus and Wilkie shook their heads.

'It's most unlikely,' Marcus said. 'You must put ideas like that out of your mind. Remember your promise.'

Agnes was about to speak but Wilkie interrupted her.

'We have a future to plan,' he said firmly. 'Let the past rest now. It was your mother's wish. Let's just wait and see what Aaron Marks has to tell us.'

Nonetheless, it proved difficult to resist speculating on the meaning of the visit and it was with some impatience that they awaited the evening and Aaron's arrival. At eight o'clock he arrived with Emma Varley and was invited into the lounge. Aaron remembered his last visit to that room and the frailty of Mrs. Waterson as she leant on his arm until she overcame the pain that momentarily wracked her. He recalled her words, her manner and her looks.

'Your mother was a remarkable woman,' he said to Agnes. 'I met her just once but her character and integrity were immediately impressed upon me. I liked her immensely.'

As they sat in the quiet lounge of the White House Aaron gradually unfolded the plan he had developed. The others listened to him in silence. When he concluded, the silence that had gathered around them was augmented by the gathering gloom beyond the windows. The silence continued as each of them considered the implications for themselves and the others. Agnes stood up and walked over to turn on the lights. She closed the heavy curtains and returned to her seat.

'You are staking a great deal on our collective ability to influence Mr. Deitch. It may all be for nothing.'

She sat down beside Wilkie.

'It may indeed.'

'You are quite convinced that Leigh Conlon was responsible for the deaths of the two men?' asked Marcus.

'One cannot be completely sure; one can only suspect. But I believe it to be so. It would be my expectation that this plan would reveal the truth.'

Wilkie scratched a tousled head and cast a broad arm around Agnes' shoulder. 'Even if Mr. Deitch could be persuaded, and I think that is improbable, do you think he has sufficient strength to see it through?'

Aaron turned and looked to Emma Varley who had remained silent. She looked at each of them. She frowned and shook her head.

'I simply cannot tell,' she said. 'He would want to help us, of that I am sure. He would resolve to do as we ask and he would be quite sure that he would do it. Whether he would have the strength to see it through to a conclusion I don't know. Conlon has a great deal of power over him. John is also very concerned about the consequences for himself.'

Agnes moved resentfully in her seat and was about to express her opinion of such weakness and selfishness. Wilkie held her shoulder and she remained moodily silent.

'Need the consequences be so bad for him?' he asked Aaron. 'Is there nothing you can offer? No compromise?'

Emma looked at them sharply. 'I think you misunderstand,' she said, 'he has an inevitable fear of incarceration – I think that's quite understandable for a man of his sensitivity – but his greater fear is of a far more personal nature. He's terrified of the shame these revelations would bring. I think you should also admit that we would be asking him to place himself in a position of grave danger. He could be seriously hurt, even killed. Can you guarantee him his personal safety?'

Aaron shook his head. 'I can't. We would do our very best but some danger would remain.'

Marcus sighed. 'I don't think it can be done.'

They sat back in their chairs. Wilkie leaned forward abruptly.

'Damn it all,' he said, 'we've nothing to lose by trying. For what it's worth I think we are halfway there already. Think of the flowers he sent for your mother,' he said to Marcus and Agnes, 'and his constant enquiries after her health.'

Marcus nodded slowly. 'We too have made some conciliatory steps,' he said quietly.

Aaron looked at Emma. 'A great deal will depend upon you,' he said.

'I will do what I can to help,' she said, 'but I won't lie to him nor will I deceive him. I will use no trickery. If he helps us it must be because he chooses to. If we can't agree on that I will play no part.'

'We must try,' Agnes said firmly. 'Wilkie is right. I don't think I could live with myself if we didn't make this one last effort.'

'I agree,' said Marcus. If we turn our backs now it will be as if we reject any hope of justice or any belief that such a thing as justice for victims can exist.'

'So we're agreed,' Wilkie asked.

Emma Varley stood up and walked across the room. She stood with her back to them for a moment.

She nodded.

'So,' Aaron said, 'let me outline what Jack and I have in mind....'

Chapter Thirty Six

Three days had passed. Leigh Conlon was sitting by the window in the turret bedroom looking down into the garden. He was bored. He watched Wilkie working his way around the rose beds, removing fading flowers and weeds. Agnes was sitting on a bench beside a wall where rambling roses displayed pink and white flowers. She was reading a book but after a moment she put it to one side and turned to smell the delicate scent. She called over to Wilkie who stood up and rested for a moment. He called something back to her and she smiled. He pulled a handkerchief from his pocket and mopped his forehead. Beyond the garden wall a chill breeze was blowing and wisps of grass blew across the lawns but where they were standing the sun shone through broken clouds and the air was warm.

Conlon watched them with vague amusement. People in love, whatever that might mean, made such pitiful fools of themselves. Look at Wilkie now, uncertain whether to continue with his work or to walk across and sit beside her. She waves to him as if they have just seen each other after a lengthy time apart and yet they have been together for hours.

At that moment he saw the gate open just beside her and John Deitch intruded on the tranquil scene. Conlon laughed. That made Wilkie's decision for him; now he was down among the flower heads again, busily working. Miss Waterson reached for her book as if to avoid speech. Deitch paused for a moment when he saw Miss Waterson. He stood still and said a few words. He looked uncomfortable. Miss Waterson evidently replied and Deitch took a few steps. Then he stopped and turned round. He spoke again.

Conlon grew impatient. What was Deitch playing at? Had he asked if he could join her for a moment? Certainly she looked unwilling but she moved along the bench seat to allow him room to sit down. He said something and Miss Waterson replied. Then they sat silently. Deitch pointed here and there at the flowers and seemed to be asking questions. Miss Waterson's replies were obviously curt and did not encourage further speech. Nonetheless she smiled on one occasion.

After a few minutes he was relieved to see Deitch stand up and reach out a hand which Miss Waterson. He was about to turn away again and return to the house when she spoke. Whatever she said seemed to please him; he smiled and nodded. When he walked back towards the house his steps seemed lighter and quicker.

Conlon frowned and his mind turned to loose ends.

He didn't speak to John Deitch for the rest of the day but he saw his car pull away from the house and head down the driveway. At the end of the drive it turned right, towards the village. He saw it return after an hour. His buoyant step had gone and he walked heavily across the lawn and into the hall.

'Normal service,' Conlon smiled unpleasantly.

'You've been busy today,' he ventured over dinner. He reached for a vegetable tureen and ladled roast potatoes beside his beef. A variety of home grown vegetables and deep, rich gravy joined them. 'Mrs. Davidson may be the most dreadful busybody and an awful bore but she does cook a fine meal.'

'Emma Varley asked me to take some things over to her studio. I spent an hour there.'

'Is her mood much improved?'

'We spoke much in the manner that we have always spoken but I don't think she's ready to return, not yet.'

'But she may eventually, do you think?'

'She may; one can never tell. Perhaps we could speak of other things.'

'I saw Miss Waterson in the garden this morning,' Conlon watched Deitch closely.

'Yes, she was with Wilkie, enjoying the sun and the scent of the roses. Did you know that one of those rose was named after Mrs. Waterson?'

'Should you encourage her to visit the garden?' Conlon asked. 'She has little enough to say that is flattering or generous, after all. Besides, she keeps Wilkie from his work.'

'She is to marry Wilkie. They like to be together; it's only natural. Besides, I've never had any reason to question Wilkie's devotion to his work. He's an excellent gardener. I invited Miss

Waterson to use the garden whenever she wished.' He paused for a moment and then looked at Conlon. 'I extended the same invitation to her brother though I doubt he'll make use of it.'

'I cannot see the wisdom or the benefit of such an offer but it's a matter for you, not for me. I would banish them if the choice were mine. I have no time for such people.'

'You have little time for anyone who doesn't bring you some advantage or gain.'

Conlon nodded. 'That is very true.'

The next day after breakfast a note arrived. Mrs. Davidson brought it to the breakfast table as she arrived to clear away the crockery. She lingered, watching Deitch, evidently intrigued by the missive. He looked at the letter languidly, turning it slowly in long fingers.

'I wonder who could possibly want to correspond with me in such a manner?' he said drily. 'How very intriguing it is. Look, Conlon. It's hand written and in a very fine hand too. I shall open it very slowly so that the mystery may last. No doubt the contents will be a great disappointment.'

Conlon looked up from his newspaper. 'It will be from some little, old lady, probably, over whom the age of technology passed without pause. She will require a donation for some worthwhile cause - shire horses or the church probably. Perhaps it's an invitation to a coffee morning for the old and useless.'

'Oh no, no indeed,' Mrs. Davidson interrupted. 'I would recognise that handwriting anywhere. It is so well formed and so very neat. There's an assurance about it, don't you think? It's very typical of the writer. 'You can learn so much about a person by their handwriting,' Mr. Davidson said to me. 'You are quite right,' I said to him. 'Take my handwriting, for example. It flies about all over the page. It has no consistency and little form.' Mr. Davidson and I mourn the passing of hand written messages. You can learn very little from an email, don't you think?'

'For goodness sake, Mrs. Davidson, can you cease from your endless, pointless rambling and tell us who it is from?'

Conlon slapped his newspaper down in exasperation.

'Well, I'm sure there's no need for you to speak like that, Mr. Conlon, but since you press me it's Mr. Waterson's handwriting.'

'Yes, it's from Marcus Waterson,' John Deitch said calmly. He looked at the neatly folded paper with some amusement. 'How very entertaining,' he laughed slowly, 'it's an acknowledgement of his gratitude for my generous permission for them to visit the garden and it contains an invitation to dinner at the White House. It will be a very informal dinner, he tells me, a family affair with just one or two friends - how very quaint!'

'Will you attend?'

'No, I shall politely decline but I shall acknowledge my gratitude for their kindness.' He handed the letter casually to Conlon. 'They will have performed a necessary but not altogether pleasant duty and I can reflect that I have saved them from the discomfiture of an unwelcomed evening. What do you think? Isn't that a satisfactory outcome for us all?'

Mrs. Davidson bristled with irritation. She collected the breakfast crockery with a deal of impatience and rather more noise than was customary.

'You mistake them completely, Mr Deitch, if you believe they would invite you merely as a matter of politeness. They aren't so unfeeling as to affect a friendship they don't feel, unlike some folk. Mr. Davidson would tell you the same if he were here. 'Marcus and Agnes Waterson say what they mean,' he would say. 'People may not always like what they have to say but you could never accuse them of falsehood.' 'Indeed no, Mr. Davidson,' I would tell him. 'I have never heard a critical word from either of them that was not well earned.'' She nodded emphatically.

Conlon interrupted her impatiently. 'I think we may consider ourselves blessed that Mr. Davidson is safely at home. I can't take too much home grown wisdom so soon after breakfast.'

Mrs. Davidson turned to leave. 'I'm sure neither Mr. Davidson nor I would waste our words where they weren't wanted,' she said. The door closed heavily behind her.

'I don't know how you put up with that woman, Deitch. In past times she would've been burned at the stake.'

'There's no-one better at her work. One must tolerate her eccentricities in order to enjoy her cooking. It's a small sacrifice. What are your plans for today?'

'I have none. I shall return to the city very soon. I can only take so much fresh air and boredom before I crave the crowded streets. I don't know what you see in this ghastly, rural life. There's not one moment of excitement from one week to the next.'

'Oh, I'm not sure of that. Take today, for example. Already I've received a most interesting letter. Later our two detectives are to return, no doubt to draw a concluding line under their futile investigations.' He spoke with casual indifference. Conlon looked up. 'Be careful what you say to them. They're irritatingly shrewd.'

'I'm always careful, Leigh. I've learned to weigh my words to within a grain.'

'Notheless...'

It was just as Deitch thought, however. Aaron and Jack arrived with their apologies. Their enquiries had met with no success. There were no further routes to pursue. Since there had been no further incidents in a number of weeks they would cease their enquiries unless something further occurred.

'Nothing more will occur,' Deitch said to them, slowly and without interest. 'These moments were mere ripples on a pool, quite striking for the time we could see them but of no lasting significance.' He held out a pale hand. 'Now, if there is nothing more, I have to see Wilkie about some small maintenance matters relating to the garden. Can I see you out?'

'We'll accompany you to the garden, if you have no objection,' Jack said. 'Mrs. Munro asked me to speak to Wilkie to get some advice about pruning. Mrs. Munro loves her garden; she has green fingers. Mine, alas, are contaminated by death and kill whatever they touch. I wonder if plants are sensitive to such things. What do you think? Do the plants in your room fade when Mr. Conlon has been near them? It would be an interesting experiment, don't you think?'

He took Deitch by the elbow and walked beside him towards the door. Aaron followed. He could not prevent a smile from flickering around his eyes. Jack Munro really knew how to push the boundaries.

They saw Conlon on the drive as they crossed the lawn towards the garden. As they walked through the gate he turned and watched them then he hurried to the tower room from where he had a view down over the garden. From there he could watch carefully, half hidden beside the deep, granite window frame.

Deitch walked across to Wilkie who was working by the trellis where the sweet peas bloomed. He spoke to him for a few moments and gestured towards different parts of the garden, giving instructions. Then the two men walked back across the garden to Aaron and Jack who were standing beside the greenhouse. They spent some minutes in casual conversation before Jack and Wilkie moved away towards the rose garden, deep in conversation. Aaron spoke a little longer with Deitch and then he retraced his steps through the Waterson Gate and towards the hall. Deitch remained still for a moment and then walked slowly towards the bench by the yew hedge and the bushes of rambling roses. He looked as if he was waiting for something. Conlon watched impatiently. What was he playing at?

Now Deitch turned away from the bench and drifted towards a bed of pink and red roses. He cupped one in his hand and sampled the fragrance. Aaron returned through the gate with a small springer spaniel at his heels. He was evidently planning to walk down towards the shore. He spoke to Deitch. Conlon saw them look towards the house and then glance towards the window where he stood. He stepped back quickly so as not to be seen.

'What is he thinking?' Conlon muttered. 'What's he doing?'

He moved cautiously towards the window again and looked out. Jack and Wilkie were walking towards the greenhouses now; but where was Deitch and where was Aaron Marks? He looked round, forgetting for a moment to remain hidden behind the stone window frame. He saw them at last, walking together down towards the shore. The dog ran ahead of them over the grass and down to the sand. It stood and waited and then ran towards them and jumped up and down. Aaron Marks threw a ball. The springer spaniel set off after it across the beach and returned panting to drop the ball at his feet. Deitch was not speaking but he was listening as Aaron Marks spoke. Occasionally he nodded.

'What are they talking about?'

Deitch stopped and seemed to laugh gently. The dog stood in front of him. He reached down and picked up the ball and threw it across the sand. The springer raced after it and scooped it up from the sand and raced into the shallow water, breaking through the low waves. She emerged and shook herself and ran on down the beach, circling, with her nose low over the ground gathering scents to bring back to the two men.

They reached a point where some black rocks protruded from the sand. Beyond the rocks the beach became increasing stony and the sand gave way to pebble, shell and weed. They paused and sat down on the rocks.

'What are they talking about?' Conlon muttered again, under his breath.

He looked back towards the walled garden and was startled to see Jack Munro standing beside the roses. He was alone now; Wilkie had returned to the sweet peas. Jack was staring directly at the window behind which Conlon was standing. He slowly raised a hand and waved. Conlon gripped the sill. He struggled to prevent himself stepping back. He raised a hand and returned the salutation. Jack didn't move. A moment later Conlon turned away and returned to the drawing room.

Chapter Thirty Seven

'I see you were speaking to Detective Inspector Marks,' Leigh Conlon said after dinner. They were sitting at the long table in the dining room. Conlon held a brandy glass cupped between his hands. A cigar lay burning on an ash tray its spire of smoke shifting suddenly as if to escape his words. 'You seem suddenly very friendly.'

John Deitch picked up a napkin from the table. 'I must compliment Mrs. Davidson on that meal,' he said, 'it really was exceptional.' He wiped his mouth and cast the napkin aside. His voice was unemotional and cold. 'Yes,' he continued. 'It was rather strange. I anticipated further questions about Barden and prepared myself accordingly but his conversation related only to the landscape and the walks hereabouts. Munro was speaking to Wilkie but all he seemed interested in was the garden. The two of them wandered around the flower beds. I chose to walk down to the shore with Marks. I had little else to do.'

'You chose to walk with him?'

'It would've been discourteous to refuse his request, don't you think? I had no real desire to go and I doubt he had any real desire for my company. He enquired politely about the walk along up to the mountain ridge you can see from the village. Apparently he'd heard about it from Wilkie and was planning to go there himself. I can't think why. It's just another piece of blank moorland capped by rocks, just like so many others. I found it quite tedious.' He yawned in a desultory manner and sighed. 'His dog was impatient to reach the beach so we continued our conversation as we walked to the sand. The walk was barely palatable for both of us, I suspect.' He turned away. 'I'm dreadfully bored, you know, bored half way to death.'

He spoke again after a moment. 'They've arranged to walk it together one day, Wilkie and our detective.' He laughed dryly. 'I asked if I might accompany them.' He laughed again. 'Don't you think that was amusing of me? He agreed, of course, out of politeness.'

'You did what?' Conlon stared at him in disbelief. 'Can you not see that this apparent friendliness is just a ploy to soften you up and persuade you to reveal more than would be sensible?'

'Oh I assure you I shall never go. His words were courteous but they were empty. He has no more intention of walking the hills with me that I with him. He seems a very polite and approachable young man, nonetheless. He appears to have a sympathetic nature. He listens. It's a rare quality nowadays, don't you think? Most people only want to talk about themselves. They don't hear what others say.

I think we should appreciate those few people who take a genuine interest in our words, don't you think? Emma is like that, you know.'

'Emma Varley wants to know everything about you,' Conlon said sourly. 'She won't have been happy until she has stolen your soul.'

'I have no soul, Leigh. I sold it to the devil many years ago.'

'Emma Varley will see you incarcerated.'

She is my friend,' John said quietly. 'We shall try to rebuild our friendship, I think.'

There was something different about Deitch that evening, something Conlon found quite disconcerting. He spoke in the same languid and indifferent manner and he gazed lazily around the room as he spoke. His words were typically slow and without emotion. There seemed, however, a greater resolve, a firmness of tone that was unusual.

'Are they coming back?'

'No, they have no need to return unless they wish to speak to you again. I don't think they are convinced by your protestations of innocence, Leigh.'

His voice was as monotonous as the ticking of the grandfather clock by the wall, his movements as lacking in emotion as the movement of the long pendulum in its case. His face, like the clock, was without expression or change.

'I shall have some company for dinner tomorrow evening, Leigh, I must ask you to take your meal in the drawing room if you have no objection. It's most discourteous, I know, but it is for a particular reason.'

He seemed disinclined to explain.

'May I enquire who is joining you?'

'Of course.' He paused and did not speak.

'Then who is it?' Conlon spoke with scarcely veiled irritation.

Deitch turned his dark eyes fully upon him. 'Emma has agreed to join me. Given the manner of your last meeting I think it would be better if you were not present. I'm sure you understand.'

Leigh smiled coldly. 'I have no more desire to dine with Emma Varley than she has to dine with me.'

Again that monotonous, emotionless laugh drifted across the table like a chilling breeze.

'Be careful what you say to her,' Conlon said. 'She's not as trustworthy as she may appear.'

'I'm always careful what I say. It's a habit built over many years. I'm an inveterate and accomplished liar, as you know. Even now you cannot be sure if I am speaking the truth. You taught me well, Leigh, very well.'

Conlon did not see him again that evening. The two men went their different ways. The next day Deitch slipped out before Conlon rose from his bed. Conlon strolled down to the kitchen where Mrs. Davidson was talking to Wilkie. She grunted an unwilling greeting.

'You catch us at our mid morning break,' Wilkie said, pleasantly enough. 'Mrs. Davidson has just baked some scones. With a bit of butter and a little jam they're the best food you can get anywhere. My mouth waters at the very thought of them.'

Mrs. Davidson was aware of the proprieties but she managed the courtesy with difficulty.

'Would you care to try one?' she asked as pleasantly as she could.

Conlon shook his head. 'I'm looking for Mr. Deitch. I think I must have missed him. Do you know where he went?'

'He left about half an hour ago. He called in to tell me that Emma Varley will be here for dinner. I am so pleased. I feared for a time that we might not see her again. I said to Mr. Davidson, 'I think Emma Varley and Mr. Deitch may have had a falling out but I do hope not. They are very good for each other.'

'Did he say where he was going?' Conlon asked impatiently.

'No, I'm afraid he didn't.'

Conlon turned to leave.

'I know where he is,' Wilkie said. He turned back. 'Agnes told me last night. They couldn't persuade Mr. Deitch to come for dinner but he agreed to call this morning for a short time, just a social call. I believe that Mrs. Waterson was very keen that they should build bridges, get over any past misunderstandings and so on. Agnes and Marcus plan to honour her wishes.'

Conlon turned sharply away and left them. He pulled the door shut rather more angrily than he had intended. The sound echoed.

'Was it something I said?' Wilkie asked.

'It wouldn't matter what you said to that man. He would take exception if you told him the weather forecast. As I said to Mr. Davidson…'

Chapter Thirty Eight

Conlon was not a man who dreamed. When the full moon drew on the tides of other minds and filled them with pictures and stories Conlon slept undisturbed. He slept and he awoke. That was all. No moon could draw dreams, like gravity draws the deep sea, to overflow onto the shore of his consciousness. Where others might lie in light sleep and see their minds create strange scenes as on a blank canvas, Conlon simply awoke.

Recently, however, he awoke in a most unsatisfactory manner. He felt as if he had left some matter incomplete. He was conscious of feeling angry and frustrated and his head ached. He was aware of a niggling irritation which had been festering in his mind during his hours of sleep.

'I must take my dinner earlier,' he muttered, 'or my brandy later.' But he knew that was not the cause.

The image of John Deitch recurred during his waking moments and somewhere, as if in peripheral vision, he could see Agnes Waterson and her brother, Emma Varley and the two detectives. He got the impression they were on either side of Deitch and they had been speaking. They had seen him and, as they saw him, they had turned away and faded into silence and shadow.

'Something's wrong. I don't dream.' he muttered to himself.

His restlessness remained with him for much of the day. He found himself watching other people very closely. To make matters worse, Deitch seemed strangely cheerful. It rubbed against him like sandpaper on a wound.

'Where are you going today?' he asked over breakfast.

'Out.'

'Anywhere special?'

'No.'

Of course he was going somewhere special; he was going to the Watersons again or to Emma Varley's studio. Why could he not just come out and say it? Why was he so secretive about it? Conlon was suspicious.

'I hardly see you nowadays. You are a very poor host.'

'I have been rather preoccupied since Emma left. You must forgive me. I am very poor company. I thought it best to remove myself from the hall and to spend more time alone. I'll try to make amends.'

Again that strange smile; he looked almost cheerful. Conlon found himself obliged to feign an unnaturally sympathetic enquiry.

'How is Emma? I was as good as my word last evening and hid myself away.'

'I've attempted to rebuild our friendship. My efforts have not been entirely without success.'

'I feel some responsibility for causing difficulties between you. Perhaps Emma doesn't plan to return again whilst I am here?'

'Perhaps,' Deitch replied with apparent indifference, 'Emma has very strong opinions on some matters which may well conflict with yours.'

'And with yours too,' Conlon added.

'Perhaps, perhaps.'

Conlon found it difficult to settle that morning. He wandered down to the kitchen and then out into the garden. He spoke to Mrs. Davidson and then to Wilkie. Nothing they said reassured him. As he turned away he felt their eyes watching him; he felt their distrust, their dislike. As he walked along the pathways between trees and lawns he glanced to left and right as if checking that no-one was watching him. He walked to the end of the drive and stood by the road side. A solitary car drove past. The driver glanced towards him and raised a hand. Conlon glared at him angrily. From the other direction a second car approached. It was a small, blue car and Conlon felt a surge of anger as it closed on him. Was it Marcus Waterson? The car approached and then passed. It was not the same car. The wrinkled face of an elderly woman broke into a smile. Conlon turned away and ignored her.

He walked back to the house and hid himself away in the drawing room. He passed the rest of the day in an unfamiliar state of irritability which was not improved when Deitch failed to return until just before dinner. Over dinner they spoke of mundane matters and Deitch said little of interest. It was only as they settled in the drawing room over brandy that he mentioned, almost casually, a matter which did little to improve Conlon's mood.

'Emma and I spent a very pleasant morning by the harbour and on the cliff,' he said. 'She had her sketch book and made some preliminary pencil drawings. She plans to convert them to watercolours at a later date. W spent an hour at least simply sitting on the cliff top overlooking a narrow cleft of rock where a pair of fulmars was nesting. She made a particularly fine sketch of them. I've asked for the watercolour for the hall.'

Conlon grunted but did not respond.

'On our way back we met Agnes and Marcus Waterson in the village. Miss Waterson remains rather cool towards me but Marcus was really very polite. He renewed his invitation. We're to go to dinner on Sunday.'

'You've accepted the invitation?'

'Emma was quite insistent. She felt it would be discourteous to decline a second time. However, I have insisted that we shall stay only for an hour or two after dinner. I don't wish to expose myself any more than is absolutely essential. I pleaded a long planned and very inconvenient conference call with an old acquaintance in the U.S. I shall be back as darkness falls.'

Conlon looked up but he couldn't catch John's eye. He seemed preoccupied with a novel he had selected from the bookcase.

'What are you reading?'

Deitch turned the cover towards him. 'Dostoievsky,' he said, 'Crime and Punishment.' He laughed lightly as if at a private joke.

That night Conlon slept poorly again and he was beset by a recurring dream from which he could not escape. He was in a rowing boat. He was fleeing from Portskail along the sea loch. He was heading inland to where the loch narrowed below dark mountains. Deitch was at the tiller.

'I can't see where we're going,' Conlon was shouting to him, as if through a fog. Deitch smiled but he did not look towards him.

'I know where we're going,' Deitch said.

'I want to know where we're going,' Conlon shouted to him.

Deitch's mouth widened into a silent laugh.

'They're listening,' Conlon shouted. 'They're following us. They're out there but I can't see them.'

'I can see them,' John Deitch said with a strange smile. 'You're safe. Trust me.'

The dream changed and he was alone in the boat and the tiller moved listlessly from side to side at the whim of the waves which tapped against the side of the boat, like messengers at a door.

'They're all around me,' he cried. 'They're closing in, closer and closer. I can't escape them. There are too many. Where are you, Deitch?' His words echoed back to him accompanied by a sinister and mirthless laughter. 'Deitch? Is that you, Deitch?' he called, 'Where are you?'

He drew the boat up onto a lonely shore and fled into the darkest of woods which flanked its edges; he buried himself deep in the leaf litter beneath moss and stone. He could feel the damp penetrate his clothes until he was soaked and shivering. He held his breath but his heart beat like a signal.

Then he heard them. At first it was just a gentle movement of leaves as if on a breeze. It was shapeless and without form. The sounds gathered as if drawn together by a magnetic force. They had a rhythm, they beat to a pulse. Footsteps were heading towards him. He could hear a strange snuffling as of an animal leading the hunters forward. Conlon scratched at the earth and buried himself deeper and deeper. Then he lay still and closed his eyes. Perhaps they would pass him by.

The snuffling beast drew closer and closer and its breathing grew louder and louder. He imagined now he could smell the foul breath emerging between dripping jaws. Behind the regular, beating rhythm the hunters were gathering. They were near him, they were around him and at their heart a huge, monstrous beast was drooling.

Then silence – an awful silence that lasted minutes. He couldn't breathe. Then the beast moved a paw and then moved another. It was scratching. It was tearing at the ground above his head. It's snuffling and scratching grew louder and faster. Then, just as he felt the claws tear at his back to reach, it stopped.'

Conlon wanted to wake up but he couldn't. He reached out a hand. Instead of silk sheets he felt the damp grass of the forest floor. He felt the leaf litter and the soil on his arms and legs. He turned slowly over and found himself face to face with the beast that pursued him.

It had the body of a terrifying wolf – but the face belonged to John Deitch.

'Trust me,' the face said and it smiled through foul, dripping teeth.

At that moment Leigh Conlon knew true terror and he awoke sweating and breathing hard.

Chapter Thirty Nine

Even before he overhead Deitch and Emma Varley Conlon knew what he would have to do. The nightmare and then the conversation confirmed its inevitability. He would never be free if he didn't act now. Emma was in the drawing room with Deitch. They were whispering earnestly. He could hear them as he walked along the corridor. He paused outside and listened.

'Then you are resolved to act,' he heard Emma say in a hushed tone.

He could imagine her holding Deitch by the hands and looking softly at him from those ageing, wrinkled eyes. He leaned against the wall adjacent to the door to listen more closely. 'You're a fool, Deitch,' he muttered.

'I am resolved,' he heard him say. 'It has taken me a long time but I'm sure now.'

'Then you'll speak to them?'

Conlon listened more intently. Speak to whom?

'I contacted Aaron Marks this morning. He'll call this afternoon and we shall discuss matters in the walled garden. It will be more private there. We shall discuss the general issues relating to my disclosures. He will be disappointed I think at how little I have to tell him. I explained that I must speak to the Watersons before I commit myself to paper or make a full statement. There are matters I would wish to disclose to them first. I think I owe it to them. He was very understanding. He suggests we speak briefly today. We can conclude matters the morning following our dinner engagement.'

'That's very understanding of him,' Emma said.

Deitch laughed softly. 'I think he fears I might change my mind. I have something of a history in that respect. He'll come here today to bolster my flagging courage and to ensure I remain committed.'

'And will you?'

'I shall,' he said. 'I'm uncomfortably aware that my life will have little value if I don't. I shall lose things that I now realise are of more importance than anything else. There are things, people, I cannot live without,'

He must have looked at her gently, his eyes conveying a message that required no words. Conlon grimaced. It would be unwise to remain beside the door any longer. They might emerge at any moment. He slipped quietly along the corridor, carefully avoiding the one step where a loose floorboard creaked. He reached the safety of his room.

The next morning he told Deitch he would be leaving.

'I see no reason to prolong my stay,' he said. 'Perhaps in my absence you may repair your friendship with Emma. I shall return to the city and spend a few days there before I fly out to the continent. It's time I retired. I'll see out my life sipping wine and absorbing the sunshine in the finest landscape I can find. I would invite you to visit me but I doubt you would accept.' He smiled coldly.

'I would acknowledge your offer with courtesy and gratitude,' Deitch smiled, 'but you're quite correct. I would never visit. I think we must allow our history to become precisely that – history. Perhaps we'll both do less harm in the future.'

'By choice in your case, by necessity in mine,' Conlon laughed. 'I'll leave shortly after lunch so that I can be in the city by the evening. It would be foolish to miss dinner when there is no need and the hotel serves a particularly fine salmon.'

He held out a hand. John Deitch shook it without much enthusiasm.

'Perhaps I'll see you before you leave,' he said.

'Perhaps you shall.'

In fact Deitch did not see his guest again that day. Conlon made sure of that. He packed his bags and loaded them into the car before lunch and then retreated to his room. He sat by the window and watched and waited. He saw Wilkie several times as he wheeled a barrow between beds or stopped to tighten a trellis or tidy a path. He watched curiously as Wilkie bent over a particular rose and smelt its scent. He must have liked it because he cut it carefully on a long stem and took it to the greenhouse, for Agnes, no doubt.

Conlon smiled cynically. Marriage, children and a home near Strathan – that, no doubt, was the extent of his ambition, the poor fool. It wouldn't last; love could never last. Love was destructive. It wormed away inside you, eating at your strength, your independence. Before you knew it you were no longer able to act or think for yourself. You were vulnerable. Look at Deitch; he used to be strong once. Look at him now. Emma Varley had identified her prey and had grasped him firmly in her talons. He was bleeding slowly to death.

'It'll be an act of mercy to kill him.'

He turned his head slowly and watched the garden. A light breeze passed over the bushes. They seemed to shiver momentarily. In the distance gulls cried and rose from the shore. The tide was quite high now and a number of birds had been driven up onto the fields. Leigh Conlon watched these things coldly and dispassionately. He glanced back towards the garden gate and the area of gravel and lawn directly below his window.

Eventually he saw Wilkie look up from his work. He had heard something. Conlon peered down. It was Aaron Marks. He was walking towards the garden, his dog at his heel and a black stick in his hand. He leaned on it lightly. When he turned along the path and through the gate and crossed to the small bench seat in the arbour Conlon slipped out of his room and headed down to the garden. He followed the wall round to the side gate and slipped inside. He knew just where he was going; he could hide himself quite easily behind the box hedge and against the wall near the arbour. He would hear what was said but he would not be seen.

He paused; a mobile phone rang. He heard Aaron answer it. The conversation was brief and functional. It was obviously someone at his office. He arranged to see them later and closed the phone.

'So you're quite resolved,' he said.

It was Deitch towards whom he had turned, Deitch to whom he had spoken, Deitch who had secreted himself in the arbour to wait for the detective. They were sitting together on the bench beneath the yew hedge. Where was Wilkie? He listened carefully. He could hear the snip, snip, snip of shears tidying a hedge across the garden, beyond the sweet pea trellis. It was careful work, meticulous, leaf by leaf, branch by branch. Conlon understood that sort of work.

'I'm quite resolved,' Deitch drawled. He sounded tired again and disinterested. It was just a process he had to go through. 'I have only one condition; I'll tell you everything, every sordid detail, but I'll say it only in the presence of Marcus and Agnes Waterson, - and Emma, of course. My humiliation must be complete. I want nothing in return for my revelations; I don't ask that we reach some negotiated deal that protects me from prosecution. On the contrary, I want no special treatment. I must pay for what I have done.'

'And Conlon?'

Behind the hedge Conlon tensed and held his breath.

'He will be guilty by implication and no doubt I shall add considerably to your supply of circumstantial evidence. I may even be able to point you in directions you have not previously considered. Whether that's enough I don't know.'

'You have no doubts about betraying him?'

'I have no more doubts than he had about ensuring my culpability in the event of a moment such as this. There's no bond that ties us other than one of mutual guilt and mutual fear.'

'What about Barden?'

'Conlon killed Barden, I have no doubt about that, but you know that already. I can offer no evidence. Conlon is far too clever to leave himself vulnerable. I'm afraid that I can offer you nothing with regard to Barden.'

'Then we must settle for what we can get. There's no way you can find evidence to incriminate Conlon in the murder, I assume?'

Deitch must have shaken his head. 'No, there isn't. Conlon is suspicious by nature. He would know at once if I tried to draw it from him. Besides, there's no time. Conlon leaves this afternoon. And you forget that I am fundamentally a very selfish man. I am concerned to find my own redemption. I despise Conlon for his treatment of Barden and Harmison and I would see him imprisoned without hesitation but I will do no more than I've already said.'

'Then we must use the evidence you provide and do the best we can.'

'Yes.'

Conlon heard Aaron stand up. His feet disturbed the soft gravel. He paused and reached down to stroke the springer spaniel at his feet. Conlon heard the dog stir and rise to its feet.

'It's high tide. I shall take Rosie along the grass above the shore,' he said. 'She'll be disappointed at the absence of sand but I'm sure she'll find some scent to follow. Would you care to join me?'

Conlon experienced a moment of anxiety when Rosie stopped a few feet away from where he was hiding. She sniffed at the ground and the air and rumbled strangely in her throat. Then Aaron called her and she moved on. Conlon waited for a few minutes. He could no longer hear Wilkie. The garden was silent. Only the breeze disturbed the grasses and flower heads and stirred the sweet peas on their trellis. He listened carefully and then looked carefully across the garden. He slipped out of his hiding place and made his way quickly to the gate. A moment later he was walking across the lawns and the gravel. Half an hour later, without having spoken to Deitch, he climbed in his car and drove away.

In the garden Wilkie emerged from behind the vegetable beds as Conlon closed the gate. He smiled. Inside the kitchen Ruth Davidson wiped floury hands on her apron and glanced with satisfaction at the mobile phone which lay on the table. Down on the shore Aaron and Deitch were staring out to sea.

'I love this place, you know,' Deitch was saying. 'I shall miss it.'

Aaron looked at him closely. 'You know there are risks involved in what we plan.'

'There are greater risks involved in doing nothing.'

'Conlon is unpredictable. We can't be entirely certain how he will react. All we can do is to eliminate as many variables as possible – and then hope.'

'You are quite wrong, you know.' Deitch continued to look out to sea. 'Conlon is entirely predictable, at least in as far as he will plan meticulously how best to rid himself of me without incriminating himself. What remains unknown is how he will do it.'

He turned slowly and for the first time in their brief acquaintance he looked Aaron directly in the eye and did not waver. 'First of all he will provide himself with an alibi. It will be unshakeable. Then he will choose a time, a place and a method. He will telephone me, of that you can be sure. He will want a clear picture of my proposed movements. You must reduce his options and be as meticulous in your planning as he will assuredly be in his.'

'He will have to act quickly since the time scale is narrow. That applies a considerable amount of pressure. We need to narrow the opportunities even more. I suggest we direct his attention to a time and a place of our choosing.'

'You may try. Conlon is not easily manipulated. He sees conspiracies at every turn. He is quite paranoid.'

He turned away and stared across the white lines of foam. 'It's never still, is it,' he said, 'the ocean, I mean. It toils restlessly and endlessly. Even in its greatest depths it moves and stirs. It's like some great beast moving and rumbling in the deepest of sleeps. I wonder what it will do when it finally awakes.' He laughed. 'You must forgive me. I'm prone to such reflections nowadays. I find echoes of the sea resonate in my mind. The weather forecast is good for the next few days. I think I'll walk along the cliff when I return from the Waterson's. No doubt Conlon will prize that information from me. I'll indicate that it's my intention to stop near the cliff top to watch few remaining auks and kittiwakes in the failing light. He won't be surprised. He will already be anticipating that I'll regret my decision to visit the Watersons. It will be quite typical of me, once the evening is over, to choose to clear my mind, to procrastinate, to reflect on my situation. He'll find it laughably predictable.'

'It's a very exposed route. It'll be difficult to keep a close watch on you.'

'It will also be difficult to approach me without being seen.'

'It has the look of a very obvious trap, don't you think? Will he fall for it?'

Deitch turned sharply. 'Oh no, of course not; you must plan for the most unexpected of strategies. Conlon will already view this as a test of his particular genius. It's just a game to him and he likes games and he likes to win. He'll cheat if he can.'

Aaron did not reply. Rosie, bored with their conversation and longing to run, barked restlessly. John Deitch reached down and stroked her head. She accepted the gesture then drew away, watching and waiting. Someone would throw a ball soon.

'It would be very foolish to underestimate the extent of Conlon's paranoia,' Deitch concluded.

'You think he will try to intercept you before you reach the hall,'

Deitch nodded. 'I'll walk through the walled garden. That will be where we'll meet, Conlon and I, and it's there that you must set your trap.'

'Can you get him to speak about Harmison and Barden, do you think?'

'I can try. At the very worst he will attack and kill me before you reach me and you will convict him for that.' He laughed dryly.

'Wilkie will provide us with suitable hiding places. We'll be within yards of you. There should be little danger.'

'There is always danger where Conlon is concerned.'

Aaron reached in his pocket and drew out a small, orange ball. He threw it and Rosie sped across the rough tussocks of grass. She retrieved it and sped back, dropping the ball at his feet. She waited, her eyes fixed, her tongue lolling from the side of her mouth.

'You have every right to change your mind, you know. We're expecting far too much of you.'

'I shall not change my mind,' He looked up and his eyes searched the sea like beacons. 'I have too much to lose.' he murmured. 'I'm an old man in love, you see, for the first time in his life.' He laughed strangely. 'How very foolish I sound. You must think me a maudlin, sentimental, old fool.'

'Indeed I don't,' Aaron said, 'and neither does Rosie. Look, she trusts you.' Indeed Rosie having collected her ball from Aaron's feet, had dropped it beside Deitch and now looked at him and waited.

'An omen, do you think?'

'Rosie is never wrong.'

John reached down and threw the ball. 'Then we must act without hesitation. Will you speak to the Watersons and Wilkie?'

Aaron nodded.

'Then there is no more to be said.'

They turned and walked slowly back towards the house.

Chapter Forty

It was Friday. In another two days the trap would be sprung. Aaron and Jack grew more and more anxious.

'There are an unfortunately large number of variables,' Jack scratched his head and leaned back in his chair. 'Too many I think. We're relying heavily on our ability to restrict Conlon's opportunities and to shepherd him into our trap.' He paused and shook his head. 'I feel ten years older today,' he muttered, 'I should be retired.' Then he brightened. 'If it goes wrong I will be, think of that,' he said. He leaned forward and drew some papers in front of them. They were covered in sketches marked with arrows and circles in different colours. 'Let's go over it just once more,' It was the third time that day. He poured over them for a moment and then frowned and sat back and threw the papers heavily on the desk. ''No, there's nothing more we can do. We've covered everything.'

'Then why do I feel as if we have missed something?' Aaron looked towards the window. Outside, the streets of Portskail were growing quieter. The occasional tourist voices drifted through the open window as if carried on air. A car accelerated away. Gulls called.

'That, my boy, is the consequence of the one true variable – Leigh Conlon. We simply do not know that he will behave in the way that we anticipate or that he'll be guided quite so easily into our trap.' Jack walked over to the window and looked down onto the street. 'Conlon is a clever man, whatever else he is and whatever we may think of him. His senses are particularly acute at the moment. He'll sense a plot even where one doesn't exist. We must prepare for him choosing an alternative strategy.'

'What alternative could he choose? Deitch is locked down as tight as if he were in a safe. The only time he is vulnerable is when he takes that walk home.'

Jack nodded. 'Nonetheless,' he said. He breathed deeply and looked across the rooftops towards the bay. 'I love this place, you know. Even the air smells homely. I never regret moving here. I could have lived in a city and been wealthy beyond my wildest dreams but it had no appeal for me, none whatsoever. I had my Kate and my home and my work. That was always enough. What about you?'

'I don't mind so long as I still have a job on Monday. I don't want to think any further than that.' He paused. 'Rosie would hate a city. She likes mountains and moorland and quiet beaches. I think Andrea and Jacob are the same. We'll never go far away from here. It's our home.'

Jack paced the room and paused at the window. 'I have tried to train my mind to think like our target. It's not pleasant, though, putting yourself in the mind of a sadistic, emotionless psychopath. I gave up in the interests of my sanity. We must focus on opportunity and cover as best we can each likely point of attack. Eliminate Conlon from your thoughts, Aaron. Eliminate him. Focus on opportunity.'

Aaron lay awake that night and his mind churned and threw up new and more complex problems. Perhaps Jack was right. Perhaps trying to read the mind of a man like Conlon wasn't helpful. They would have men by the harbour, men on the cliff and in the garden. They had arranged for cars to watch the roads. They even had a couple of men on the hillside with binoculars. Maybe that was enough.

He turned over in bed and groaned.

'What's the matter?'

Andrea, tousled and bleary eyed, awoke and turned towards him. Aaron switched on the light.

'It's not enough,' he said. 'I can't sleep. I need to go downstairs. I need to think.'

'Do you want me to come with you?'

'No, you go back to sleep. I won't be long.'

If he was Conlon, what would he be thinking? If he was Conlon, what would he do? Conlon was suspicious and he was very careful. He would see plots even where they didn't exist. If he was Conlon, what would he anticipate? Would his paranoia be sufficient to anticipate even the complex plan they had evolved? Slowly he began to picture the problem as it would be seen by the predator rather than the prey. An hour passed.

He picked up the phone. The answer came quickly. 'Jack? Yes, I know what time it is. Were you asleep? No, neither was I. I was just thinking...'

'...me too,' Jack murmured. 'I've had an idea...'

'...So have I -let's talk.'

Half an hour later he returned to his bed and slipped in beside Andrea. Her warmth wrapped round him and he held her close. Her sleepy fragrance seeped through him and he absorbed her presence as if it could permeate his skin. He was asleep within moments. His mind was at rest. He knew now as clearly as if it had already happened what would unfold the next day. He slept deeply until morning.

Sunday evening eventually arrived. The weather was fine with only a light breeze. Deitch set off to walk to the Waterson's along the cliff. It would take an hour perhaps but he wasn't expected for dinner until seven. He had plenty of time. He felt strangely calm. He carried a small pack with his shoes in it. When he arrived at the Watersons – if he arrived at all, he thought, if Conlon believed, as he had told him, that he would drive to the White House and walk back - he had no intention of arriving in muddy footwear. He wore boots which could be changed for clean shoes on arrival.

'I'm becoming quite fastidious,' he mused.

He crossed the lawn down towards the shore and then turned to head away from the beach up the gradually rising cliff.

In his fisherman's cottage, Wilkie paced the tiny living room. He glanced at his watch.

'Time to go,' he said. He checked his collar and his coat and brushed some invisible speck from his sleeve. He looked in the mirror. 'You'll do,' he told himself. He took a deep breath and turned to the door.

Jack, Aaron and Sim checked their preparations. They were in the tiny office beside the greenhouse in the walled garden. They had been there since morning, their car securely hidden in an outbuilding. Everything was in place. The cars were positioned strategically near the village and on the road; the watchers were on the cliff and hillside. It would be a long, uncomfortable wait.

'Time to go,' Jack said. 'You know what to do, Sim?'

Sim nodded. His eyes shone with anxiety and excitement. This was a new experience for the young detective. He shuffled anxiously and looked around as if expecting to see Conlon appear at the door.

'You're looking forward to this, aren't you?' Jack observed. 'Ah, the enthusiasm of the young; do you remember what it was like, Aaron, when you ventured out on your first significant arrest?'

Aaron grinned at Sim. 'The excitement will wear off after three hours hiding behind a bush. 'You'll just want it to be over so you can go home.'

'Exciting nonetheless,' Jack said.

'And frightening,' Aaron added. 'But the worst of it is over. I hate waiting.' He laughed suddenly. 'Good God,' he said. 'I sound like you, Jack.'

They opened the door slowly and checked the garden. Everything was still and silent. Even the birds seemed to have disappeared into the shadows to watch and wait. They slipped out. In a few moments the garden was as silent as if no human life existed within it. The blackbird and thrush dropped down onto the grass beside the fruit vines. A willow warbler sang from a tall shrub in the corner of a wall. A robin pecked for food amongst the stones on the gravel path. An hour passed. A squirrel scurried along the wall. It paused and rose on its hind feet, dark, sharp eyes watching, ears and nose flicking this way and that. Hearing and scenting nothing of concern it moved forward, step by cautious step before it dropped into the garden and hopped away between the flowers. A few moments later it reappeared on the furthest wall, its tail curled and feathered over its back. It dropped out of sight, back towards the trees. Only Sim could see it from his vantage point behind the bushes near the arbour. He was sitting now, his knees tucked up, his back resting against rough stone.

Another hour passed.

Emma Varley was in her studio, standing beside a canvas, scrutinising an unfinished portrait of John Deitch. She was working quickly and intently in oils and had lost all track of time. She would be able to finish this portrait now. She knew what she needed to do to make it complete. Eventually she glanced at a clock on the wall.

'Oh dear,' she cried, 'Oh dear me, look at the time. John will be here in half an hour and I've not even started to get ready.'

She laid her palette and brushes unwillingly aside and hurried to her first floor rooms. Five minutes later the sound of water could be heard from the shower.

Agnes Waterson was busy in the kitchen at the White House. She had little to do but she wanted to keep busy. She couldn't remain still for more than a minute. The food before her was nothing more than a side show to the main event but it felt at that moment like the most important thing in her life. She fussed over every item and then walked through to the dining room to check the table. Marcus was standing by the window looking towards the trees and the driveway.

'Here's Wilkie.' He raised a hand and waved. Agnes hurried to the door.

'Thank goodness you're here,' she said as he held and kissed her. 'I couldn't go through this without you.'

'I must speak to Marcus,' Wilkie said. Agnes led him through to the dining room. Marcus was turned and grasped his hand.

'Are you prepared?' he asked.

Wilkie nodded.

Deitch stopped only briefly to watch the lingering rafts of auks on the water beneath the once teeming cliffs. There had been barely a sound as he approached up the steep slope and now, the summer having passed, only the wind and the restless waves could be heard below. Perhaps there would be a day, he thought, when he would be able to stand here on these cliffs with an untroubled mind. That would be good, very good. He turned away and the sound fell away just as quickly as it had arisen. He walked on now until he reached the village. He stopped only at the door of Emma's studio. He knocked and entered.

In the garden Sim carefully stretched out one leg and then another. He rubbed his calves. He glanced at his watch. They would be eating at the White House now. He felt envious of the warmth, the comfort and the food. In another two hours Deitch would set off to return along the cliff. In two and a half hours, maybe three, he would be back. When would Conlon appear? It could be any time now. Sim resettled himself. In his ear he heard Jack's voice. The earpiece was working fine. He whispered a brief, hushed reply. Even the blackbird failed to hear him. The sharp eyed thrush hopped close by but saw nothing.

At the White House the evening passed slowly. No-one felt much inclined for conversation. Agnes engaged Emma with questions about her work. Marcus spoke of his time in different countries. The conversation was briefly enlivened when he and Deitch discovered a shared liking for a particular area of Spain. Then their words died away and silence hung around them as if it too was waiting for the evening to be over.

The meal completed and compliments offered and received they adjourned to the sitting room. After some time Deitch looked at his watch.

'Is it time yet?' Marcus asked. His voice betrayed his anxiety. Emma looked up as if startled.

Deitch was remarkably calm. He felt no fear and only a tremor of anxiety. In fact he felt strangely elated, even excited, and that was all. What would happen would happen. He was caught up in a wave that would not cease rolling until it hit the shore. He could do nothing now to control its path. There was no point in worrying.

'Not yet,' he said. 'I would prefer to leave just as the sun drops to the horizon so as to arrive back as darkness overtakes the garden. It's important to make this as easy as possible for Conlon, don't you think? There's no point in putting a cage around the tethered goat.' He laughed dryly.

It was the first time anyone had mentioned Conlon or the purpose of the evening.

Agnes looked at him closely. 'Aren't you afraid?'

'I don't know. I'm not sure.'

'I think you're very courageous,' she said.

John Deitch looked at her and at the others. 'No,' he said, 'please don't think of this as courage. It's mere cowardice that obliges me to act in the way I do. I simply couldn't continue to live as I have for the past few years. My fear of living as I have is far greater than my fear of anything that may happen tonight.'

He paused and looked at Emma. 'I feel strangely contented,' he smiled.

'I'm very proud of you,' she said, 'very proud indeed. When you return, I shall have a gift for you.'

'Then I shall take particular care,' he smiled.

Silence fell around them like an impenetrable fog. Each of them sat alone in their private confessional, aware only of their own thoughts and their own hopes.

'I'll be glad when this is all over,' Wilkie said at last.

John Deitch looked again at his watch. He glanced out of the window. The evening light was growing dim. To the south west the sun was sinking slowly into the ocean and steam-like clouds fled in wisps or burnt red.

'It's time to go,' he said. He stood up and brushed his sleeves. 'Do I look suitably prepared?' he asked Emma with a short laugh. 'It's taken many years to achieve this particular eminence. I must look the part.' She helped him on with his coat. At the front door he replaced his shoes with boots.

'You look very refined,' she said and leaned forward to kiss his cheek. 'Be careful, John. I...'

'I know,' he said.

Aaron Marks looked at his watch. The sun had fallen below the horizon and the sky was blistered red. He spoke in a low voice. Jack was motionless beside him.

Sim listened. Nothing stirred now. Even the air around him seemed to be holding its breath. He too held his breath and listened for any sound. He heard nothing and released his breath slowly and carefully so as to make not the slightest sound. Each time he breathed he was sure his hoarse rasping could be heard across the darkening flower beds.

Minutes passed.

'He's not coming,' he murmured. He wanted to move his legs now but he dared not. He wanted to turn his neck but he could not. The stone wall pressed in his back but he couldn't move. Away to his left he heard the gate click open. Footsteps ground on the stone path. Someone had entered and was walking towards the arbour. In a moment whoever it was would pass him. He whispered a hushed warning to Aaron and Jack.

'He's here.'

He waited.

The footsteps approached closer and then stopped just beside him. He shrank back into the darkness as if it could absorb him. He dared not blink an eye. He looked slowly towards the dark figure as he paused and removed a cigarette from a case in his pocket. In the flame from a lighter Sim saw Deitch briefly illuminated. He inhaled deeply and then turned towards the house. If it was going to happen, it would happen now.

There was a sudden movement on the path to his right. A figure, a shadow, a dark shape moved quickly past him and followed Deitch. In four steps he was on him. He caught his shoulder and spun him round. Sim was two steps behind him. There was a flash of silver, a movement of an arm through the air, a heavy blow and a groan.

Deitch took a torch from his pocket. Sim had struck a hard blow against the attacker's arm and a sharp, narrow bladed knife lay helplessly some yards away. Sim had pinned his victim to the ground. Two officers, who had shared Sim's vigil, emerged from the darkness of the greenhouses and descended upon the attacker.

Sim stood up and turned the figure over. He stood back; his face was white as if suddenly deprived of blood.

'It's not him,' he hissed. 'Jack, Aaron, it's not him!'

Deitch looked down in confusion. 'I know him,' he said. 'That's Carlton Brooke. He's a friend of Conlon's. He married Agnes

Waterson.' He grabbed the prostrate man by the throat and screamed, 'Where's Conlon? Where is he?'

The figure on the ground laughed. He tore away from Deitch and leaned on his elbows. He wiped away the blood which trickled down his face. He laughed again loudly and nastily.

'He's too good for you,' he laughed. 'He's beaten you. He's beaten all of you. Look.'

He nodded a bloodied head towards the sky beyond the garden. Above the village a plume of grey smoke was rising and the black sky shone with a strange light. 'It was the Watersons and Emma Varley he was after all the time. He didn't fear you.'

Deitch stood up. 'No,' he moaned, 'Oh. Please God, no.'

Jack Munro emerged from the darkness by the Waterson Gate.

'It's the White House,' Brooke laughed. 'You're too late.'

Deitch turned to run towards the gate.

'Emma!' he screamed. 'Emma!' Jack caught him by the arm and pushed him back towards the house.

'You must leave this to us now. There is nothing you can do. Go back into the house and stay there until we call you.'

Deitch looked frantically round. He tried to pull away but Jack held him. 'Emma,' he sobbed, 'Emma.'

Jack spoke hurriedly in his ear and pushed him unwillingly him towards the gate and the hall.

'Get Brooke in the car!' he shouted back to Sim. 'You can explain to him just how foolish he has been. Conlon has set him up well and truly. Tell him he can be proud to know that he is the single stupidest person I've met this year. Well done, Sim, young man.' He nodded to the officers. 'The same goes for you. Well done. I'll get Aaron to buy you a drink.'

'What a bloody mess,' he muttered. He pushed Deitch towards the hall. An officer was standing in the shadows by the stone steps. 'Take Mr. Deitch to the house,' he called. 'Take him to the drawing room and lock him in. Don't let him out. Then come back to the outer door and stand very visibly at the top of the steps. Keep a close watch. I don't want anything else going wrong tonight.'

As he turned to leave the only sound he heard was the coarse laughter of Carlton Brooke as he was led towards the car.

Chapter Forty One

Wilkie waited for half an hour after Deitch left the house. He watched impatiently as the night grew gradually darker. Marcus sat at the window looking out. Emma and Agnes flicked through pages of magazines without recognising a single word.

They waited.

Wilkie glanced at his watch. 'It's time, I think,' he said. 'Let's hope Jack and Aaron were overly cautious, shall we?'

Marcus stood up and closed the curtains. Agnes turned off the light. The darkness that surrounded them was heavy with fear.

'Do you think…?' Emma began.

'I'm trying very hard not to,' Agnes sighed.

Wilkie and Marcus turned towards the door.

'Be careful,' Agnes whispered.

The lounge door closed behind them. Emma and Agnes heard the soft sound of the back door opening and closing as quiet as a whisper. Then there was only silence. Just outside the door the two men parted to left and right. Wilkie crept towards the driveway, carefully masked from sight by the trees. His footsteps made no sound. He stopped by the wall and sat down, his back pressed against the stone, his eyes firmly fixed on the front of the house, the lounge window, the kitchen beside it. Behind the house Marcus would be doing the same.

Only a few minutes had passed when a car drove slowly along the lane. Its headlamps illuminated the trees momentarily and passed across them like a search light. It slowed down as if someone was looking carefully at the house, checking it. They would see the whole house in darkness as if the occupants had retired for the night. The car moved slowly past. As it approached the harbour it turned and returned and the lights caught the trees and the passed across them. The driver was careful. He didn't want to make a mistake. It was better to check and check again.

Once more the car gradually increased its speed and moved away. Behind the wall Wilkie held his breath. Above him the branches and leaves were silhouettes. A half moon broke from the clouds illuminating them momentarily, charcoal grey, sketched clearly on the sky. In the distance an oystercatcher called. He could see the house clearly now in the moonlight. Behind the lounge curtains Agnes and Emma waited in silence.

'I hope Jack and Aaron are wrong,' he thought again.

The car seemed to have disappeared. Perhaps it was simply a neighbour or a late arriving visitor searching for their lodging. He stared across the drive towards the side of the house. There were pale shadows now, cast by the moon, but nothing moved. He shuffled to relieve the pain in his back. Then he froze. Something by the corner of the house caught his attention, a movement perhaps, something in the darkness which had slipped silently across the path with no more presence than a ghost. He watched carefully, scanning every shadow, every bush and every tree for the slightest movement. His heart beat rapidly.

Then he saw it; a fox emerged from the undergrowth a few metres away. It paused and scented the air. It knew something was wrong. Its narrow muzzle twitched. Its eyes turned. Then it vanished through the trees beside him and hopped silently over the wall and across the road.

Minutes passed before Wilkie saw further movements. These were larger shapes. Their movements were heavy and coarse. There were two distinct figures. They were dragging something between them. They paused below the window and seemed to be occupied unfastening whatever they were carrying. They turned round and shuffled backwards towards the door. Here they paused again.

Caught on a soft wisp of air a sickly, pungent smell reached out to Wilkie. He leaned forward, suddenly alert, suddenly scared. Agnes! Emma! The two men were laying a trail of petrol under the window and a round the wooden front door. There wasn't a second to lose. He rose to his feet like an incarnation of vengeance. He was no longer concerned about silence; he didn't care if he was seen; he was without fear. His stocky frame emerged from the trees and he headed towards the intruders with his head lowered. As he emerged he shouted as loudly as he could for Marcus! Marcus! The two intruders had barely time to turn before he hit them and threw them to the ground. The petrol can slipped from their hands and fell. He pinned one of them to the ground and parried his flaying arms but the second figure quickly regained his feet and rained blows and kicks on Wilkie until he rolled to one side gasping for breath and crying out in pain.

The two men stumbled towards the side of the house from where they had appeared. They met Marcus at the corner and there was a fierce struggle. Marcus held them up for sufficient time for Wilkie to regain his feet and stumble towards them. Together he and Marcus fought off the ferocious attack of the two men. One of them fell to the ground from a thunderous blow levelled at his head by Wilkie. The second man struggled free, struck Marcus a disabling blow, and fled towards the car parked further up the narrow lane. Wilkie turned to give chase.

'No,' Marcus called after him. 'Leave him. He won't get far.'

The front door had been flung open. Light burst out like a flood. Agnes rushed out angrily, brandishing an old cricket bat that belonged to Marcus, followed more discretely by Emma, carrying a large umbrella in two hands.

'Is it him? Is it Conlon?'

Marcus struggled to his feet and turned the figure over.

'No,' he said. 'Damn it, no.'

'Has he got away?'

Wilkie shook his head.

'That wasn't him either,' he gasped. He winced with pain and held his ribs. 'I think I may have a couple of cracked ribs.'

Marcus held a handkerchief across a bleeding nose.

'So he got someone else to do his work?' Agnes cried out. 'He's escaped us.'

'Perhaps,' Marcus said, 'or maybe he followed Deitch to the Hall after all. Perhaps they've already got him.'

Wilkie looked around. 'I don't think so. I don't understand this. Why was it necessary to kill us and why go to such trouble?'

'Revenge,' Marcus said darkly. 'A man like Conlon doesn't need any other reason.'

Wilkie shook his head. 'Conlon is just the sort of man who does need a reason,' he said. 'Aaron was right. Quickly,' he said suddenly, 'Help me gather some leaves and branches together. Make a pile here on the drive. Quickly, there's no time to lose. Marcus, get the petrol. Quickly now! No time for questions!'

Agnes reached the petrol moments before Marcus and they carried it heavily across the gravel. Emma and Wilkie pulled together leaves and branches and formed them into a rough bonfire.

'We need more,' Wilkie shouted. 'Quickly!' He dragged a large, fallen branch and flung it on the pile. 'Agnes, get me newspapers, magazines, anything that can burn. Marcus, Emma, look in the shed. There are some logs there.'

There was a flurry of movement. Behind them by the window the intruder was slowly struggling to his knees. Wilkie stopped. 'If you move one more inch,' he threatened. 'I'll set fire to the petrol myself.' The man looked at his hands, his feet and his clothes. All around him the petrol was soaking into the ground.

'You wouldn't.'

'Try me.'

The man cowered back against the wall. He did not move.

'They were right,' Wilkie shouted as he threw the final items on the bonfire. He was almost laughing. He picked up the petrol and scattered the contents freely all over. 'Aaron and Jack, they were right. This was nothing more than a distraction. Our deaths were to be a welcomed bonus, that's all. This has got to be a big fire. They need to see it at the castle. Stand back.'

He struck a match and threw it into the fuel. An explosion of flame threw itself into the air, arms wide and waving like a frantic, manic dancer. Smoke billowed after it. A wave of heat beat them like a sudden wind. The crouching figure by the wall whimpered in fear and shuffled further away.

It was five minutes before Wilkie's phone rang. He fumbled to open it hurriedly. He listened. It was Jack.

'Deitch was attacked in the garden,' he repeated, above the roar of the flames. He hurriedly gave Jack his news.

'So they've got Conlon,' Agnes cried. 'It's all over. Thank goodness.'

Wilkie shook his head. 'Conlon wasn't there,' He glanced at Marcus and then put a strong arm round Agnes's shoulder. He hugged her tightly. 'It was Carlton Brooke.'

In the distance a police siren blared and behind it a fire engine. They were coming closer.

Chapter Forty Two

Deitch hurried up the steps two at a time. He ran into the drawing room and picked up the phone. He waited impatiently, breathing heavily. In the lounge of the White House Emma Varley's phone rang and rang unheard in the pocket of her coat which lay silently across a kitchen chair. She was outside in the garden.

'Come on!' he muttered as it went to answer phone. He rang again and then again. Behind him a key turned in the drawing room lock and the door opened quietly.

'I'm trying to get through to Emma,' he said without turning.

'I think it's most unlikely that you will succeed,' a voice behind him said icily. He span round and grasped the table behind him.

'You were expecting one of your detective friends I assume.' Conlon pointed a small hand gun at him. 'They have hurried rather foolishly towards the village leaving a single officer at the door. It wasn't difficult to hide myself in the cellar without anyone seeing me. Let's sit down, shall we?'

He motioned with the gun towards an arm chair. Deitch sat heavily down.

'If you've hurt Emma,' he began.

'You'll do absolutely nothing,' Conlon snapped. 'Not because you wouldn't – I'm sure you would happily see me dead at this moment – but because you can't. I estimate we have at least thirty minutes before those fools decide to check your safety. I doubt you are high on their list of priorities at the moment. I doubt you ever were. When did you become such a fool, John?'

He spoke with a chilling calm. There was no emotion in his voice, not even anger or hatred. He was as cold as a pillar of ice. The chill that emanated from him seemed to penetrate Deitch. He shuddered involuntarily as if fingers of permafrost had scraped deep beneath his skin. Conlon glanced at his watch.

'You should have retained incriminating documents,' he said. 'That's what I would have done. You were always too trusting, John.'

'You had nothing to fear. The evidence I hold is contained only in my head. I told you that.

'Yes, we'll come to that in a moment.'

Conlon laughed.

'I have no fear, John. You, of all people, should know that.'

'Then why?'

'I don't like loose ends.'

John Deitch looked round the room frantically. 'You'll never get away with it, not this time. This isn't like Barden. The police are everywhere.'

Conlon laughed even louder. 'I know where the police are,' He said. 'I can tell you where every car is situated and every officer is hidden. I can even tell you that at this precise moment Marks and Munro have arrived at the White House to find it engulfed in flame.'

Deitch lurched forward as if to grasp Conlon by his throat and shake the life from him. His eyes were wild and frantic. Conlon levelled the gun.

'Sit down,' he snapped. 'I have no doubt your precious Emma and her friends have found their way out and are securely blanketed in the garden awaiting an ambulance. The ambulance will take a little while, of course. The health service is not what it was. Most ambulances are now guaranteed to arrive just after the casualty expires. It's a money saving strategy. They'll be disappointed to find the occupants of the house all alive.'

'They'd better be alive. I warn you, Conlon.'

Conlon smiled patiently and shook his head. 'There you go again making idle threats you have no possible chance of carrying through. You really are a very boring and predictable man, Deitch. I hadn't realised it before.'

'So now you will kill me just as surely as you did Barden.'

Conlon smiled patiently, as if at a child. 'Oh no, this is quite different. I actually planned to reason with Barden. I didn't plan to kill him. The man just wouldn't see reason. He pushed me. He even tried to threaten me. It was a foolish gesture, don't you think.'

'So you beat him to death.'

'I suppose I did, after a fashion. But, do you know, his departure was rather less satisfying in many ways than Harmison's. A few blows, a few kicks and the poor fool expired on the floor in front of me. I had to work on Harmison. It took time and considerable effort. The poor fool was actually happy; imagine that. He had lost everything but he had found some strange contentment. He was weak though, frail, vulnerable. Step by step I tore him apart. I left him with nothing. I got so deep inside his head there was no room for anything else. I knew even as I drove away from the croft that he would be dead within a couple of days.'

'And now me,' Deitch said slowly.

Conlon smiled that same cold smile. He moved casually towards the brandy decanter. 'There's time for a farewell drink,' he said, 'for old times' sake.' He poured it slowly. 'Here,' he said. He looked at the clear liquid and swilled it round the glass and offered it to Deitch. He poured a malt whisky for himself and raised it in a toast.

'We made a good team while it lasted.'

'We were never a team. You know that, Leigh.'

He raised the glass to his lips but before he could drink the door behind Conlon clicked open. Conlon glanced up and in the pier glass above the mahogany table he saw the wiry figure of Jack Munro enter the room behind him. For a moment he was stunned and incapable of movement. Why was he here? He should be floundering in smoke and water at the White House. At the same moment the small door to the ante room opened and Aaron Marks entered. He swung his walking cane hard on Conlon's wrist. The gun, which he was raising, dropped uselessly on the ground and span for a moment before it lay still. The cane lay beside it, cracked and broken.

'I knew that cane would be useful one day,' he said.

Jack held firmly to Deitch's arm. He indicated the brandy. 'I wouldn't drink that if I were you. I don't think it would agree with you. I expect it contains a rather unpleasant additive.'

Conlon looked frantically around him. There was no escape. The tall, solid frame of Aaron Marks now stood by the door. Jack, who had retrieved the gun from the floor, stood in front of him. Deitch sat back on his chair and leaned his head against the back rest. He closed his eyes momentarily.

'Is it over?' he asked. He sounded tired.

'It is,' Jack told him.

'And the recording?'

'First class,' Jack smiled. He looked at Conlon and the smile fell away from him. 'I hope you haven't anything arranged for the rest of your life, Mr. Conlon,' he said. 'What was the plan? I assume you intended to poison Mr. Deitch here with his own brandy and to slip away unseen?'

Conlon dusted his sleeve. He smiled. 'I was never here,' he said. 'At this moment I am playing cards with some friends in the city. I believe I'm winning quite heavily. They will all remember it quite clearly because I had a run of luck. The cards fell my way – two pairs in one hand, three of a kind in another, all court cards as well. I'm doing very well, I believe. It must have been Brooke who caused all the trouble here. He probably broke in this room earlier and poisoned the brandy in case his attack in the garden failed. No doubt he would have tried to blame me but that was just malice. He never forgave me for persuading him to marry Agnes Waterson, you know.' He laughed again, dryly. 'It was a disastrous match.' He looked at Deitch. 'You were party to all of this, I assume?'

Deitch nodded. There was a glint of triumph in his eyes which drove away fatigue.

'I congratulate you. I am particularly pleased that I have been defeated in such spectacular fashion. I anticipated my little diversion would have been sufficient to draw you away.' He nodded at Aaron and Jack. 'A few casualties would have made it all the better but you must understand that it was not my intention to kill anyone at the White House. I merely assumed that if casualties occurred the blame could easily be directed once again at Brooke. I even persuaded him to hire those two thugs as arsonists. You see, nothing could possibly have come back to me. I salute you.'

He reached out a hand towards Jack as if to congratulate him. Jack did not move.

'We should be going,' Conlon sighed, lowering his hand. 'There's really nothing more to be said. Perhaps I can just finish my drink. It will be some time before I shall enjoy another fine brandy.'

He reached for the brandy glass on the table but Aaron stepped forward and held his arm. For a moment their eyes met and locked. Conlon relaxed and smiled.

'I think the whisky is your,' Aaron said. He handed the glass to Conlon who studied it for a moment and then threw back his head and drank it.

'I see there is to be no dramatic ending for me. Perhaps I shall spend the rest of my life writing my memoirs. I shall gain a certain notoriety, don't you think? I shall be very flattering about the skill of my adversaries, of course. The more skilled I make you, the more imaginative and intelligent my own plan will appear. In order to have an evil genius one must present a righteous brilliance in one's adversaries, I think. Holmes had his Moriarty. You shall have me.'

He turned to Deitch and his smile vanished. 'I shall take pleasure in knowing that you are not far away. Perhaps we can arrange to share a cell. That would be very fitting, don't you think, although the part you play in my memoir will be less than flattering, I expect.'

Aaron opened the door behind him. Two officers stood outside. Conlon turned and walked out between them.

'Emma?' Deitch asked. 'Agnes? Wilkie? Marcus?'

'They are all safe and well,' Aaron said. 'They caught the intruders before they could do any damage. It was Wilkie who started the fire and gave the signal.'

'You caught the intruders?'

'We have one in custody. The other won't get far.'

'Then it really is over.'

'It is.'

Deitch stood up. 'It's strange,' he said, 'I've been terrified by the thought of this moment for years. Now it's arrived I am unconcerned. I'm indifferent to the consequences. I merely feel relieved. I feel free. It is most strange.'

Chapter Forty Three

A year had passed since the events at Strathan Tower and the White House. The turbulent weeks of press intrusion, local and national television and radio, had come and gone. Life was returning to normal. A year's waves had broken on the harbour walls scratching deeper into their pitted surfaces, eroding and wearing them down, grinding away their resistance, prying patiently into the cracks and searching them for any weakness. The season of sunshine and white cloud had given way to the gales of Autumn. Flowers had faded and died, their seeds hiding in the earth for the spring sun and the warmth of longer days. The cliffs had emptied of their breeding colonies and the seas of their passing flocks. Only the gulls remained around the harbour walls and the fishing boats, patiently riding the storms and waiting for better days. The clifftop grew red and then grey and then white as winter frosts gripped the low grass.

Then the spring gradually returned. The sea outside the harbour sank a little into its bed and slumbered. The white wisps of foam grew more brilliant and the aquamarine sea grew deep and rich.

Early primroses grew along the stream and by the waterfall on the hills. Then the summer returned at last.

It had been a difficult year. Agnes had suffered particularly. The trial of Carlton Brooke had inevitable consequences. The brutal treatment she had received at the hands of her ex-husband provided column inches for the newspapers. The accounts were sympathetic but that was no compensation for a sensitive woman who shied away from such exposure and who suffered agonies as each day of the trials occurred and each headline appeared. Throughout it all Wilkie stood at her side, as solid as an oak against which she could lean, in which she could trust, without fear of falling. The days passed. Brooke was tried and sentenced. It would be eight years before he would be free.

Conlon would never be free. The sentence imposed on him would end only with his death. He showed no remorse; he showed little feeling. The same enigmatic, indifferent smile lingered on his lips throughout. He spoke only to laud his own genius and to compliment his captors.

Deitch was adamant that he should face prosecution but it did not happen. There was little appetite for it after the manner in which he had trodden such a dangerous path in order to assist the police. Conlon, who could have incriminated him, remained stonily silent. In the end it was decided that it would not be in the public interest to continue and Deitch had to accept it. Shortly after the trials he and Emma departed for the continent. Emma rented a villa for them in a small resort. The warmth and the peace would help restore John and the light and colours of the neighbourhood would provide her with material for many weeks and months of painting and sketching. They talked of marriage.

Jack Munro and Aaron Marks received praise and censure in equal proportions but they remained unchallenged at Portskail. It seemed the authorities believed they could do some good and the least harm in their chosen location and that it would be easier all round to leave them there.

Yes, a year had passed; only one short year. To the participants in the story it felt as if they had ended one lifetime and begun another. Something beyond the harbour, deep in the ocean, had stirred and awoken. They had been caught up in the flow of its ominous, rolling tide. Now they were on the sand, gasping for air but alive, alive. It was time to stand up and begin again.

Aaron was in the walled garden of Strathan Tower. He was sitting on the bench in the arbour and removing a pair of mountain boots. A small day pack lay on the ground before him. Wilkie was sitting beside him. Some distance away, beside the greenhouses and in front of the wall of rambling roses, a table had been set. There were crystal glasses, a decanter and plates of sandwiches and cakes. Mrs. Davidson looked it over with a professional eye. She seemed pleased. Behind her on the seat by the wall Agnes was reading a book. Marcus and Jack walked towards her from the house and she looked up and smiled. Wilkie and Aaron joined them.

'Help yourselves, help yourselves,' Mrs. Davidson said to them. 'Oh dear,' she added, suddenly raising a hand to her mouth, 'how very presumptuous of me. It is hardly my place to invite you to table. It must be the excitement of the day. Imagine!'

'Come, Mrs. Davidson,' Marcus smiled, 'you are a guest here today.'

'It's such a special day,' she laughed. 'I feel as if I'm twenty again, though twenty is a long way behind me now.'

'Yes, we have much to celebrate,' Marcus said.

'Then the hall is finally yours,' Wilkie said, 'and I have a new employer.'

Marcus nodded. 'John Deitch has been more than generous. There have been many legal hurdles to cross but we would appear to be there at last. The lease for Strathan Tower is now mine, and at very little cost. Deitch has refused to emerge with even a pound profit. He would appear to have disposed of most of his wealth to a number of worthy causes. He has retained only what he felt he honestly earned.'

'Will he return to the village, do you think?' Aaron asked. 'Emma Varley has retained her studio and house I see.'

'I hope so,' Agnes murmured. She sat beside Wilkie now and bit into a small sandwich. Her appetite was only now returning. 'I believe they plan to marry. I like happy endings, don't you? Mother would have been most pleased.'

'What about you? Do you plan to move into Strathan Tower with Marcus?'

Agnes smiled demurely. 'Wilkie refuses to commit himself. I would like to remain in the White House. It has become my home. I have a lot of fond memories. Wilkie says we must wait until tomorrow. He refuses to say anything until then and he won't explain why. He is being very mysterious.'

Aaron turned and looked at Wilkie who was blushing deep red. He smiled and then laughed.

'It's a promise I made,' he said, 'to a very dear friend. Tomorrow we are going to a very special place. We shall walk along the beach, barefoot in the sea. I shall probably fall in the waves and, if the sun shines, we shall sit on the shore amongst the flowers. Mrs. Davidson will prepare some sandwiches for us, some special sandwiches.'

'And then?'

Wilkie laughed and then laughed again so loudly and deeply and with such good humour that the others could not help but laugh with him.

Rosie looked up from beneath the table and turned her head to one side. She saw that everything was good and yawned deeply. She curled round in a ball, sighed softly, and closed her eyes.

END

If you enjoyed this novel you can find out more about the author and his other books on his website, **www.bleaknorth.net**, or on his Amazon Author Page.

The author would welcome reviews of the book which can be posted on Amazon.

Other works by the same author include 'The Cave' and 'A Tale of Shadows' available as e-books or in paperback through Amazon or any good bookshop.

Made in the USA
Charleston, SC
01 September 2016